Barbados Joy

by

GWENYTH CLARE LYNES

Grosvenor House
Publishing Limited

This book is published by
Grosvenor House Publishing Ltd
Link House
140 The Broadway, Tolworth, Surrey, KT6 7HT.
www.grosvenorhousepublishing.co.uk

This book is a work of fiction. Any resemblance to
people or events, past or present, is purely coincidental.

A CIP record for this book
is available from the British Library

ISBN 978-1-83975-876-8

Books in the Newton Westerby Series

Because of You
Out of my Depth
Broken and Lost

Also collated by Gwenyth-Clare Lynes
A Godly Heritage
Love Letters 1939-43
(Written by her father A.D. Butler to her mother)

The characters, events and places in this book, other than well-established towns and countries, are entirely fictitious and any resemblance to actual persons or places is purely coincidental. Some events are based on the author's experiences.

Any mistakes are the authors entirely.

Acknowledgements

My warmest thanks to Trevor's Cousin, Derek and Brenda, who treated me royally and introduced me to so many people and aspects of Barbados.

The warmth and hospitality of the Bajan people is second to none. Wherever I was taken I was accepted with kindness and affection. People, too numerous to mention, opened their homes and their hearts to me. My thanks to you all.

Fond memories of Brenda's brother Derek and the times we spent together as he reminisced and regaled me with fascinating anecdotes.

My thanks to Jon, who persuaded me to venture abroad and write a story based upon my adventure, then valiantly ploughed through the resultant manuscript.

How I appreciate the technical skills of Andi and Oliver. My grateful thanks to you both for your advice and expertise.

My gratitude to the Staff of Grosvenor House Publishing.

Dedication

Brenda and Derek Briggs

who insisted I obtain a passport and
visit their home in Barbados

And
A Tribute to the Memory of
Derek Williams

who shared with me so many of his memories
which have been woven into this story

GLOSSARY

Inspired by the bustling anchorage of Newtown, mentioned in Gillingwater's Mediaeval History of East Anglia, Newton Westerby has been placed on the coast somewhere south of the Norfolk/Suffolk border. This fishing port has long disappeared so today only exists in the imagination of the author and reader. The local inhabitants speak with a Suffolk dialect but only a few of the residents have been depicted as using such in the text.

On my visit to Barbados I discovered that many of the residents make an imperceptible use of d/de instead of th in conversation i.e. de for the and dis for this. Mostly only Mumma Madge and Connie have been portrayed as using this in speech in the book. The phrase 'you know' is frequently added on to the end of a sentence in conversation by countless people.

Ow/ou pronounced ew i.e. you – yew, snow – snew.
O pronounced oo i.e. so – soo, Go – goo.
A'ciding – deciding.
Afore – before.
Agin – against.
Aloan – alone.
Allus – always.

A-tween – between.
Bin – been.
Bor – boy.
Dew – do.
Ent – is not, isn't.
Doan't – don't.
Fer – for.
Foller – follow.
Funny – odd/strange.
Fust – first.
Git/gits – get/gets.
Gor – got.
Gorn – going.
Hum – home.
Int – is not.
Juss – just.
Loines – lines.
Med – made.
Mek – make.
Nivver – never.
Noo – no.
Oi/oi'll/oi'm – I, I'll, I'm.
Ole/owd – old.
Pretty – rather.
Roite – right.
Rud – road.
Rum ole do – strange happenings.
Sin – seen.
Squit – nonsense.
Suthen – something.
Taak/tek – take.
Thass – that's/ that is.
Tonoite – tonight.

Yew're – your.
Yewsel – yourself.
Yew've – you have.
yow'n/yourn – your/yours.
Wuz – was
Yus/yup – yes.

CHAPTER ONE

29 Degrees and rising!

The latch on the garden gate clicked. Madge Foster glanced up from the sink as she rinsed the breakfast dishes under a running tap. Across her eye line, through the kitchen window, she caught the flight of a hummingbird as it landed on the deep orange flower of the Pride of Barbados, a beautiful, crested Antillean. Fascinated she watched, as with wings flapping furiously the small bird dove beak down to suck out the sweet nectar, a movement so quick it would have been easy to miss.

"Mornin' Miz Foster," Jethro hollered as he lolloped up the steps of the veranda towards the open door, wafting an envelope high above his head. The startled bird flew away to safety.

Madge pushed back wisps of hair that had fallen across her face, briskly wiped her hands on the nearest tea-towel and moved forward to greet the postman.

"Mornin' Jethro, how's de world treatin' you today?"

"Fine, Miz Foster, just fine. Letter from foreign parts."

Oh, no! Her heart dropped to her feet like a stone.

Hastily she plastered a smile in place and reluctantly reached out to take the missive Jethro held out to her.

"Hi, Mumma, has it come?" Connie called out later that afternoon as she skipped up the steps from the road to the veranda two at a time and rushed through the front door into the family home in the parish of Christchurch, Barbados. A door that was ever open, not only to let in whatever breeze there might be to relieve the stifling heat that built up in their living quarters, but also as an open invitation to all who passed by to "come on in and rest awhile, as de Good Book says."

These were always her mother's words of invitation. Madge Foster had a kindly heart, a broad smile and affectionate embrace. She drew everyone in by the genuine warmth of her relaxed, big-hearted hospitality. Cool refreshing drinks were continuously on offer, mostly home-made sorrel or mauby. The whole neighbourhood knew that, if you were hungry, there was always an abundance of food available at Mumma Foster's house.

When the tantalising smell of her corn pie and chicken stew cooking on the stove drifted out of the open doors and windows, amazingly, additional feet found their way across the threshold and a welcome place at the table. Madge was generous to a fault but, my, was she strict! Growing up, her children knew it was schoolwork before play and household chores before leisure pursuits, and woe betide any of them if they forgot their P's and Q's, whatever the day or occasion.

"Sunday is de Lord's Day," Mumma insisted. "There will be no work dis day, school or otherwise, but you wear your Sunday best with shiny shoes dat you polish on Saturday night." She would always check that all was as she expected before Connie and her siblings went to bed. On Sunday morning Connie cooked breakfast to give Mumma a break, usually fried plantain and fluffy egg with corn bread. When the washing-up was done Mumma would declare, "We's ready!" and they all piled into Daddy's 26year old car, spotlessly cleaned by whoever had been allotted that task on Saturday morning before sun-up, to attend the worship service at the church in Bridgetown.

Madge, along with Connie and Jacinth, sang in the choir and as they had to robe up after their appearance at church, were anxious never to be late arrivals. The boys were not so keen on the structured singing element of church so, after meeting up with their older brother, they gravitated to the pew they generally shared with their father and some of their aunts, uncles and cousins. Clyde had a beautiful tenor voice. He and Connie sometimes sang duets together, her natural contralto pitch harmonizing perfectly with his voice, but he was not always available to attend choir practice or services on Sunday, so he chose not to be a member of the choir.

Connie, a primary school teacher, still lived at home along with her younger siblings, Luther Garfield, Jacinth Monica, and Deighton Joel, but her twin, Clyde, a qualified doctor, had his own home in the district near to his Doctor's office.

Connie hovered around her mother as she stood by the stove cooking flying fish for her family's evening meal. Anxious for a positive reply Connie asked again, "Mumma, did the postman call?"

"Calm down, girl. Quit your pestering. Remember what de Good Book says, 'Who of you by worrying can add a single hour to his life?'"

"I do not want to add another hour to my life, Mumma, I want to know if it's come."

Madge turned over the flying fish in the pan and gave a good stir to the green pea rice before bending down to open the oven door to check on the corn pie.

Connie sighed.

"You need to learn patience, Constance. Why do you want to go all dat way, anyway? You have a good job at de school and a good home with Daddy and me. Don't de Good Lord need you here? What makes you think He wants you over there?"

"Mumma, we have been through this so many times. You know that I have always wanted to teach in England and go there to learn about de birthplace of our ancestors."

"We live in de here and now, what does it matter dat our Greats live someplace else many years ago."

"Mumma, we are where we are and who we are because of these people. I majored in History and Geography in order to learn more about de world and our past and how it impacts upon us now."

"Pshaw!" Madge banged the fish slice so hard that the flying fish almost flew out of the pan.

"You are always telling us to read de Good Book and I find it also reminds us that God told the Israelites, 'Remember... my words...Don't forget... Teach them to your children and to their children after them.' I think He taught that truth to our ancestors to pass on to the next..."

"But He do dat here. You do not have to go thousands of miles away to find dat out." Madge swished the tea-towel across her shoulder. "And de cost!"

"Mumma, I have saved de fare to get me there."

"And to get back?"

"I will put aside an amount from my salary every month so that I can return home in de holiday."

"Humph!"

"Mumma, you could visit me..."

Madge turned from her task and wagged the fish slice at Connie to emphasize her words. "No! No! No! You's not getting me in one of dem flying monsters. It just might drop me in dat big, big ocean and it's too big for a sea bath."

"Oh, Mumma," Connie flung her arms around her mother, fish slice, tea-towel and all. "I do love you so, but you have to trust in that Good Lord you are always talking about to keep you safe. And if that is what worries you about me going, well, I will trust Him to keep me safe, too, and you must do de same."

"Go on with you, let me get on with de tea. De boys and Jacinth will be in from de bus soon, starving as usual and Daddy has called to say he is on his way, too."

Connie did not budge.

"Mumma, you haven't answered my question."

Madge turned back to her cooking. "What question was dat?" she asked as she commenced to lift each individual fish on to a serving dish.

"Mumma, don't be so obtuse."

"Obtuse? What kind of word is dat? Don't come your school teachering with me."

"Teachering, Mumma? You rewriting de dictionary?"

A clattering on the front veranda announced the arrival of her brothers, Garry and Joel, along with their sister, Jacinth. They did not often manage to catch the same bus home from school and college so when they did it was a bonus having them arrive together, Madge did not have to hold back the meal.

Madge looked up and gave them each her broad smile. Whenever she was asked why there was such a gap between the twins and the rest of her family Madge replied with a big smile across her face, "One baby is a blessing, two is mighty hard work and I have only two knees, where would I sit a third?" neglecting to mention that between the twins, Constance Joy and Clyde Josiah, and Garfield, she miscarried six babies. Madge loves babies so much the loss still grieves her which is why her arms are ever open to all who come to her door. She turns no one away, particularly the young ones.

"Shoes off!" she directed the new arrivals.

"Yes, Mumma," the teenagers chorused in unison having already slipped out of their footwear when they reached the veranda, knowing what Mumma's first words to them would be.

"How did cricket practice go, Garfield?"

"Good, Mumma, real good."

"You in de team tomorrow?"

"Yes, Mumma."

"Go check your whites, then," she instructed. Garry rolled his eyes at Connie, a wide grin across his face knowing that his mother would have already washed and pressed his cricket gear after the match the previous week and put it onto his hanging rail. The only time it had not been ready for the next match was when he had disobeyed her instruction to drop it in the laundry basket on washday. My, oh my, he not only got a tongue lashing from his mother but also from his father, who had turned out on his day off to watch his son play, as well as the team coach, who had not been best pleased with him for appearing in dirty, crumpled gear. "You're a disgrace, Foster. You've let your team mates down by such a slovenly appearance." Garry made sure he never forgot washday again.

"Do you have homework, Jacinth?"

"Yes, a little, Mumma," Jacinth replied as she reached into the fridge for a jug of iced coconut water.

"Get to it, then, tea in thirty minutes."

With an eye on the stove Madge nodded at her youngest son. "Who's dat with you, Joel?"

"Fruendel, Mumma."

"Hi, Frue, you want flying fish?"

"Yes, please, Mumma Madge."

"Sit down, boy when you's washed your hands. Joel, show him de bathroom," she instructed as she stirred, even though Frue was a frequent visitor to the Foster home and well acquainted with the lay-out of the house.

"You boys got homework?"

"Yes, Mumma. Information Technology. Me and Frue are working on a project together."

"Me and Frue? Me and Frue!!! I mean proper schoolwork."

"This is proper, Mumma, set by our tutor, Mr Clayton."

"Humph!" Madge clattered the serving dishes, "not what I call proper. I meant Maths and English."

"This is English based, but we are doing it on the computer," explained Joel frantically pushing Frue towards the door. "We will go start it now and get washed and changed for tea." The boys beat a hasty retreat.

"Will it teach you to say, Frue and I?" she called after them.

With the influx of hungry young people Connie knew it was useless trying to pursue a conversation with her mother until everyone was seated at the table with a full plate of food in front of them, so she turned towards the en-suite room she shared with her sister, Jacinth, but her mother called after her.

"Constance, when you have showered, come prepare de salad."

"Yes, Mumma."

Resignedly, Connie sighed and murmured, "My question will keep." She de-robed from her classroom attire, turned on the shower, and allowed the water to wash away the grime and heat of the day. It felt good to plunge her bronze body beneath the cascading shower head. Once dry, and deliciously refreshed, she donned white shorts, and a lightweight aqua blue, sleeveless top. She combed through her springy, dark hair and went to give her mother a hand leaving her sister to complete her assignment.

"So, no news?" Jacinth called after Connie as she exited the door.

"Not yet."

"No hopes of an English young man on the horizon, then?"

Connie turned and wagged a finger playfully at Jacinth. "I am not looking for a young man, English or otherwise. When de Good Lord wishes it to be, then, we will meet."

"We shall see," her sister chuckled as Connie made her way to prepare salad for their evening meal.

Jacinth loved her older sister, thought her great fun and an ideal confidant but she could not wait for Connie to move out so that she could have a room to herself but that seemed a long way off since her sister did not even have a boyfriend! The boys, however, would still have to share because Mumma insisted they always have a spare room for whoever might need a bed for the night.

Jacinth turned back to her books. She worked hard at school and attacked her homework with diligence, completing much of it in free periods while still at school or travelling home on the bus leaving only a small amount, if any, to finish off at home. She already had her future clearly mapped out. Her ambition was to go to University and then follow in her mother's footsteps and train as a nurse. She was undecided about whether to stay on the island as Connie did, or go to Canada like her eldest brother or even to England like her father, to do her training. She still had a year or two ahead of her before she was required to make a final decision so was keeping her options open but considering all possibilities.

So far, their youngest daughter had not caused her parents any anxious moments beyond the usual childish ailments while she was growing up, for which Madge and Wilson gave the Good Lord thanks. Jacinth had developed into a pleasant, attractive young lady. She had inherited her father's compassionate nature and her mother's organisational abilities. She was thoughtful, focussed, and adept at presenting reasoned arguments for her decisions and actions and competently tackled any task assigned to her. She was fond of her siblings but not so openly demonstrative with her affections as her older sister.

On the other hand, her fun-loving brothers were a different kettle of fish much to Madge's displeasure. They had become masters at procrastination over anything to do with lesson work unless it involved sport, cricket-in-particular. Madge blamed the influence of her father, aided and abetted by her father-in-law, who were both cricket mad. The men spent hours regaling their grandsons with stories from the heydays of the West Indies team, and constantly encouraged Garry in his technique when he was a young boy, taking him off to matches when his focus should have been on academic studies. To stem her frustration Madge frequently enlisted Connie's help to encourage Garry and Joel to address their college and schoolwork.

Madge was determined her children should make the most of the education possibilities available to them. She and Wilson had struggled hard to achieve academic attainments in a society riddled with racial prejudice. "Don't squander de gifts de Good Lord has given you but use them well and wisely," she constantly admonished them, particularly when they were 'messing about', as she called it, on laptops, iPad or cell phones instead of catching up with homework.

Clyde, the elder of the twins, was a quiet, studious young man, gentle in nature but always ready to lend a hand or listening ear wherever there was a need. He had attended University and Medical school in Canada and returned to Barbados to practise as a family doctor. How proud Madge was of his accomplishments. He had no wish to emulate or compete with his father who was an eminent orthopaedic surgeon at the Queen Elizabeth Hospital in Bridgetown. Young Doctor Foster had a leaning towards childhood illnesses and had specialised in paediatrics in his last year in Canada before coming home to Barbados. A Doctor's office where he attended to the needs of the whole family, particularly the children, was the focus of his life.

Connie, with her bubbly nature was quite the opposite to her reserved twin, and like her mother exuded warmth and friendliness. She had elected to attend the University of the West Indies to study the humanities. Following this period of learning she had gone on to do her teacher training concentrating on the education of primary aged school children. On qualifying she had obtained a position at a school not too far from home. The children loved her engaging manner and responded well to her style of teaching.

Garry, named for Garfield Sobers, the Barbados and West Indies cricketer, had won a sports scholarship to the local college but to the dismay of his father and grandfathers he was not achieving his original potential. In recent weeks, his attitude to practise in the nets was inconsistent so that at times his performance on the field was erratic. To the chagrin of his mother his whole approach to life was becoming somewhat lazy and haphazard and he tended to think that his skill on the cricket field was all that mattered. However, Madge was adamant he knuckle down to concentrate on other subjects that she felt could be important, even in the cricketing sphere, and essential whatever avenue his life took in the future beyond his cricket career.

"You need Maths to keep tally of de scores and English to write up de reports and make intelligent conversation," she told him. "History is necessary so that you learn what past cricketers have achieved and know who to emulate. You require Geography to enable you to know where to find de ground of de next cricket match especially when you go overseas. RE is de most important because it teaches you to know de words of de Good Lord which will help to keep you on de straight and narrow, how to behave and how to treat other people. You require Science because it will make you aware how man thinks dis world ticks."

Discussions with Joel about his prospects always ended in disagreement, frustration for Joel because he felt his mother never really listened to him and annoyance for Madge because she was out of her depth as far as the subject matter was concerned. She always lost. That never pleased her. So, she always brought the conversation to a close with the words, "We will talk about dis later, Joel."

"Daddy's home!"

CHAPTER TWO

Sunshine and Showers!

In his late fifties, Doctor Wilson Everton Foster, BS. FRCS. was a tall striking man with a keen mind coupled with a sense of humour and a compassionate nature. He had broad shoulders, a shock of dark brown, wavy corkscrew hair dusted with grey above handsome facial features and displayed expressive hands of highly developed dexterity, but he was a great disappointment to his cricket loving father. He had been named after his father's great friend, Everton Weekes, in the hope that he would follow in the cricketer's footsteps. Although he loved the game it was more as a spectator rather than a participant. It was not Wilson's ambition to use his long fingered, elegant hands to swing a bat or bowl a ball but to wield a knife and stitch a fine line. He sought to mend bones and bring healing to broken bodies in more ways than one.

As a young lad he had passed the 11+ and gone to Harrison College, the boy's grammar school. He had subsequently gained a place at Cambridge University in England and gone on to Medical School in London. Whilst in London he attended services at Westminster Central Hall where he came under the influence of the ministry of RT Kendall which had a life changing impact upon him. After qualification as a doctor, Wilson moved back to Cambridge, to gain more surgical experience at Addenbrookes Hospital, before returning to his beloved Barbados to practise at, what was always referred to by the locals as, the 'new Hospital' opened and named by a young Queen Elizabeth II in 1964. Here, Wilson met and fell in love with the diminutive nurse who ran the operating theatre with the precision of a battleground campaign.

Her deep contralto voice belied her stature but reached his heart with its cadences and pure notes as he listened to her sing solos with the church choir. Over time, as he got to know her, at events held at church as well as in the day to day running of the department at the hospital, it was evident that Madge had a sweet fragrance about her that drew people to God. All that she did and said displayed His beauty. Wilson was irresistibly drawn to her. He was aware that some of the junior members of staff lived in fear of her and called her a 'bossy dragon', but he felt her desire to have everything done properly and correctly at all times was essential to the safety and wellbeing of his patients as well as the staff. She was not afraid to speak her mind, yet it was never careless speech, but always carefully considered and reasoned.

Her heart, fragrant with the love of Christ, captured his and within ten months of meeting he had proposed and by the end of the year they were wed.

They started married life in a one-roof house and, like their parents before them, extended the property as the need arose and funds allowed. Madge, too, expanded in girth, love and warmth with the arrival of the twins and each subsequent child. Now, with the numerous additions, they had a three-roof house with a large living room divided from the cooking area by a waist high bench over which were built cupboards to house the crockery and glassware. To the side was an archway leading to a corridor off which were a bathroom and four bedrooms, two of which had en-suite shower rooms. The veranda stretched across the breadth of the living area with a balustrade wall either side of the steps. It sported numerous chairs upon which to sit and chat, eat or simply enjoy the view which included a distant glimpse of the Caribbean Sea framed by coconut palms.

Connie completed her chores, but before she could approach her mother with the all-important question the others had washed, changed and gravitated to the dining table. As they each stood behind a chair at the table, Wilson, reached out his hands in blessing. "Father God, accept our grateful thanks for the bounty of this day. May we now enjoy the company and conversation of one another as we eat this delicious meal together and bless the hands that so lovingly made preparation for our needs. In the name of Your Son, we pray. Amen."

Eagerly, chairs were scraped back, and bodies quickly seated in order that the process of eating could commence. Instantly, many hands dived in to pick up dishes overflowing with food that set the taste buds tingling.

"Help yourself to de dish nearest to you and pass it on to de person on your right," Madge explained to Frue. He nodded and for the next few minutes, along with the others, he was busily engaged in filling his plate with the delicious food that was passed to him.

When the fish platter reached Madge she remarked, "Oh, one flying fish left, who can that be for?"

Joel eagerly raised his hand to claim it when a knock, followed by a call at the door stopped him in his tracks.

"Hello there, may I come in?"

"Yes, yes Pastor, do come in," Madge welcomed. "Garfield, reach me another plate," she gestured with her hand. "Pastor, draw up a chair. You's just in time for tea. Jacinth another place setting, please. Joel, grab a glass for de Pastor."

"Sorrel or lime?"

"Your own make?"

"Of course. Help yourself, now." Madge indicated the spread before him.

"Then sorrel, please," Pastor Desmond said as he accepted the plate and the glass the boys passed to him.

"Homemade sour dough rolls, if I am not mistaken."

"Of course, nothing but de best for you, Pastor."

"And your family."

"Always," Madge beamed at those seated around her table pleased to see everyone tucking in heartily to the meal she had prepared. However, while food was being served and Pastor's needs attended to there was no opportunity to engage in conversation. Both Connie and Joel were itching to return talk back to earlier discussions they had been having with Madge. After making inroads into the food on his plate Joel keenly sought eye contact with his mother but it was proving impossible, so he gulped down a mouthful and took the plunge.

"Now, what about I.T. Mumma?" He held his breath, but with Pastor there and Frue on his side Mumma was unlikely to be quite so adamantly against his request to add I.T. to his studies.

"It?"

"No, I.T."

"Oh, your 'magic' machines – well, if you do good at all de other subjects, I suppose you can tag dat on at de end."

"But Mumma, computers are important, they are involved in all aspects of life. Frue is taking I.T. studies as well as the other subjects, aren't you Frue?" Joel turned to his friend for support. With his mouth full of food Frue simply nodded vigorously his assent.

"But, but but's never got man anywhere!" stated Madge emphatically.

"But Daddy uses computers every day at work," Joel muttered to himself.

Joel felt he was losing the argument before it ever got started and groped for a lifeline.

He turned to Desmond whom he knew prepared his sermon notes on an iPad. He also knew the church accounts were done on a laptop, too, by the church treasurer. "What do you think, Pastor?"

Desmond smiled and weighed his words carefully before replying to the eager young man. The pastor was aware that Wilson supported Madge to a certain degree believing his children should use their brains, "or they will turn to mush", before delving into the mysteries of the computer world but Desmond also knew that Information Technology was very much a part of the doctor's day to day life in the hospital. Madge had ceased working at the hospital some years ago when she was expecting the twins. At that time, the use of computers in the hospital was in its infancy, so she was not as familiar with their use as the rest of her family.

"That is a difficult question to answer, young man, but I'm glad you've asked it. I.T. has its place and we all know that much of life is now governed by computers and the wide scope the internet offers. However, while it is important we understand the role they play, it is equally important we control the use of them, not the other way round. Your parents are anxious that you use the intellect of your mind rather than depend solely on machines for problem solving in your schoolwork and leisure pursuits. Used wisely the internet can be a useful tool, used irresponsibly it can destroy a life."

"I see, so you don't think I would use it responsibly?"

"I did not say that, nor do I think your parents are implying that," Desmond looked towards Wilson and Madge for confirmation. They both shook their heads.

"We are anxious, my boy, to know that you can differentiate between the two and get a right balance between them," Wilson gently interjected.

"I see, I think," Joel looked down at his almost empty plate, toyed with his cutlery and sighed as his shoulders slumped in his chair.

Connie saw his crestfallen face and kindly asked on behalf of her deflated brother, "You are not entirely opposed to Joel taking I.T. studies next year then, Daddy?"

"Not at all. Correctly used they are an essential asset to daily life, but I want you all to realise they are not the essence of life."

"De Good Lord, He is de mainstay of life not machines. Would anyone like something more to eat…" Madge, determined to have the last word and close the subject, quickly cast her eyes around the table. Seeing numerous nods in reply to her question she proceeded "...then, Jacinth will you pass de dishes round, please." With a shrug Joel flashed Connie a look of thanks for her intervention on his behalf.

As youthful appetites were satisfied Desmond, anxious to broach the difficult topic for which he had called upon the Foster family, felt this was the moment to open the discussion that laid heavily on his heart. He turned to Garry and asked, "Have there been any drug issues at the College?"

Garry coughed and spluttered as the food he was swallowing went down the wrong way. Joel got up and thumped him vigorously on the back.

"You have specific reasons for asking that question of my son, Pastor?" Wilson calmly enquired, giving Garry opportunity to recover.

"Yes. Officials have reason to believe that persons connected to drug cartels are luring unsuspecting youngsters outside education establishments and grooming them to act as runners..."

"Runners?"

"Go-betweens, carriers for the drugs from supplier to user. Monetary rewards can be significant but the greatest incentive to participate is to prevent the promised threats against family and friends being carried out. Enormous pressure is exerted on those who are singled out. Fear makes them give in to the demands. It seems the drug bosses do their homework well and know what will have a weighty hold over their quarry."

"I see," Wilson replied ponderously. A lengthy silence followed his words and a pall hung like a heavy blanket over the table. No one dared to move let alone continue to eat. Joel felt a tickle in his nose. It itched to be released. He wiggled it and held his breath. He surreptitiously tried to sniff. It simply would not be held back. "A-A-Attishoo!"

"Are you suggesting my son is involved?"

"No, no, Wilson, not at all." Desmond ran a finger round the inside of his collar. "Following a chat with the police inspector I am asking all the boys in church if they have heard anything. This is a problem that needs to be nipped in the bud before it gets too great a hold. I feel we need to do all we can to safeguard our young people. I am sorry, my friend, I should have approached you first."

Desmond, aware that Garry had not answered his question, but anxious to lift the sombre mood that seemed to have descended upon the company sat at the table, turned to Connie on his right, "And what is your news, Connie?"

With a mouth full of food, Connie simply shook her head.

"Oh, well, we shall have to wait and see," remarked Madge.

Connie swallowed quickly, "Mumma, what do you mean?"

Madge shook her fingers dismissively. "Finish your tea, Constance, just finish your tea."

"But Mumma…" She followed her mother's eyes.

"Remember, Connie, but, but buts never got man anywhere and I expect the same applies to women." Garry, having recovered his equilibrium, teased, mimicking his mother's earlier expression. Everyone laughed and eased the tension that had built up around the table.

"Mumma!" Connie saw where Madge's eyes rested. Her cutlery clattered as she jumped up from the table. Then remembering her manners, she turned rapidly to her father, "Oh, Daddy, please excuse me."

Wilson smiled benignly. Connie ran round the table and flung her arms around his neck. "Thank you, Daddy."

"What is it Mumma?" Jacinth enquired.

An envelope was lodged on the bottom shelf just inside the glass cabinet above the workbench where Madge normally placed important documents and correspondence for their father.

Connie whisked it out. "A letter, Mumma!"

"What does it say?" clamoured her siblings.

Wilson reached into his pocket, "Here, Constance, open it with my penknife." A gift from his father on his 21st birthday.

"Oh, Daddy, thank you." A special implement for a momentous occasion.

Carefully, Connie slit the buff-coloured envelope along the top of the seal. With trembling fingers, she opened it up.

The only sound to break the silence was the croaking frogs accompanied by the singing crickets heralding the fall of night.

Connie gasped then flung her arms wide into the air.

"I've got it, I've got it, I have got it!" She jumped up and down unable to contain her excitement.

Daddy rose from his chair and put his arms around her and hugged her to him. "Congratulations, my precious girl, you deserve it." Jacinth, the boys and Pastor Desmond joined in with their congratulations.

"Mumma?"

"Mumma, aren't you always saying that remembering God's faithfulness in the past strengthens us for the future?"

But Madge just sat as still as stone, staring in front of her.

CHAPTER THREE

Storm clouds brewing!

Jackie Cooper sat with her head on her hands as she contemplated the documents on the desk, her face pale and pinched with concern. She had worked so hard during the past year with her staff, as well as the pupils, yet the Ofsted report she had just read did not attest to that fact. It was quite critical of her efforts and most condemning of the learning environment the school offered, considering some areas and aspects of teaching to be below par. How could standards have plummeted so drastically in the last year? How could she have missed the slump in targets?

How on earth am I going to turn this situation around? The criteria will have to be addressed and addressed now.

If only Miss Pedwardine were here. She would know what to do. But then if she were here Newton Westerby Primary School would not be in this predicament.

Jackie massaged her temple with her fingertips as she considered an approach to the solution. *A reshuffle, maybe? Perhaps one or two members of staff would have better results with a different year group.* A face loomed in her mind. *Someone will definitely have to go!*

But replacements are hard to find. It is so difficult to recruit teachers to a rural location. Advertising further afield might be the answer.

A sunbeam danced on her desk as the sun shone through the recently cleaned window of her office. Her fingers slowly traced around the refracted colours as she pondered the dilemma before her. Perhaps there was a ray of light even amongst the gloomy words of the report. Jackie grabbed a pad of memos, checked her diary then quickly wrote a name, along with a time, upon several separate pages. She folded the sheets in half then swiftly stepped along the corridor to the staff room. Straightening her back she walked tall, held her head high, displaying a confidence she did not really feel. Once through the staff-room door Jackie glanced round at the group taking a well-earned break, while the children were letting off steam in the playground, then smiled as she handed a memo to each one.

"I've received the Ofsted report which I'd like to discuss with you all. Miss Stafford, could I see you in the office in 5 minutes, please? And I would be pleased to see the rest of you at the times indicated on the slips of paper, today or tomorrow, if possible."

"Of course, Miss Cooper," Kerry Stafford responded promptly and most of the others nodded assent over their cups of coffee after skimming the contents of the notes.

"In the doghouse, are we?" smirked Dillon Brankscome, his bulky form slouched in the corner, till he saw the time he had been allocated. He preened himself and sat upright. "So, I'm to be last."

"Yes, Mr Brankscome, if that is convenient."

"That's fine by me."

"Good."

"See you anytime, my lovely."

"Now, now, Mr Brankscome that's no way to speak to the head," chided Mrs Beckett.

"4 o'clock! In our own time," whinged Tina Morehouse.

"Quit your squawking, Tina, you never stay late," Dillon bellowed across the room.

"Why should I?" she snapped. "Neither do you."

"Do pipe down, Tina, I'm sure it's for the children's good that we're being asked to see the head," Mrs Camberley gently admonished.

"Do you have a problem with that, Miss Morehouse?"

"No, Miss Cooper," Tina muttered discourteously.

Jackie returned to the office mulling over a fitting tactic to deal with the problem ahead of her. *Maybe, just maybe, we can turn this situation around before the end of this school year if we all pull together. It's a big ask but we have the whole of the summer term ahead of us. So, time to put changes into place.* Every member of staff was uniquely different so her approach to each would need to be different.

Mrs Beckett taught year 6 and was a rotund motherly figure who had been teaching for over 30 years. She was dependable, but not open to new ideas and at times lax with discipline. Although she was reluctant to utilise the wealth of material now available for use on the computers so kindly donated by the parent's association, she had immeasurable patience with the slow learners. *The wellbeing of the children is always her priority, and her support is invaluable. However, I am glad I have Emma's flare to counterbalance Josie Beckett's negativity.*

In complete contrast was petite, fair haired Kerry Stafford who had been qualified for 4½ years. *What an asset she is to the life of the school. She is energetic and very au fait with modern methods of teaching, computer literate and able to direct the early learners in her care admirably.* Kerry not only knew her children but also their siblings, as well as their parents, and had taken time to learn something about their background and home life. She was very innovative, willing to discuss new procedures and put them into action.

Dillion Brankscome was a different kettle of fish. *He is a nightmare! He is overbearing and in this age of equality he, surprisingly, carries considerable resentment that a female is head teacher at this school. I really do not like his leering attitude towards the female members of staff, and his language, I wouldn't call it conversation, is often lurid and suggestive. He gets under my skin, makes me feel uncomfortable. Emma warned me to be on my guard after that incident in the village shop involving RK, as well as his unpleasant remarks aimed at Rosie Jenner and the part-time Saturday girls in the Tea Rooms.*

He had come with impressive credentials at the beginning of the school year, but his lazy work ethic did not support the glowing references he presented with his application. He appeared to make no preparation for each day's class work. He arrived late at school most mornings in a dishevelled state of dress and departed as promptly as possible at the end of the day. "Sorry, no time for extra-curricular duties," was his constant mantra as though it was beneath him to spend extra time with the children, developing social and sporting skills. This had a devastating effect on his class. In fact, his whole demeanour and slovenly appearance created a 'don't care' attitude in his pupils, behaviour was disruptive, written work messy and at times illegible, project work non-existent. Daily, the classroom looked and sounded as if World War 3 had broken out. *He does not seem to care about the pupils in his charge at all. He is certainly not an asset to the school! He will have to go. The children's work is suffering. But it is so difficult to remove incompetent teaching staff.*

On the other hand, Marianne Worsley was a hard-working, cheery, buxom young lady, who was sharing playground duty with Tim Draycott, this morning. She was a level 3 Teaching Assistant currently working with nursery and reception children. *What a boon she has proved to be. She is adaptable, willing and able to help in all the classes as the need arises, particularly with the most challenging children. Despite the funding cuts I will fight tooth and nail to retain Marianne. She shows genuine care and concern for all the children, has their wellbeing at heart and is always ready to go the extra mile for their benefit.*

Tim Draycott, a brisk, balding man, moved into the village along with his wife, two boys and a girl on his appointment as deputy-head. *The whole family has integrated nicely into village life and are well liked. He is always smartly dressed and tidy in appearance, a stickler for accuracy, punctuality and spelling. His classroom is the tidiest room in the whole school. No one can go home till every book, box, chair etc is in its rightful place.* Tim expected forms to be returned by their due date and homework to be completed within the time set. He was able to keep a tight rein on the behaviour of the more recalcitrant pupils but the timid were somewhat afraid of his sharp tone of voice and crisp, precise manner. However, the boundaries he set enabled most of the children to produce good quality work and he rewarded those who tried to do their best. *Tim is a great encourager, listener and always willing to go out of his way for the sake of the pupils. Without his input, after school clubs would have folded but, with the help of Noreen, he has introduced extra ones like the chess and gardening clubs. He has been such a support to me in his role as deputy-head. I cannot manage without him.*

In contrast, Mrs Noreen Camberley, was a softly spoken, newlywed young woman. She exuded warmth and caring yet looked for and stimulated the best from each child. Slight in stature, when she wore her flaxen coloured hair up in a ponytail, she could easily be mistaken for a teenage older sister to the children instead of their class teacher. Rather than issuing orders she would reason with the children about their behaviour, attitude to class work and their fellow pupils. Her smiling, calm demeanour had a settling effect on each child. *Noreen's classroom is always a quiet, industrious haven. I know the parents grumble because they are always the last to depart at the end of a school day but it's only because she is meticulous and wants to ensure they are not leaving anything behind. Her thoroughness means she's not always up to speed with the curriculum timetable, but she has a good influence. I don't want to lose that.*

However, flamboyant Tina Morehouse, excited turbulence with her flowing auburn locks and high pitched, penetrating voice. Brightly coloured, ill-matched apparel, daily, adorned her 5'10" frame. Dangling earrings and multiple rings on her fingers and large stoned necklaces completed her ensemble.

Her classes were always chaotic, but the children adored her. She firmly believed the children learned best by expressing themselves freely and no matter the subject or topic it generally involved paint, lots of it, splodges ending up on the floor, tables and chairs, much to Michelle Cook's dismay, who, as school cleaner was expected to clear up the mess.

With commendable restraint Jackie held her tongue but when it became a daily issue and a possible resignation on Michelle's part when she threatened to hand in her notice, even though she desperately needed the money to make ends meet, Jackie knew she would have to act. Complaints from, not a few, irate parents at the state of their children's clothes at the end of a school day also swayed the balance. Jackie invited Tina into the office and had a quiet word about the waste, as well as the constant chaos and mess. For a few days, the situation improved but very soon returned to its usual state. It was an ongoing battle.

Tina was also very keen on amateur dramatics and with considerable exuberance had the children learning and reciting things like Edward Lear's nonsense poems, 'The Owl and the Pussy Cat' and 'The Jumblies', Hilaire Belloc's 'Tarantella', chunks of Psalm 107 and 'From a Railway Carriage' by Robert Louis Stevenson. With exaggerated movement and dramatic gestures, they demonstrated their achievements, Miss Morehouse's voice booming out in full flow and the children copying, frequently at falsetto. A din which reverberated throughout the whole school building, much to the chagrin of other members of staff who were trying to instil a calm, orderly approach to learning in their charges.

As soon as the bell indicated the end of the school day Tina was off in her Mini, apart from the occasions when she was coaching her class in the Christmas Nativity play, or producing the end of year performance.

Emma Cooper, married to Jackie's cousin, Doctor Roger, did job-share with Mrs Beckett but was not in school today as she also ran the village store. Jackie found her a staunch ally and a dependable, efficient member of staff. *I must ring Emma and apprise her of the situation regarding the Ofsted report and arrange a time to talk during the next 24 hours.*

There was a tap on the door. Kerry Stafford walked in.

The following afternoon, Dillon Brankscome waited restlessly in his classroom.

"That big hand is taking forever to reach the six."

He fiddled with some books on a shelf. He drank from a bottle inside his case.

"Will 4:30 (his appointment time) never come?" he blurted out impatiently.

"Unlike most women Miss Cooper is a stickler for time-keeping. That is commendable," he thought sarcastically.

He wandered repeatedly between, around and through the gaps separating the children's tables and chairs. Then he lounged indolently at his own desk with his legs crossed across the top and took another swig from the bottle. He fished out his mobile phone from his pocket and scrolled down the screen.

"She'll soon be mine – all mine!" he posted.

He got up, looked out of the window, his face flushed. Smacked his lips in satisfaction, rubbed his hands gleefully, almost dropping his mobile. He did an ungainly twirl and slapped his thigh. He glanced through the open classroom door towards the clock in the hall. Three minutes to go. He kicked impatiently at a box left out on the floor.

"Not long to wait now." Miss Cooper was always punctual. He dashed to his briefcase, grabbed a bottle of Boss. He tipped some out into his hand and sloshed it on his cheeks.

"She'll like that. Girls swoon at such evocative smells."

He heard a door click as the clomping of Tina Morehouse's footwear echoed along the corridor.

"This is it! Wa—hoo!"

With a closed fist he punched the air. With air-born feet he ran along the corridor. Breathlessly he knocked on the Head Teacher's door and without waiting for the command to 'enter' he barged straight in.

Jackie was busy writing notes and seemed unaware that he was in her presence. Dillon rushed forward and grabbed her arm.

"I'm here, my darling, just as you requested. I knew you left me till last so we could have this special time together." His silky words dripped like treacle over the desk.

Startled, Jackie looked up and tried to pull her arm from his grasp but the more she pulled the tighter Dillon's hold became. He lurched closer and plonked his free arm possessively around her shoulders, hauled her towards himself and nuzzled his nose in her hair.

"Mmm, my dearest Jackie, that smell is so enticing. I'm all yours and soon you'll be all mine. You will be mine, won't you? Just set the date. You won't have to do this tedious job any longer. They can get a man in to do it. He'll have more authority."

Jackie gulped. *What is he talking about?* She wriggled her shoulders and jerked her body to get free. Unsuccessfully, because his grip was immoveable. *Stay calm,* she charged herself. Adopting Miss Pedwardine's best headmistress voice she said, "Mr Brankscome, thank you for coming to this meeting. Please sit down." The calmness of her words belied the fear her pounding heart indicated at the irrational behaviour of Dillon Brankscome.

"Oh, my darling, you have such authority. I like that."

"Mr Brankscome get a hold of yourself," Jackie again struggled to shake off her assailant and stand up. "Please release me, Dillon," but despite her plea his grip tightened and became more vice-like.

"Never, you're going to be mine for always." They grappled for a few moments. Jackie's chair tilted precariously with the force of his weight. She grabbed the edge of the desk with her free hand to prevent the chair from tipping over. As she clutched at the wooden perimeter her forefinger hovered over a hidden button. She pressed it hard. The stench emanating from his mouth and cheeks from the amalgam of excess Boss and alcohol was overpowering and nauseous. The closer he got to her the more her stomach revolted. She pulled and pushed to lessen his hold on her, but he would not relinquish his grasp. When Dillon tried to kiss her, Jackie shook her head as vigorously as she could, catching his mouth and knocking off his glasses. Dillon yelped. Immediately he released his hold to put a hand to his face.

"You vixen! You like it rough, then I can give it rough," he shouted. Jackie seized the opportunity to rise from the chair but quick as a flash Dillon viciously lunged his bulky figure at her, his outstretched fingers groping the front of her body, ripping her blouse, intensity blazing in his eyes. Nothing was going to prevent him from claiming her as his own, but his sudden action caught Jackie off balance, tipping the chair over. She fell heavily to the floor her arm bent awkwardly beneath her. Paying no attention to the ominous crack or Jackie's gasp, Dillon blindly pounced on top of her with his 17 stone weight, his hands mauling her indiscriminately.

Jackie called out in pain. Dillon ignored her cry.

"Meeting?" he smirked. "Meeting?" He guffawed loudly. "That's a good cover for a private tete-a-tete."

"Not when you have an audience," a voice barked from the doorway, astounded to see a colleague in such a compromising position.

"What are you doing here?" Dillon shouted back at the figure silhouetted in the doorway.

"I suggest you get up, Mr Brankscome."

"Oh, Tim, thank goodness you're here." At the sound of the deputy head's voice, Miss Cooper, uncharacteristically, burst into tears.

"Came as soon as I could." Tim Draycott strode further into the room looking to see where Jackie's voice was coming from. "Michelle heard the buzzer as she was cleaning the staff room and ran to your door. She saw the commotion, thought things were not right so called the police then remembered I was still in school and fetched me from the che..." Horrified by the spectacle before him Tim stopped in mid-sentence.

Speedily he moved closer shocked at the ungainly body mass between the desk and the metal filing cabinet. Perturbed by Mr Brankscome's predatory posture sprawled over Jackie moved Tim briskly into action. He yelled loudly, yanking vigorously on Dillon's uppermost arm. "Get up, Mr Brankscome," he shouted as he pulled with all his might, "you're hurting Miss Cooper." He managed to marginally shift Dillon's position. Jackie cringed and gritted her teeth as pain shot through her.

"Rubbish! You're only saying that to take her from me. You're not having her. She's mine," he ranted at Tim.

"Dillon, please, get off me," Jackie begged. But he obstinately refused to release his hold or stand up.

Using as much force as he could muster Tim pushed and shoved to remove Brankscome's bulk to one side. He reached out to assist Jackie to get up from the floor. When she did not respond he looked at her with concern. "Are you OK?" At the slight shake of her head he pulled out his mobile phone and rapidly tapped in numbers which connected him to the surgery. "Miranda, Tim Draycott here. Would it be possible for Doctor Roger, to come to the school, at once? There's been an accident." Kicking at Brankscome's limpet-like hold on Jackie's arm Tim quickly took off his jacket, rolled it into a ball.

"Hey, hey, hey, you get out, mister, she's mine." Rattled that his plans had gone awry, Dillon Brankscome levered up his ungainly body, pressing down on Jackie's hurting arm in the process causing her to call out again in agony.

Concerned by Jackie's anguish Tim's slight frame bent forwards to cushion her head elbowing Brankscome as he did so. He was alarmed when he saw blood and again pulled hard at Brankscome's arm.

"Mr Brankscome, get up at once!" PC Prettyman commanded from the doorway.

Tim turned his head. "Glad you could get here, constable."

"Couldn't leave a damsel in distress, though I didn't anticipate this debacle."

Defiantly, Dillon Brankscome eyed the constable with disdain holding more tightly onto his prize.

"Get up, Mr Brankscome," PC Prettyman reiterated his order reaching out to forcefully raise the man to his feet.

Once erect Dillon approached the constable with fists a blazing, punching out viciously at his chest, curses emanating from his mouth, but PC Prettyman stood still and towered above the angry man.

"I'd like you to come with me, sir."

"I'm not going anywhere. You'd take advantage and you're not having her, she's mine."

"Mr Brankscome, I am arresting you..."

"What for?"

"Causing bodily harm to a lady, for one thing, impersonating a schoolteacher for another, attempting to attack a police officer and finally being under the influence of drink whilst at work." Jackie's eyebrows rose. The constable proceeded with the arresting protocol, but Dillon Brankscome was not listening.

"Don't talk rubbish, Miss Cooper arranged our meeting."

"I asked you to come and discuss the Ofsted report as I did with all members of staff," said Jackie in a shaky voice. She attempted to shuffle into a sitting position but was hampered by her injured arm and an excruciating pain at the back of her head.

"Will you, please, come quietly?"

"'Course I'm not," Brankscome shouted aggressively, doing all he could to resist the handcuffing process, but PC Prettyman kept an arm firmly locked behind his back. "I'll show you the note she gave me to arrange our meeting." Dillon fumbled in his pocket with his free hand.

"See!" he said triumphantly, displaying the crumpled missive in front of the constable. "Handwritten, too."

"I gave one to every member of staff," explained Jackie in a broken whisper. "I had no idea he would behave like this."

PC Prettyman nodded in acknowledgement as he handcuffed Brankscome, but his brow furrowed with concern as he observed Jackie's predicament. "I am sorry you've had to endure this."

"I'm fine, thank you," but her pasty face belied her brave words.

"We've had our eye on this gentleman for some time. I regret we didn't act sooner to save you this distress, but it does provide concrete evidence for an investigation being conducted by colleagues in another force."

The arrival of Sgt Catchpole with the squad car and Doctor Roger Cooper with a paramedic meant that both Mr Brankscome and Jackie were dealt with appropriately.

It would be some time before Jackie and her staff learned the details or ramifications of that investigation.

Chapter Four

Inclement weather!

The news that Miss Cooper had been attacked at the school soon travelled across Newton Westerby and surrounding hamlets quicker than an express train. Of course, the story got embellished in the telling, to such an extent, that some heard it was a crime scene, so the school was closed for the foreseeable future.

"Noo such luck," grumbled Joss Brady to Ricky Saunders next morning after their mothers sent them off to school as usual and they found the gates open and the other pupils running around in the playground. "If there's noo one to tek our class we can play footy all day," the boys planned gleefully.

"Miss Cooper's nearly dead an' Mr Brankscome's been done fer murder."

"Hear they only juss got her to hospital in time."

"Nivver did like that chap."

"Too slimy and wouldn't look yew in the eye."

Gossip was rife throughout the community. Young and old discussed various options for dealing with the culprit and sorting out the dilemma the incident created for the school.

The absence of two teachers caused difficulties which required unprecedented steps to temporarily rectify the situation. Tim Draycott, as deputy-head, was legally bound to take responsibility for the school in Jackie Cooper's absence so called a meeting extraordinaire of staff and governors that evening.

With characteristic efficiency he rapidly formulated a plan of action though not before he had sent the chess club home, instructed Michelle Cook not to touch the head's office till the police had finished their examination and informed his wife he would be late home for dinner.

He sat at Mrs Scholes's desk in the general office, pen and paper to hand, bullet-pointing ideas and tasks. The easiest option would be to call in temporary agency staff, but he knew that would overstretch the school's budget. However, he was reluctant to add further pressure to Jackie's aggravations when she eventually returned. He rang Lord Edmund, as chair of governors, to acquaint him with the situation. They briefly discussed balancing the cost of agency staff with other possibilities.

"Aren't there a number of parents holding safeguarding checks who already assist in various capacities? I'm sure if they were approached one or two might be able to help as this is an emergency."

"That is one option. Mrs Prettyman is Nursery trained and frequently leads story time sessions for pre-schoolers and Reception at the library. Perhaps she would be willing to hold the sessions at school instead and so free Kerry Stafford to teach another year at that time. With Marianne Worsley or a parent helper in situ that should work well."

"Excellent idea. Miss Pedwardine seems the obvious choice to fill the teaching gap." Lord Edmund left his recommendation in the air, but Tim Draycott noted his comment intending to act upon it.

At the emergency meeting all suggestions were thrashed out. Most members of staff agreed with the proposals Tim presented and were prepared to be flexible apart from Tina Morehouse, who, angry at missing her amateur dramatic rehearsal that evening, emphatically refused to do more than she was contracted to do. "We need a replacement teacher ASAP not a hodgepodge."

"Mrs Scholes, will you kindly draft an advertisement to that effect. We will circulate it as far and wide as feasible," Tim instructed.

Following the emergency staff meeting Tim Draycott approached Jennifer Pedwardine about temporarily helping at the school.

"I am willing to fill any teaching gaps until such time as Miss Cooper is fit and able to return and resume her responsibilities, as long as I am not stepping on anyone's toes."

With relief he accepted her offer. As the recently retired head she was familiar with the school routine and knew most of the children.

Mrs Scholes, the school secretary, co-ordinated the revised timetable and temporary staff schedules which ensured smooth running of the school with the least disruption to the children's education as possible. RK Prettyman and the parents holding up to date safe-guarding certificates were acquainted with the situation and with their agreement and availability woven into the amended arrangements.

It had been decided to keep Jackie in hospital overnight, mainly for observation. The break in her arm was a nasty one and on examination it was discovered that when Mr Brankscome felled her to the ground, not only were her ribs bruised but she had hit the back of her head on the corner of the metal filing cabinet causing a gash which required stitches. So, there was concern that she might be suffering from concussion. However, the enforced rest gave her too much time to reflect on how she had landed in this predicament and how she was going to sort out staffing problems at school and raise the benchmark before the next inspection. *While I did not particularly like Dillon Brankscome, I had no idea he had developed such an obsessive fantasy relationship about me. I never gave him any reason to suppose I reciprocated his feelings. I always treated him, as I treat all the staff, on a professional level. He was a dreadful man and a shocking teacher. Whatever did Dan mean when he mentioned that Dillon was an imposter? Did he say imposter or impersonator? I can't remember. What am I going to do about that class? They have become so unruly while he has been their teacher. I can hardly ask Emma to come in full time she has too much responsibility at the Stores. I need to turn things around. I must find a solu..."*

When Jackie began thrashing about on the bed the night nurse came over to her bedside. "Jackie, you really do need to rest and give your body time to heal. I have something here the doctor has prescribed that will ease the discomfort and help you sleep." Within a short time, the breathing of her patient indicated a relaxed slumber had claimed her.

Jacqueline Cooper, middle daughter of Billy and Pauline Cooper who kept the butcher's shop in the village, was an energetic young lady, 5'7" in height, had an enviable slim figure and nutmeg brown hair which she wore pulled back into a French pleat for school.

"Very school marmish," teased her sisters Miranda and Hilary. "But, very practical and suitable for my position as head," Jackie retorted. She had always wanted to teach, to broaden minds of children to the world around them.

As a child she ran carefree along the beach near her home, pigtails flying behind her in the wind. She would plunge into the North Sea in summer months when others would only timidly dip their toes in at the water's edge. She brought home all sorts of creatures, crabs with missing claws or seagulls with damaged wings and even a beached baby seal and nurture them until they were well enough to be set free again. Her father helped build cages and pens in the back yard behind the butcher's shop where they lived, whenever the need arose.

So, carefree in attitude and caring in nature, Jackie was inquisitive, always asking questions, wanting to know how everything worked and why. If her father did not know the answer, he would find someone in the village who did.

Jackie was quick with figures and so keen to help in the wooden payment booth situated in the corner of the butcher's shop between the wall and the serving counter. From early childhood she revelled in that little triangular space with its hatch window for customers to pass through their money to pay their bills, an intriguing relic from her great grandfather's day. She loved organising the shelves above the counter so that all the paperwork was kept neat and tidy. There were no discrepancies in the change she gave to customers and her figures in the account books were always accurate. Her father decided when everything needed to be computerised, to be in line with his suppliers, Jackie was to be the one who taught her mother the rudiments of the 'contraption', as Pauline named it, rather than the other way round. "Computing seems to be a sixth sense to youngsters of today," remarked Pauline to one of the customers when they were discussing changing trends as she weighed out some braising steak.

It seemed there was no end to Jackie's insatiable appetite for learning. Her father was glad when Jennifer Pedwardine took Jackie under her wing and channelled her learning in a positive direction. It was a foregone conclusion that Jackie would leave home and go to university but in the sixth form she fell in love. No one took her feelings seriously. "Just a schoolgirl crush," "You'll get over it," "Concentrate on your studies," was the advice that was thrown at her. But she was adamant. She was in love.

Her aptitude for figures gained her a place at Cambridge University to study Mathematics but she really did not want to go. Although interested in her immediate world and workings of things around her Jackie was at heart a home loving person and had no desire to venture further afield. The pull of her heart towards Lord Edmund's son almost made her turn down the place offered to her. In consternation Billy rang the primary school head teacher for advice. Miss Pedwardine arranged for Jackie to call in to her office one afternoon when she got off the bus bringing her home to the village from the sixth form college in the city.

"God has given you this gift of learning. Do not throw it away. It would be selfish and unworthy of you not to take this opportunity to get your degree and qualify to impart the knowledge you gain to other young enquiring minds. Children just like you were, infused with curiosity and inquisitiveness. What an exciting prospect you have before you to develop your skills then pray how best you can use them."

Jackie started to interrupt but Miss Pedwardine raised her hand to silence her before she could begin. "I know, at the moment your heart says otherwise, but if what you feel is real it will endure and in the time of separation, deepen, but if it is a passing phase, it will fizzle out and you'll wonder what all the fuss was about. In any case, now that Eddie's got his degree, he needs to put his mind to learning the business ready for when he takes over at the helm when Lord Edmund eventually decides to retire. So, each of you has something important to focus on which involves your future."

Jackie looked up at her mentor. "I respect your wise counsel, Miss Pedwardine. You have always been a great encourager not only when I was in primary school but all through my secondary school years and while I've been at the sixth form college. You were strict but straight with me. I appreciate that, now."

"You didn't always." Jennifer laughed.

"That's true, I didn't. But I've always known that your advice was sound and for my own good."

"Take it a semester at a time. Cambridge is not so far away. We have the postal service, but don't spend all day scribbling when you should be studying. You both have mobiles but set times for your calls and limit their duration, so they do not interrupt the flow of your studies or Eddie's work schedules."

Jackie nodded. Miss Pedwardine's reasoning made perfect sense, in her head, but oh, how her heart said otherwise.

However, that evening she and Eddie met up on the beach, talked through their feelings and made plans. Jackie went to Cambridge and Eddie got to grips with the workings of the family firm. They kept in touch frequently and met up as often as possible by arranging to be at home in the village at the same time. She gained her degree and he gained experience and knowledge of the company founded by his great, great, great grandfather. Jackie returned to Newton Westerby when she completed her teacher training and accepted a job in the nursery/reception year at the village school. Eddie came home to live at the Manor, had an office there where he was able to work on his computer, commuting to the factory in West Yorkshire at least twice a week and travelling the country, and sometimes abroad, meeting business contacts and customers.

In the intervening years, their relationship matured, and love deepened, and on Jackie's birthday Eddie proposed. But two days later as Eddie was riding his motor bike to the factory after meeting with a client he was in a head on collision and killed outright. A drink drive accident which his mother never got over. The sentence meted out to the perpetrator was paltry and in no way compensated for the loss of her son.

Jackie, too, was devastated. She felt her broken heart would never mend. Her personality seemed to change overnight. She clammed up, would not socialize, but concentrated solely on work. Joy and light were gone from her life. Even as she struggled with the "Why?" God extended His unfailing love towards her, but she brushed it aside.

When Jennifer Pedwardine retired as school head Jackie, who had by now become deputy head and teaching year 4 was appointed head teacher. As years passed, although she mixed more with family and close friends her focus was entirely on the wellbeing and education of children in her care. She attended church and went through the motions of worship only because it was expected of her as head of a church school.

She was still angry with God for taking so fine a young man as Eddie de Vessey who had much to offer, to her, the church, the village, the family firm and society as a whole. Her heart was hardened and unreceptive to the father-love of God. He had deprived her of the joys and fulfilment of married life, therefore, she wanted nothing more to do with Him. "If You're in control, why didn't You prevent the accident?" she shouted at God.

Her life became a monotony of work and sleep, sleep and work till a few years later when she was in her office preparing for the commencement of a new school year following her leave of absence after the incident with Dillon Brankscome, seemingly, out of the blue, a new colourful member of staff walked through the door of the school, accompanied by her cousin, Stephen, laden with a bundle of cases.

"I found this delightful young lady at the bus stop looking for the school," he explained with a grin.

"Hi, I'm Constance Joy Foster." A broad beam filled the face of the person accompanying him, parted full lips revealed gleaming teeth that sparkled like jewels. She dropped down the suitcase she was carrying and rushed forward with arms spread open wide, the bag upon her shoulder falling to her elbow, as she embraced the startled head then proceeded to kiss her on both cheeks in greeting.

"I have come! Where do I go?" The newcomer looked round eagerly. She pushed the errant bag back onto her shoulder, picked up her case and prepared to walk wherever Jackie directed her.

Stunned, it took a moment for Jackie to regain her equilibrium. *Oh, my, it's the replacement teacher. I'd forgotten she was arriving today and that she was from the Caribbean.*

She reached out her hand in welcome. "Hello, I'm Jaqueline Cooper, head teacher. Welcome to Newton Westerby Primary School. The children do not return to school till Wednesday. Tomorrow is a staff training day, but I can show you your classroom."

"Oh, dat is good."

"I'll leave you two to get acquainted." Stephen smiled at the newcomer. "Hope to see you around."

"Yes, dat will be good. Thanks for your assistance."

"You are very welcome. 'Bye," Stephen raised his arm in farewell and exited the door.

"Excuse me a moment, Miss Foster," Jackie darted after Stephen.

"Stephen, do you think you could get some of the gang together for an impromptu supper to welcome Miss Foster to Newton Westerby."

"Sure, Jack, when and where?" He addressed his cousin with the shortened version of her name that remained from his toddler days when he couldn't pronounce Jacqueline.

"Sevenish, tomorrow evening, preferably. Venue will depend on who's available."

"So, six or so, meet at your place. Anymore, I will chat to Mum or Aunt Bernice. That, OK?"

"Thanks, Stephen, you're a pal. I'll ring Jilly about some eats."

"I get the feeling this is all rather unexpected."

"Not exactly. I was aware a new teacher had been appointed. Tim Draycott, in consultation with Lord Edmund, oversaw the interview process while I was off sick. They did keep me informed by sending me transcripts of all the interviews and asking my opinion, but I've been so busy I had forgotten that she was due today."

"Nor that she was coming from overseas?"

"It slipped my mind."

"The village is good at welcoming strangers, so we'll make sure she soon feels at home. Where will she stay?"

"I guess the governors will have sorted that out. It's not as if we're short of accommodation. I'll make a few calls."

"See you tomorrow, then."

CHAPTER FIVE

Chilly Winds!

The following morning Connie was introduced to the other members of staff at the Primary school. They each welcomed her, some with open arms, others with reservations.

"Hi, Tina Morehouse." A bangled arm was thrust towards the newcomer. "Glad you could make it. Hope you've got spunk. You'll need it in this God-forsaken place."

"Hello, I am Connie Foster. Very pleased to be here. I find de Good Lord, He is everywhere."

"Don't take any notice of Tina's nonsense this is a lovely village and a super school to work in, with smashing kids to teach. There are challenges but the rewards are worth it. I'm Kerry Stafford, by the way." Her warm, cheery smile was returned by a radiant beam from Connie.

Josie Beckett took her arm and led her towards some chairs.

"Welcome, my dear, we've had a rough, few months and are so pleased you've come to ease the strain, though I'm not too sure how you are going to fit in."

Connie beamed. "De Good Lord, He told me to come so, I came."

Some eyebrows were raised, and tittering circled the room. Tim Draycott cleared his throat rather noisily and drew the session to order. He formally welcomed Miss Foster to Newton Westerby Primary School and introduced those present who had not yet spoken to her. Throughout the day she had opportunity to interact with everyone and gradually became acquainted with her new colleagues. If they were surprised at the choice of Dillon Brankscome's replacement no one voiced a comment. Kerry stayed close by and explained unfamiliar procedures to her. Emma Cooper also kept a watchful eye on her, but Connie seemed able to hold her own joining in the friendly banter with her distinctive repartee. Her openness and naïve charm endeared her to them. She also learned much about the differences in teaching between the two countries. But, frequently throughout the day she reminded herself that she had set out on this adventure knowing that there would be hurdles to cross and challenges to overcome and was prepared to meet them believing she was in this place in answer to prayer. Initially, she thought in answer to her own prayers but as she listened to staff chat throughout the day of events at the school, in the not-too-distant past, it seemed some felt she was an answer to their prayers.

"Your predecessor was a really bad lot."

De Good Lord knows what He is at, so I'll trust Him, she wrote to Mumma later that afternoon as she penned a note to her family. She described her flight, her first impression of *this new land*, the manner her fellow schoolteachers had received her and the house where she was staying which was so very different to her home in Barbados.

50

When Stephen Cooper called for Connie that evening, she had already showered and dressed impeccably in one of the two best dresses she had brought with her, sleeveless with a flared skirt. White open-toed sling back sandals on bare feet completed her ensemble. As she opened the door Stephen saw before him a brightly coloured vision of yellow, orange and red topped with shining eyes, a beaming smile revealing gleaming, even teeth and a white, light weight cardigan draped around her shoulders.

"Hi, you look nice."

"Thank you, Stephen. See, I remembered your name."

Stephen laughed but was perturbed that the new teacher might catch a chill in the cooling night-time air of an early September evening so asked, "Do you have a coat or a fleece? The wind is getting up and it already feels a little nippy out here."

"No, I only have de jacket I travelled in."

"I should bring it. The temperature will be even cooler when we come home. Can't have you catching cold when you've so recently arrived here."

As he stood in the hallway waiting for Connie to return Stephen reflected that he would have to mention Connie's lack of warm clothing to Jackie or Emma or perhaps the vicar's wife. *I am surprised no one warned her when she was offered the job that England is colder than the Caribbean, even at this time of year.*

After his conversation with Jackie yesterday Stephen had managed to contact quite a few friends who happily agreed to come to Green Pastures to meet the new school mistress. The young people were always glad of any excuse to have a get-together and Bernice Durrant liked nothing better than hosting events of any sort, but social gatherings of young people always cheered her heart.

By the time he and Connie walked down the lane Annette and Nicky Andaman had joined them and quite an animated crowd greeted them as they arrived at the Durrant home. Bernice in her inimitable style ensured that Connie was comfortable and well fed throughout the evening, everyone circulated and had opportunity to chat with her. There was much teasing and laughter as Connie was persuaded to sample buffet food with which she was very unfamiliar.

"In Barbados buffet is a type of banana." She explained at one stage which caused great hilarity.

Connie was pleased to meet up again with Stephen Cooper, Jackie's cousin. He seemed a nice young man and she was delighted to learn he was a cricket enthusiast.

"Do you play cricket?"

"Yes, I'm currently captain of the village first X1."

"Would you be willing to lend a hand with an after-school activity if I were to set one up?"

"You know anything about cricket?"

"Of course! All my brothers are named for Barbadian cricketers."

"No!" Came the exclamation of disbelief from most corners of the room.

"In my country nearly all de boys, and some girls, play cricket at all times and in all places. One of my brothers aims to play for our island team. He already plays for de youth team. In fact, it is de ambition of most Bajan boys to be good enough to be chosen to play for de West Indies team."

"Can you keep score?"

"My Daddy made sure I could keep score before I went to school."

Before Connie had finished her sentence all the young men eagerly gravitated to where she was seated, crouching, kneeling or sitting at her feet.

"Miss Foster, are you free on Saturday afternoon?"

"Now, dat is a hard question to answer."

"Why is that?"

"I am so newly come I do not know what my schedule is for dat day."

Stephen looked round the room for his cousin. "Jack," he shouted, "have you anything planned for Miss Foster on Saturday?"

"No, of course not."

"Miss Foster, you are free. Would you like to keep score for our side on Saturday?"

"Gladly I'll keep score. Will you help me with de school children?" The room erupted in laughter.

"You drive a hard bargain, Miss Foster." And so, she enlisted the help of Stephen and his pals from the cricket club to teach a class, she had yet to meet, the rudiments of cricket. "The season is drawing to a close in this country, but we'll do what we can now, and start afresh when the new season opens next April," Stephen explained.

Connie clapped her hands gleefully. "Oh, dat is good."

"By the way, the match this week takes place in the village and starts at 1:00 o'clock. Now we are into September matches commence earlier in order to get play in before dusk, so someone will call for you at a quarter past twelve."

"I hope you've got some warm clothes, my dear," said Bernice with concern, "that pavilion is like a wind tunnel and can be pretty chilly even when the sun is shining."

"Oh!" Exclaimed Connie dubiously.

As was usual at many of the village get-togethers the evening ended with a singsong around the piano. When they all gravitated to the other room, as Justin commenced playing, Stephen grabbed Emma and Jackie and whispered for their ears alone, "She hasn't got a coat and I suspect no other warm clothing."

The girls looked at one another, nodded and whispered back, "Leave it with us."

Listening to the young folks sing always delighted Bernice's heart but hers were not the only eyes to light up when suddenly Connie's contralto voice resonated around the room.

Justin stopped playing, turned round and smiled at Connie. "Are you free Thursday evening?" Before she could reply Stephen shouted, "Jack, is Miss Foster free Thursday evening?"

"Of course."

"Miss Foster, you're free Thursday evening, would you like to come to choir rehearsal? I am sure Adam would be thrilled to meet you."

"Oh, you have a choir," Connie beamed and clapped her hands with joy. "How I love to sing. I sing in our church choir in Barbados."

"Good, someone will call for you about 6.45pm."

The lady who hosted the evening commented that I would not remember everyone at first, but she hoped

there would be someone I would gel with and, as you see, I have found some cricket pals already. And I am going to church choir practice so I will make some more friends.

They were all so warm and friendly, Connie continued to write in her letter home. *I think I am going to like it here, but it is too cold.*

The remembrance of talk about cricket and the easy banter between the young people, whom she was discovering were mostly related in one way or another, brought a lump to Connie's throat. How she missed her family, her brothers' teasing, Mumma's cooking, Daddy's words of encouragement and the girly chats with Jacinth, the walks and supper meals shared with Clyde, her twin. The crashing waves of the inhospitable, angry grey North Sea onto the shingle beach was not a patch on the enticing silver sand and warm azure blue of the Caribbean Sea. Already she longed for home, and she had only been in this new country a few days.

Connie's greatest comfort came in prayer, wrapping her in a blanket of assurance.

I will trust de Good Lord to take care of them over there as I believe He will take care of me over here.

However, as she settled down to sleep the silence almost unnerved her. Apart from the distant waves crashing on the shore there were no other sounds, none of the familiar night-time sounds of home. She tossed to and fro on the bed that felt burdensome and bulky with the unfamiliar weight of a duvet pressing down on her. *Lord grant me peace and joy in this new place. Teach me your will and guide me in my task.*

Her introduction to year 5 on the first day of the Autumn term did not go without a hitch. Dialect was the biggest problem until she identified Joss Brady as the most vociferous voice in class and Daniel Catton the most articulate and had them interpret her words to them and theirs to her. In a short space of time her new pupils did discover her clapping hands meant silence and nothing would proceed until everyone complied. That proved the hardest lesson to learn and the most difficult to implement in a class of children predominantly used to having their own way.

"She doan't shout, dew she?" observed Jessica.

"Noo, an' she be allus laughin'."

"Oi like her."

"She be strict."

"But she dew say 'er words pretty funny."

"She'll get used to ow'n ways."

"She'll dew."

Connie was not slow to mix with the village community. In her first week, outside of school hours, she was out and about in the village getting acquainted with the parents of her pupils, her neighbours, the shopkeepers and their customers and anyone else who would stop and chat with her. As they slowly got to know her, Connie's bubbly personality soon won over the hearts of most people in the village.

"There's a beam on her face every time she comes into the Stores that would outshine a Cheshire cat," commented Rosalie Andaman, the village shop manager. "She doesn't often buy anything, but I find she is quite fascinated by the variety of food we stock that is different to what she is used to in Barbados. She is always asking questions and spends a lot of time comparing prices."

"Her laughter is infectious," giggled Rosie Jenner. "When she comes into the Tea Rooms she stops by each table and chats to whoever is sitting there and soon there are ripples of laughter throughout the whole room. Even my old Aunt Jenner's stern face manages to crack into what might pass as a smile when Connie speaks with her." Ripples of laughter floated between the shop aisles. They were all familiar with Mrs Jenner's grumpy temperament. "Aunt's belligerent attitude also seems to be softening towards Miss Foster and she's no longer muttering about her going back to where she came from."

"She's an absolute joy to have in the house," Jennifer Pedwardine complimented. The school governors had decided that the Caribbean schoolteacher ought to be billeted for a time in an English home. "Just until she becomes acclimatised and accustomed to the English way of life." Although a holiday cottage let had been set aside for Connie, should she decide she would prefer to live independently, Jennifer was pleased to offer accommodation and welcomed the company now that she was no longer required to teach at the school since Jackie was back at the helm.

However, for the present Connie was content to let the arrangement stand because it enabled her to concentrate on adapting to the differences in school preparations, policies and practices without concerning herself with all that running a household in a foreign country entailed.

In fact, with each passing day, she was more than glad that the governors had made such a decision because, as she had anticipated, there was much to adjust to not least the vagaries of the English weather. "I never know when I wake up each morning whether it's going to be hot or cold, dark or light. In Barbados daylight comes at 6am and darkness occurs at 6pm every day of de year. It is always hot, so I wear de same sort of clothes every day. Here I do not know what to wear because de weather fluctuates, not just from day to day but in de same day! I am so thankful someone attended to my needs so that I can be warm on de cold days. I have no idea how to use your heating. We do not need it at home. I can plug in a fan to keep cool, but I do not know where to begin with a boiler, thermostat or radiator."

Her effervescent nature spilled over into the classroom. At first this was a problem because it created indiscipline amongst the unruly but gradually, she learned ways of dealing with this in order to bring out the best in her pupils. "Ma Mumma would not approve of such behaviour. Would your Mumma?"

The children were fascinated by her darker skin, very curly hair and obviously vastly different English pronunciation. Some mimicked at first, but she found ways of dealing with this by getting them to focus on something else that was different like food, geography, history, climate and sport. Cricket was a Barbados passion, in her family and community, so she endeavoured to foster an interest in cricket amongst her pupils knowing that she was going to get help from the cricket team.

Her foray on the cricket ground on Saturday afternoon was as successful as her inclusion in the church choir rehearsal on Thursday.

"We're really pleased to welcome you to Newton Westerby and hope you will soon feel a part of our community." Adam said before the commencement of choir practice. "Don't ever feel isolated or alone. We're one happy family…"

"Mostly related, anyway," someone muttered.

"…and you are always welcome in all our homes and at the Tea Rooms. The Village Stores, as Lord Edmund has so frequently said, is the hub of our village and since Emma has opened that marvellous place upstairs, we meet there on many occasions for coffee and conversation."

"Don't forget Bible Study as well, on Wednesday evenings."

On Sunday morning she accompanied Miss Pedwardine to church and while Connie revelled in worshipping the Lord in such a beautiful setting the congregation basked in the beauty of a voice that filled the space between pews and rafters in a joyous song of praise.

Rev Hugh Darnell was aware of the newcomer in their midst and although he had no desire to cause embarrassment, he wanted to ensure Connie knew she was welcome to their church family. So, when he announced the choir following the offertory prayer, he acknowledged her presence. "It is good that the love of our Lord spans all boundaries including the miles across oceans and we can be one in Christ Jesus. We are pleased Miss Constance Foster has come to share Christian fellowship with us." Spontaneous applause broke out led by the younger members of the Catton and Jenner families. Connie beamed. Stood and waved an arm to all before her. *Dear Lord, it is good that I am here in Your presence this day!* With a flick of his wrist Adam indicated that the choir should stand. As one they joined Connie. When the cadences of the canticle reached out across the sanctuary Adam knew he had before him a gem, a priceless gem. What a voice! What a joy!

But Connie sang as only she knew how. The last chord died away. The congregation held their breath in awe. Never had the choir sang so well. They took their seats. In the hush that followed, fisherman Mark Bemment, on shore for a few days, moved from the baritone section to the lectern to read the Gospel lesson. *My, what a big man!* Connie thought. Unaware of her scrutiny Mark read on, his rich voice resonating throughout the whole church with clarity, adding depth of meaning to the text.

Hugh rose in the pulpit. "How in touch with God are you? Have you spoken with Him today?" Silence! "Have you spoken to the person sitting next to you this morning?" A buzz of conversation rippled around the church. "Good, that's how it should be in our village each day. In our conversation and actions, in every home, in our workplace, at school, down the street, the shop, the common, the quay, on the sea, the playing field, on the bus, everywhere we are, there should be a continuous hum of communication between Newton Westerby and Heaven.

"What stops you from being in touch with God who loves you? The Bible tells us it is sin and unbelief that locks us away from God and all the promises he has for us in His Word. Why miss out on what God wants you to have? We can be very self-centred, arrogant people at times not allowing God a foothold in our lives. Paul

writes about the 'sin that so easily besets us.' How do
we deal with that sin? I am talking about that which
separates us from God in order to open the door to
God's blessings?

"Sin is deceitful because it is of Satan, and if you give
in to it continually you harden yourself to God's grace –
that which God gives so freely when we least deserve it.

"Sin tends to attack the individual, so everyone of
you must examine his or her own faith. Are you keeping
your faith fresh? What is causing you to turn away from
Jesus Christ? Why are you neglecting your daily precious
quiet moments with Him? When did you last come to
the Lord for release from that which binds your heart
and ask for His guidance and strength?

"Pray! Pray so that the thread of communication
might be restored.

"Pray for release from that which restricts you and
pray for renewal in your spirit through Him whose
grace knows no limits. In the name of Jesus Christ, by
the blessing of God, the Father Almighty and through
the power of the Holy Spirit, Amen!

"We'll stand to sing 'Tell out my soul'."

"My word that packed a punch."

"I wonder who that was intended for?"

As is the wont of congregations instead of applying
the message of the sermon to their own hearts they
considered its application to others. But one member of
the congregation knew to whom the vicar's words were
directed but she slinked away through the back door of
the church not wishing to meet anyone or address the
issues they raised in her heart. Yet, Connie was not the
only one to notice the head teacher was missing from
the coffee fellowship in the church hall after the service.

CHAPTER SIX

Season of fruitfulness!

As the Autumn term progressed Connie began to get itchy feet. She had never spent so much time inside four walls. Despite the cooling winds and lowering temperatures she bravely continued to take a walk around the village every day, now warmly clad. Emma had taken on the responsibility of ensuring that Connie had suitable clothes for English weather. She had spoken with Penny Darnell, the vicar's wife, Aunt Bernice and Trixie, her mother-in-law, about the problem and between them they had been able to provide warmer clothing without causing embarrassment yet ensuring Connie would not suffer ill-effects because of the contrariness of the English climate.

The visitor enjoyed discovering new aspects of the location in which she was living, so vastly different to what she was used to. *There are no verandas, and everyone closes their front door and locks them as soon as they pass through them, Mumma,* she wrote in one of her letters to the family. *The houses all have inside stairs. The beds are on the upper floor, so everyone sleeps at the top of the house. It is eerily quiet at night, apart from the crashing waves. You would miss the crickets singing and frogs croaking. I have not seen any chickens in the road or monkeys in gardens, though I have been told there are chickens on the farms. I have encountered a few dogs being taken for walks on what the people call 'The Common' and cats in some gardens but mostly they seem to be indoors. The seagulls make a din when fishing boats sail into harbour and on a farm nearby I have seen horses, cows and pigs.*

There are four or five small shops. One sells old books and houses a woodwork business in what was once a blacksmiths shop, though I have yet to find out what actually took place in there. Another is a butcher's shop which sells only meat. The butcher and his wife are the parents of Jackie, the headteacher. The biggest shop sells all the food you need to eat. It also has a tearoom upstairs where they sell very nice English cakes. You would really like them, Joel, all sweet and gooey! There is a Doctor's office which the English call a surgery, with a pharmacy built at the side, and down some steps near the church is another office where you go if you want to rent a house for a holiday. Two other shops are referred to as the flower shop and the hairdressers, but they look empty and unused to me. The fishermen sell their fish from a shack by the harbour, different types of fish to those we eat. A van comes round sometimes in the evening selling cooked fish with chips. Not at all like your flying fish or monk fish, Mumma, lacks your special seasoning.

The changes took some getting used to. She added a few lines about her activities in a continuous letter at the end of each day and planned to post it off every week to her family so that they might feel a part of her English life, so very different to what they knew as normal.

She was delighted with the garden her hostess had developed and enjoyed exploring the different garden 'rooms' Miss Pedwardine had constructed. *It is more like Andromeda Botanical Gardens than a normal house garden,* she penned in her letter journal. She sat pensively looking through the window. *How I would love to introduce my pupils to this enchanting setting. Such composition and order would surely instil a love of the natural environment and foster a desire* to *grow flowers and food for themselves. The lady I am staying with grows* vegetables *which she picks and cooks every day.*

Connie was pleased to be invited to participate in church activities, the choir and Bible study and house groups. *I am making lots of new friends at these groups and through them I am learning about the English life. Daddy, you would like the Doctors, a father and son. The father is known as Doctor John and his wife, Trixie, is a chiropodist, who visits clients in their homes. Their daughter, Jansy is the practice nurse, married to Dave, a fisherman. Stephen, the youngest son is the young man who met me off the bus when I first arrived. He is so kind and such fun. You would get on well with him, Garry, as he is village cricket captain and he and some of the team are going to teach cricket to my school class. Their eldest son is Doctor Roger who works one day a week at Norwich Hospital as well as the village surgery. He is married to Emma who only teaches part time at school as she also owns the Village Stores and Tea Rooms. It is taking me a long time to remember all the family connections but as I meet the same people many times at different events, I am beginning to get it straight in my head. I am invited to people's homes for meals. Not the same as yours, Mumma, quite, quite different! Some I like, some are ugh!*

One afternoon at the close of the school day Connie strolled down the lane towards the village shop in company with Emma.

"I guess things are very different here to what you're used to in Barbados?"

"Yes, there really is no comparison, architecture of de houses, de weather, food, money, de price of things, de sea, de beach, the list is endless. Even language. The children put me right when I make a mistake with my pronunciation. All so different. People are different and yet de same everywhere."

"Tell me about differences in school."

"I cannot get used to being confined."

"Whatever do you mean."

Connie proceeded to explain what happened in Barbados.

"Every day each class has opportunity to spend some time out of doors."

"Really!"

"Yes! It is built into the timetable so there are no clashes. Some days I take de children to the beach for swimming or to Miami Beach in Oistins for a geography lesson to show the increasing coastline, which has happened in my lifetime. The children are intrigued that de huge Casuarina trees growing there were newly planted when I was just a little girl. There is also a very distinct line which shows where de sea used to lash up against a wall."

"Oh, we have areas along our coast where that has happened, too, but we also have huge chunks of the coastline, which is receding, where homes are being lost to the sea."

"How dreadful, I must go and see that and take some photographs to use when I return home."

"We'll organize a time to take you. Erosion has occurred along the coast both to the north and south of Newton Westerby. Our own village has also been ravaged over time by the sea so that New Town East-by-the-Sea, Newton Easterby in local parlance, is now in the sea."

"Really?"

"Yes, truly."

"Sounds like a fascinating history lesson."

"We'll have to arrange one", Emma laughed. "In the meantime, I will search for the photos that Dad took of Alex and I walking on the beach at Easton Bavents just days after one such a storm. A house was still hanging precariously on the side of the cliff."

"Oh, my!" Connie clasped a hand across her mouth in horror.

"How else does a Barbados school engage with the outdoors?"

"We will go to Speightstown Museum in the northwest of de island or one of the few remaining plantations for a history lesson about the slave trade and growing sugar cane. Sometimes we go to the former English garrison and learn about life when Barbados was an English colony or visit Bridgetown to explore an area that has more recently been flooded, called the Careenage, and the nearby civic buildings that are built from coral."

"For such a small country you do have many fascinating places of interest to explore in connexion with the school curriculum. We have what we call field trips but usually only one class at a time, once a term, due to financial constraints."

"We, too, have similar restrictions. At least once during a child's years at primary school they have opportunity to visit de underground Harrison's cave in St. Thomas."

"That sounds exciting."

"It is believed it was first found in 1700's but was only rediscovered in 1970 by Sorensen of Denmark and Mason from Barbados. Much work had to be done before it opened to the public in 1981."

"I guess the children find that interesting."

"Yes, it is the highlight of their school year. But most of the time we do more ordinary things. For instance, each day we have out-of-doors activities that are completely free, such as, storytelling, personal reading and essay writing time, news and conversation lessons are held in an outdoor classroom in de school grounds. There are no walls just a roof to protect us from the heat and glare of de sun."

"Not really possible with our inclement weather," Emma chuckled.

"But surely, despite de weather conditions, at least one outdoor activity could take place each week that doesn't cost a cent."

"You write up a plan, organize it, that is, health and safety and risk assessment, then present it to the Head and Governors. See what they say, you've got nothing to lose."

"Right, I will."

"In the meantime, please come for supper tomorrow evening and meet some more of the young folk. They're wanting to get to know you."

"Mmm, that will be so nice."

"About a quarter-to-seven be alright?"

"Yes, thank you."

"Miranda and RK will call for you. I think you met them at church though you may not remember anyone's name yet."

"You are correct, names and faces are still a jumble. I have been concentrating on getting to know my pupils. I do remember you are married to Doctor Roger and I met your sister at church and have seen her with a little girl in the garden next door."

"Alex and Bethany," Emma chuckled.

"I do like your vicar, though. He said he would come to visit me."

"Hugh Darnell is a good, godly man and if he said he will do that, you can be sure he will. His wife Penny is also a lovely person. She runs the pharmacy. They have two children, Ellie, who's at College studying interior design and Gareth, who's just gone up to secondary school."

Over the next few days Connie gave much thought to possible outdoor activities she could engage in with her class. With this thought in her mind, she strolled down the lane one afternoon at the close of the school day, passed the former bakery which was now Miss Pedwardine's home, 'Bakers', where she was staying. *I really must ask Miss Pedwardine if I might introduce the children to such a charming garden, with its beds and borders, shrubs and trees, nooks and crannies, after Christmas. Perhaps in the Spring she will demonstrate how to grow things to eat.* Connie did not stop at the house but continued along the lane. Despite the biting north-easterly winds and fluctuating temperatures she still endeavoured to take a walk each day around the village to discover the delights of a location that was so vastly different to the one she was used to. The riverside and harbour fascinated her, and she enjoyed watching Mark Bemment land his catch earlier in the week but generally the sea and beach were a disappointment. She did miss the fine, silver sand, blue sea and warm sun of home.

She waved to Bethany who was playing in the garden of the house next door to the old bakery and called a greeting to Alex Castleton who was unpegging washing from the line. Connie paused at the Castleton's garden gate.

"You leave de washing out all day?" Earlier that morning Connie had seen Alex pegging washing on the line when she left for school.

"Oh yes," Alex replied as she bundled clothes into her arms, "and pray that the weather stays fine and the wind blows the clothes dry, especially at this time of year." She looked up to the sky and nodded to indicate black clouds developing overhead.

"At home washing dries in what Mumma calls, 'de blink of an eye'."

"What a blessing that must be. We are not so fortunate. It's going to pour soon."

"Not a quick shower?"

"Oh, no."

Alex called to Bethany and together they dashed indoors as drops of rain started to fall. "I hope you're suitably attired," she called from the shelter of the porch.

Connie chuckled, pulled her coat more closely round her, as the rain increased, and quickened her steps towards the Village Stores. She browsed shelves while she waited for Rosalie to finish serving a customer then took opportunity to chat over the possibility of bringing the children in for a lesson on the value and use of money. *I will learn about English money, too.*

Pleased with the outcome of their conversation Connie skipped up the stairs to the Tea Rooms hoping to be in time for afternoon tea before it closed. She chatted to Rosie, passed the time of day with Mrs Durrant and had the Catton children in fits of giggles. She chose a table by a window that gave her a view of the sea, a grey, gloomy sea pounding angrily onto the shore hugely dissimilar to the calm, clear, blue Caribbean Sea she could see from the veranda at home. Despite the contrast, movement of water was an attraction to her.

While waiting for her order to be served Connie made notes in her diary. She had several ideas for activities for each week following the October half-term including story-time in the library with RK, a visit to the harbour master's office to learn about his job, brass rubbing in the church, making Christmas cookies in the village bakery with Jilly Briggs and Christmas decorations with ladies of the WI in the church hall. She had learned that in English winter months outdoor activities necessarily happened indoors, partially at least, but next week she planned to take the class on an Autumn exploratory ramble. *I must also make enquiries of Stephen about opening times of the village museum.* Not simply for a class visit but for more personal reasons.

Chapter Seven

Autumnal breezes!

The following week, permission and all safeguards in place, year 5 set out on a country walk suitably clothed in hats, scarves and welly boots. They ambled towards the newly created nature reserve in the centre of the village at the bottom of the gardens of the recently restored cottages which back onto the eastern side of the de Vessey estate.

As the class made their way passed Kezia's Book Shop they spotted Adam Catton up a ladder cleaning an upstairs window. He shook his wash leather in greeting.

"That's my Dad," pointed out Daniel proudly.

Some of the children called out to Stephen Cooper, proprietor of the book and woodwork shop, who was standing in the doorway and waved to acknowledge their calls.

"Tread carefully," Connie called out as they traversed the cobbled lane to the side of the shop premises. This was a new surface to her.

"Look, Miss," pointed Keir Jenner. Connie followed his finger.

"What is it?"

"It's the old smithy where Mrs Cooper's great, great grandad worked when he was farrier to the horses on the de Vessey estate."

Connie was none the wiser so looked to one of her parent helpers for the day, Thomas Cook's Mum, Michelle.

"Thass true. Emma's ancestor, George Kemp, was a blacksmith, amongst other things. He shoed all the horses in the area as well as those on the estate. These buildings were discovered about two years ago when a derelict, overgrown area in the centre of the village was cleared," Michelle explained.

"Dat sounds an exciting project."

"It was. Lots of the villagers got involved. Much was unearthed about the history of the ancestors of our village including a number of old properties."

"We helped fill one of the skips," volunteered Daniel.

"Stephen Cooper has displayed a lot of the artefacts in the newly created museum."

"Oh, that I must see."

"Can we go now, Miss?"

"No, we will plan that for another day. We will continue our nature walk today. Keep your eyes open for something to draw or paint or can be placed on the nature table."

Connie turned to Michelle. "Does the museum only display recent findings?"

"No, Stephen be endeavouring to collect as much material as he can about people and property over the years. But he be such a busy person it will take a long time to gather all the information. He's hoping some of the older college students will be interested enough in the history of their village to give him a hand."

They reached the end of the cobbled lane and turned left into the reserve entrance.

"My Dad helped make this," quipped Ricky.

"Well, my Dad manages it, now," boasted Joss.

"An' my Dad helps Lord Edmund look after it," added Jess.

"Your fathers must have important jobs on Lord Edmund's farm," commented Connie.

"Oh noo, the farm doan't belong to Lord Edmund, the Beckingsdales have Manor Farm."

"Lord Edmund has the estate."

"Mrs Beckingsdale is Lord Edmund's youngest sister."

"An', Mrs Durrant be his oldest sister," chirped in Jess.

"Mrs Gill is his other sister but she's abroad."

"Mr Gill be a spy for the government."

"I see!" But Connie did not see at all. She was still struggling with all the village familial relationships. Even though in Barbados she was related to many on the island she was finding it difficult to remember the relational links between the English village families.

"Mr Gill works for the government," Michelle explained quietly. "He be a diplomat overseas."

Connie nodded. Ahead of her was a muddy trail through the copse which looked as though it was paved with gold. Small triangular shaped leaves drifted gently from the silver birch trees in front of them as a gentle breeze blew the yellow coins down to add layers to the carpet beneath their feet. They mingled with the russets and reds from other trees that seemed, in contrast, to gleam like jewels. Connie was enchanted. Bending to pick one up she noticed it was not pure yellow.

"Look at this rich carpet we are walking on."

"It's soft and squidgy!"

"Noo, it's crunchy!"

"It be pretty with lots of different colours."

Connie twisted the leaf aloft. "What does this remind you of?" The children glanced her way. "A green leaf painted yellow!" Some of the boys sniggered.

"Look nearer the stem."

The wind rustled and more leaves spiralled in front of them, and the children reached out to catch them. Most eluded their eager fingers with erratic twists, twirling to the ground to join the mosaic of other fallen leaves.

"Mine's got spots like a leopard," shouted Jess.

"Mine be speckled like the hens down the farm."

"Noo, it turns like helicopter blades."

"Well done," complimented Connie warmly. "What is the name of the tree?"

"Doan't know."

"Well, Joss, perhaps you can do some research and find out by the end of the week."

Joss eyed her oddly and muttered reluctantly, "Yus, Miss."

The boys scuffed their feet through the moving carpet and set the leaves scurrying to a new resting place.

Many more leaves struggled to hold fast to the branches above them, against the rising onslaught of the wind, making a mottled, moving canopy of muted greens, rich reds, bronzes as well as yellows tinged with orange.

"Remember to put into your bags anything you find interesting for our nature table or that you can use in a picture."

Some of the boys who had shot ahead yelled back, "There be loads of conkers."

"What are conkers?"

"Fruit of the horse chestnut tree," explained Thomas's Mum.

"You thread them onto string and hev a conker match to see who be conker king."

"I see. You will have to show me."

"Can't, health an' safety banned it," declared Ricky crossly.

"Oh?" Connie looked questioningly towards Mrs Saunders another parent helper for the trip, who nodded. "I'll explain later."

"Look, Miss." Joss held up a gleaming mahogany horse chestnut peeping through its spiky casing in one hand and a fist full of the shiny fruits in the other. "What a beaut!" he said with a sigh.

From the nearby bushes came a light twittering, whistling song.

"What is that?"

"A robin," several voices chorused.

"There's its beady eye," pointed out Daniel but before Connie could see, the songster flew off the twig into a cluster of remaining leaves on a higher branch in a nearby tree.

"We will turn back now. Lock into your memory what you have seen so that you will be able to paint, draw or write about it after playtime."

A grey squirrel skittered in the leaf litter not far from their feet.

"Look Miss, it be collecting nuts for its winter store cupboard."

At the childish cry, the squirrel sat and looked boldly

forward. In the seconds it remained motionless Connie could make out the chestnut tinge to its face, body and tail and the clean purity of its white underbelly. The restless scuffing of youthful feet soon sent it bounding up the nearest tree trunk.

"Come now, we really must make our way back to school."

"Aw, Miss, must we?"

"Can we do it again, Miss?"

"We will see."

"It be such fun!"

"Just thank de Good Lord you's had chance to enjoy His creation, today."

Villagers greeted the children as they wended their way back along the lane. Stephen Cooper waved again from his workshop and Billy, the butcher, stood on the step of his shop and called out, "Have you had a good time?" The reply was a resounding, "Yus."

Connie stepped to one side, "Keep an eye on the children for a moment, please, Mrs Cook."

"Mr Cooper," she called, "What time does de museum close, today?"

"Four-thirty, Miss Foster."

"Thank you, I will return after school." She quickly re-joined the crocodile of children making their way back to school.

Connie felt the excursion had been a success but realised she had probably learned more than her pupils because they were so familiar with the ways of the local countryside. At least she had managed, for a while, to get them outside of four confining walls!

CHAPTER EIGHT

Cool weather!

On the day the planned cricket experiment was due to take place Stephen and his cricketing friends devised a simple, yet what they hoped would be a workable, exciting plan which would enthuse year 5.

"Our aim is to so grab their interest, in the couple of sessions we may be able to get in before the end of the season, they'll be keen to get involved next spring," Stephen said to Connie.

"There may be some budding batsmen or bowlers hiding unawares," Connie smiled enthusiastically. "I am relying on your skill to draw them out."

At the school, expectations were rising. After morning break the children returned to the classroom in a highly excitable state.

"Now, now, boys and girls," Connie clapped her hands to quieten the hullabaloo that bounced back at her off the walls of the classroom. "I cannot possibly pick a team with all this din going on," she continued.

"Aw, Miss, we wuz just a'ciding who'd be best at wicket keeping," piped up Joss Brady.

"Was, Joss, was," Connie corrected.

"Yus, Miss."

"No, Yes."

"Yes, yes, yes," Joss mimicked.

Year 5 knew Miss Foster was a stickler for correctness, in speech as well as behaviour. She applied the same dictum to herself as to her pupils and got quite annoyed when she inadvertently reverted to Bajan pronunciations.

"Jo-o-o-ss," she drawled his name in a warning manner.

"It is just as important to pronounce your words in the right way as it is to hit through a cricket ball correctly to send it to the boundary."

"Okey dokey, Miss, Oi'll dew that when yew pick me fer the team." Giggles chortled across the room

Connie looked him straight in the eye, pursed her lips, then smiled. The class understood what that look meant. They had learned. Calm descended.

In moments like this Connie was grateful they had progressed from the nightmare of the first week of term. She had struggled to understand the Suffolk accent of her pupils and they in turn wrestled with her Bajan intonation of the English language. The children, particularly the boys, revelled at taking the 'micky' out of her and at times she became exasperated with them. Nor did they seem open to direction so that her well-structured lessons became a shambles. *The children appear to be so intent on doing their own thing, regardless of the lesson subject or topic in hand.* Then one of the more vocal boys pointed out to her that "Mr Brankscome always let us dew what we liked." She was grateful when a member of staff drew her to one side and filled her in about the lackadaisical ways of her predecessor. However, Connie remained undeterred, determined to restore a semblance of order to the children's education, so continued to prepare as thoroughly as ever but learned to adapt and be flexible.

"Like yew're woolly top knot, Miss. Yew steal ee from the sheep?" Jessica Saunders quipped cheekily. Connie gave tit-for-tat and retorted, "Same way as you acquired your ponytail from Mr Beckingsdale's horse's mane!" The children roared with laughter. Thankfully, they had moved on from the fiasco of those early days.

Her natural bubbly personality appealed to the children, and she used the differences between them to enhance the lessons. For instance, when Jessica quoted her mother by telling Connie, "Ma says yew've bin sittin' too much in the sun that's why yew's so scorched," Connie replied "That's partly right because my country is nearer to the equator than England. It is much hotter in Barbados than it is in Newton Westerby," and turned the conversation in to a geography cum science lesson about the impact of ultraviolet radiation. It was a body blow when Ricky called out, "My Dad says yew should goo back to where yew come from." She flinched, swallowed hard then explained about melanin pigmentation in the skin being in relation to where people live in the world thus affecting the colour of a person's skin.

As each new day dawned Connie remained positive in her approach to teaching and endeavoured to make learning fun. Every negative aside the pupils threw at her she turned around to make into a game or a springboard to teach something new. The topic of her skin colour and accent became a geography project about Barbados and the Caribbean which led on to a history project delving into comparisons between East

Anglia and the West Indies covering a range of topics from crops, food and menus to houses and architecture. This was followed up by discussion and essay writing on the composition of the land; sand, stony or coral and sea, blue or grey, differences in culture and the decline in historic industry such as fishing and sugar cane. This led to a sports project particularly cricket, which was dear to Connie's heart, and was the current topic they were working on.

"Mr Cooper is expecting us at one thirty sharp, so I need a team in place before we go to lunch," Connie repeated her earlier announcement.

"Me, Miss."

"Choose me."

"Noo, Me."

Feet stomped, hands shot up and voices yelled.

Connie clapped her hands sharply together, again.

"The best cricket players are those who listen to instruction, so my brothers tell me. So, shouters and stampers will certainly not be in de running, sorry, the running. On reflection, I think, as you are finding it difficult to be quiet, it might be best to leave selection to Mr Cooper."

In seconds, the class was as silent as a winter's dawn. One could hear a pin drop. Mr Cooper was great fun in the kid's club, but he was a stickler for good behaviour in the library.

Connie, unaware of this facet of Stephen Cooper's character, continued with the lesson.

"Think for a moment of de names, sorry, the names of cricketers you have heard of." Chattering moved across the room in a wave.

"I believe I said think, not talk."

Miss Foster turned her back to the class and picked up a black marker pen. Upon the white board she drew two columns with the headings, West Indies – England.

"Now, Joss, come to the front." As he sauntered towards Connie, he held his head high and smirked at his mates as he made his way to the front of the class. They sniggered in return. "Teacher's pet," they hissed. She handed the boy the pen.

"Why are you called Joss?"

"Dunnow, Miss."

"I do not know," Connie corrected.

"Thass wha'r'oi said." She chose to ignore his accentuated accent.

"Do you think it might be after de cricketer, sorry, the cricketer Joss Buttler?"

"Might be, Miss."

"His Dad's mad on cricket, Miss," muttered Archie Pickard.

"Which team does he play for?"

"Village first eleven." Roars of laughter went up.

"Joss Buttler?"

"Doan't know, Miss."

"England, England," voices yelled from the right.

"Write his name on the board, please Joss."

Laboriously Joss wrote out the name. Inadvertently he began to write his own surname till guffaws from his mates stopped his hand in mid flow.

"Oi've done it wrong, Miss."

"Then rub out and start again. There are two t's in Buttler."

"Yus, Miss."

"Now, tell me names of more English players."

"One at a time," Connie called as voices started to shout out.

"Daniel?"

"Stuart Broad."

"Anderson."

"Joe Root."

The English list grew.

"Now, what about West Indies players."

Silence hovered as tongues were stilled.

Slowly a hand went up.

"Yes, Samantha?"

"When he wuz a boy my uncle had his photo taken with Dean Hedley."

"That's interesting but Dean Hedley was an English cricketer!"

"But he is black, Miss!"

"Still an Englishman."

"Oh!"

"Oi know, oi know," yelled Rich Warnes jumping up and down, "the chap who stands an' hits the ball out o' the ground."

"And what's his name?"

"Ummm, doan't know."

"Chris somethin', oi think."

"Yup! Chris Gayle. He be bril. He can smash it anywhere," a voice shouted from the back of the classroom.

"Daniel, you play for the under 11's and have been in d, um, the cricket pavilion. Are there photos of cricketers in there?"

"Yes, but I don't know the names of players. I do know when Dad was young some West Indies cricketers played against a Norfolk first eleven at

Lakenham and he had his photo taken with Jimmy Adams."

"My Grandad saw Garry Sobers and Brian Lara play."

"Great," encouraged Connie. "When my Grand Daddy was a boy he played with Everton Weekes."

"Nivver heard of him."

"Nevertheless, he was a West Indies cricketer."

"Duane Bravo wuz on the tele."

"Soo wuz Darren Bravo an' Jason Holder."

Connie clapped her hands and looked out across her class with a broad smile.

"There's somebody called Archie," a voice called out on her left.

"Noo, his name be Archer."

"Yus, Jofra Archer."

"How come he be from Barbados, Miss, but he be a playin' for England?"

"Good, good, you're beginning to remember what you have seen and heard about cricket. Archer can do that because his Dad is English. He also holds a British passport. Lots of d, the boys in my country play cricket and their ambition is to play for the National team and maybe one day be picked for the West Indies team. I would like you all to write 5 sentences about cricket. You may use information from our conversation this morning or your own knowledge prior to today. After which we will discuss possible teams to meet with Mr Cooper."

"How many in a team, Miss?"

"Eleven."

"How many teams?"

"Two."

"How many in the class?"

Connie's smile broadened to show her white teeth.

"Twenty-two."

"But that includes the girls!"

"Of course!"

"But they can't play!"

"Why not?"

"'cos!"

"There was a time when the English Women's cricket team was more successful than d, the men."

"Oh!"

"It is a game for all those who want to play."

Connie's hands clapped together again.

"No more talking. Write!"

"She be a roite ole battle axe," muttered Jessica Saunders in a loud whisper. Miss Foster had sharp ears.

"Jessica, will you please look up the word 'insubordination' before spelling test on Friday so you can share it with the class."

"Yus, Miss," came the subdued response.

"Doan't she know it be football season now."

Adam Catton and Harry Saunders had offered to provide parental assistance when year 5 made their epic visit to Newton Westerby's cricket ground for which Connie was grateful. Many in the class were overly excited at the prospect of doing something different to the normal school timetable. Some were not so keen on the cricketing aspect of the outing but felt it was a better option to sitting in the classroom doing maths or writing.

Immediately following lunch Connie instructed her pupils to put on their sports gear and prepare to make their way to the cricket field. Harry chivvied along those lagging behind while Adam escorted the early birds. Connie walked alongside the small group in the middle, all eagerly chatting about what was going to take place.

On the cricket pitch Stephen and Graeme were setting out plastic stumps on the outfield. Whilst standing outside the pavilion a few cricketers, of varying ages, waited to greet the children. Amongst them was Doug Ransome, Nathan Jenner and Nicky Andaman. Connie was surprised to see Mark Bemment, the big man who had read the lesson in church her first weekend in the village.

"I did not expect to see you here."

"I'm a part timer at the club as I can only be involved when I'm ashore. Sam and I have come straight from the 'Seagull' after unloading the morning catch," he explained.

"Good to see you again. Thanks for giving up your time for the children." Mark smiled and graciously nodded as Stephen joined them.

"I thought initially we'd teach them kwik cricket," Stephen explained to Connie. "Get them all involved straightaway."

"I see," said Connie dubiously.

"More fun for them this way. Next spring we'll have more opportunity to see who has an aptitude for the real game."

"Good thinking." She clapped her hands. "Please listen to Mr Cooper as he tells us what to do."

The excited chatter died down as Stephen proceeded to divide the children into three groups. "Three adults to a group." Connie found herself in a group with Mark and Nicky. Mark took charge and issued instructions as he gave out red bands for each child.

"Nicky, you will umpire behind the wicket. Miss Foster, you will keep score and a watchful eye on things from square leg. Joss, you are wicket keeper. Keir, you take the bat. You must run whether you hit the ball or not."

"Yus, Sir."

Mark indicated where he wanted the rest of the team to position themselves and explained what they were expected to do.

"To commence, I will bowl to show you how it is done then, Rich, I'd like you to bowl 6 balls. Remember it is underarm. You will all have opportunity to bat, bowl and field. Then we shall have a tournament with the other two teams. Are you ready? Play!"

From then on, the afternoon seemed to take wings that carried them on a flight of sparkling enthusiasm. Even the least interested became animated when it looked likely their team might win the impromptu competition. Their clapping and gleeful shouts drew several supportive spectators from the village who stood around the edge of the pitch despite the drop in temperature as a brisk north-easterly blew in across the sea.

All too soon, for some, the fun ended, and it was time to make their way back to school.

"What do you say to Mr Cooper and his team?" Connie prompted.

"Thank yew."

"Yeah! Thanks, mate."

"When can we dew it again?"

"It wuz great," they chorused all at once.

"It has been our pleasure, glad you enjoyed it. We'll do it again next week if Miss Foster and the weather is agreeable." Stephen inclined his head towards Connie.

"Oh, she be agreeable," shouted Joss, "She likes cricket an' if yew like it she might like yew."

Connie looked directly at Joss.

"Yew've got the look, Joss bor, yew're in for it now," muttered Archie.

"Mr Cooper, is the museum open on Saturday morning?"

"Why, yes, would you like a tour?"

"If I may, I would like to learn more of the history of this area. I did not have sufficient time on my last visit."

"It opens at ten in the morning. I'll meet you there."

Joss looked knowingly at his classmates and winked saucily.

On Saturday morning dawn broke over the North Sea with blue sky and sunshine, the promise of a mild, dry day. The bitter wind had turned into a light, southerly breeze. So it was with a spring in her step that Connie made her way to the museum eager to delve more deeply into the secrets it might hold.

On her previous short visit Stephen had enthusiastically explained the clearance of Kezia's Wood and the exciting discovery of derelict dwellings some of which had been painstakingly restored including the one that now housed artefacts that had also been found on the site. When Connie explained her desire to trace her ancestry, which the family believed to be linked to

Newton Westerby, Stephen's keen interest knew no bounds and he offered his help.

Anticipating her arrival Stephen kept an eye on the door as he answered queries from one of the early morning visitors to the museum. He had unearthed some documents which he hoped would hold interest for Connie.

Her delight as she held the yellowed scripts that depicted the extent of the 18th/19th century village of Newton Westerby and remains of Newton Easterby was immeasurable. "My ancestors may have walked across this land," she whispered incredulously. Her fingers slowly traced the coastline and hovered over the de Vessey estate boundary. When she quietly explained a possible family connection to the de Vessey family Stephen looked at her disbelievingly but promised to speak with Lord Edmund. "I know he holds extensive records in the family archives. He's loaned a few of general interest to the museum but has retained more personal documents. If he's aware of your interest he may be willing to allow you access to them."

CHAPTER NINE

A blast from the east!

"Does it get any colder?" Connie's muffled voice asked Rosie as she rushed into the Tea Rooms one afternoon after school. Inside, the soft hum of chattering customers mingled with the occasional clink of teacups. On one wall a flickering wood burner sat inside a Victorian fireplace, in the room that had once been the bedroom of Emma Cooper's great grandparents, Kezia and John Durrant. "My word, that creates a warm, enticing ambience which is so welcome on such a cold day," she mumbled.

Rosie smiled in welcome as she added more logs to the fire. "Gosh, you are bundled up to the eyebrows. I guess you've been fighting against that biting north easterly."

"The weather changes so rapidly here." Connie shivered and clamped her arms around her body. "Does it always blow this cold?"

"Quite often. I reckon we're used to it but, today, the wind is coming in off the sea and you'll feel the bite more than we do coming from such a hot country."

All that could be seen were the whites of Connie's eyes peering out from the window created beneath a knitted hat and a bright pink, woollen scarf wrapped around her neck covering both mouth and nose.

"Brr… I have never felt so cold."

"Come and sit nearer to the fire. I'm afraid it could get colder as we move deeper into winter." Rosie indicated a vacant table next to the blazing log fire that was throwing out comforting warmth.

"Thanks," gasped Connie as her teeth chatted together. "My brother said it got cold in Canada when he was there studying some years ago, but I did not expect it to be as cold in England."

"You're right, English temperatures don't plummet as low as they do in Canada but when the north wind blows along the east coast it feels colder than the thermometer indicates."

As heat reached out its welcome Connie absorbed its warmth. She looked across the restaurant. Scrutinising the clientele, she slowly unravelled the scarf from her neck as she took the seat Rosie offered and stretched her hands towards the fire. She had come to the Tea Rooms in response to a text message from Stephen.

"I am meeting someone for afternoon tea, but he is not here at present."

"Then I'll bring you a coffee to warm up while you're waiting."

"That sounds a good idea, thank you." Connie settled herself by the fireside, her eyes drawn to the dancing flames. *Whatever would Mumma think of this? Sparks pirouetting from side to side while others spiral upwards from the blazing wood.* Her mind jumped to the letter she had so recently received from Mumma full of family news and picnics at the beach. She regularly received notes as well as the local paper from someone in the family, so she still felt part of the community. Many of the articles were about people and places with which she was familiar; accidents on the roundabouts on the ABC road; kite surfers in difficulties; an explosive in the entrance to the hospital; sewage problem at Hastings; horticultural show, where uncles Lennie and Peter both received rosettes; vandalism on a doctor's office; wrangling between politicians about the economy.

Almost subconsciously she clasped the cup in her hands that Rosie placed in front of her and sipped the burning liquid. Its warmth penetrating the depths of her being and easing the numbness in her hands. Her nearness to the fire soon caused a rosy glow to heighten her golden-brown skin.

The changing colours and mesmerising movement of the flames so held her attention that she failed to hear Stephen as he drew up a chair, sat down beside her and placed a bundle of files on the table in front of her.

Startled from her reverie she looked up and beamed at her companion.

Stephen grinned. "Log fire another new experience?"

She nodded. "Fascinating!"

"Are you thawing out?"

"Gradually." Connie placed a hand on the files. "Lord Edmund agreed?"

"Yes."

"And you found something relevant?"

"I'm hoping so."

"Tea, Stephen?" Rosie hovered to the side.

"Mmm, please, Rosie."

"Top up, Connie, and scones for the two of you?"

"You know us so well, Rosie, thanks."

Stephen took some papers out of the blue file. "You might find these interesting reading. After our chat in the museum I spoke with Lord Edmund and explained what you were researching. He graciously gave me access to some letters and documents from his family archives."

"I am so grateful."

"Initially, he was cautious, but I think your story intrigued him which is why he gave his consent."

"That is so good of him."

"Yes, when I was a boy, I was scared of him. His voice boomed out when he spoke, sufficient to blow a ship out of the sea."

Connie laughed, "You are exaggerating!"

"No, ask anyone. He seemed so stern and unapproachable. I guess the tragedies in his life made him so aloof. Probably it was his way of coping with things, I suppose. I'm sure he always had a softer side, but we never saw it. As the years have passed, he seems to have mellowed. We certainly see a more caring side to him these days and I think your landlady has much to do with the change in his demeanour."

"Really?"

"Mmm, love changes people, no matter what their age."

Connie chuckled, "You are matchmaking?"

"No, it's a fact. I'm sure before too long we'll be hearing wedding bells."

Connie glanced at him and smiled. "Mr Cooper, you are quite the romantic."

"A realist. I simply keep my eyes open to happenings in the village."

"Tea and coffee, plus scones for two." Rosie served them with expertise gained from experience then quietly withdrew.

For a few moments, the couple concentrated on their repast then Stephen passed a sheet to Connie.

"Read this one now, then take the rest home to digest on your own. Some of this documentation goes back to 1831. I believe Lord Edmund has bundles of papers in his attic that go back even further."

For some while Connie's eyes were glued to the letter Stephen handed to her, but as they moved across the pages, they began to puddle till rivulets trickled over her cheeks.

He passed across his serviette. "Can't have tears splodging such important evidence."

Breathlessly she whispered, "So sad, so sad. This could be my great, great, great, great, great Grand Daddy."

Stephen nodded. "Incredible, isn't it?"

Connie wiped away the tears falling uncontrollably down her face.

"As I explained when I came to the museum this is the reason I wanted to come to England. Mumma did not want me to delve into our family history, but I had this deep desire inside me that simply would not go away. I had to find out. De Good Lord, He knew my heart and has made it possible for me to discover the roots, find my ancestors."

She placed a hand on his arm. "I appreciate what you have done on my behalf."

Stephen shook his head. "It's been my pleasure. I enjoy delving into the history of our community. I see the possibilities of a new exhibition for the museum."

Shocked, Connie looked straight at him, "No!" She shook her head vehemently. Although she wanted to unravel her roots, her heart at this moment, was unwilling to have the suffering, shame and indignity of her Great grands displayed for all to see.

"Oh, yes!" He replied with confidence. "Read through all of these and you'll see that I'm right." He pushed the files further towards her. "There's an unbreakable link between Newton Westerby and Barbados that bridges miles and centuries. History impacts undeniably on our life today. We can't let that go undocumented or kept out of the public domain. Once events have happened they can't be erased."

Connie sat staring thoughtfully at the fire, her hands fiddling with the folds of the winter skirt Emma had helped her to choose in Norwich when she had been taken on a shopping expedition.

"This has happened more quickly than I expected."

A lopsided grin crinkled Stephen's lip. "You were clever enough to ask help from the right person."

A smile sneaked through the corners of Connie's mouth as she shook her head at him. "Stephen Cooper!" She exclaimed. "My Mumma would say you was arrogant!"

"No, it's the truth. As museum curator, amongst other things, I'm fortunate enough to have access to many historical records or I have contacts who have answers to things I don't know."

Eyebrows arched Connie looked at him. "Thanks, I guess."

Stephen inclined his head with a grin. "You are most welcome, ma'am."

"I would like to speak with Lord Edmund," she shuffled uncomfortably, "but it might be a little awkward. I am unsure how he might view our common ancestry. I only see him from a distance at church and even though he was on the panel at my interview on Zoom and welcomed me when I first arrived in the village, I do not really know him."

"As I said, he really is more approachable these days," he patted her arm. "Don't worry. I'll get in touch to arrange a meeting."

Connie looked up at him. "Sure?"

"Of course, and I'll come up to the Manor with you, moral support and all that."

She let out the breath she had not realised she was holding in. "Thank you." Relief lifted from her face like a cloud moving across the sun. Her countenance shone.

She grabbed Stephen's arm. "Oh, thank you, thank you. I am so excited." She clapped her hands together. "I can hardly wait to read through these files."

Stephen pushed back his chair. "I have to go. Work awaits me. I'll pay for our drinks, but we can meet again to chat through your findings and see how you want to proceed." He fastened his coat, tightened his scarf and turned up his collar. "In fact if you've nothing else planned I'll ask Rosie to bring you another coffee. It's quiet in here this afternoon, why not stay in the warm and peruse these in this cosy spot."

Eyes wide open Connie looked up at him in disbelief. "I can do that?"

"Of course. Why not?" He patted her shoulder.

"Enjoy!" He called as he made his way to the counter.

That man has gone to so much trouble for me, I will do just that.

In no time at all she was immersed completely in what could be the story of her ancestors.

What will Mumma make of this?

She became so absorbed that she was unaware that Rosie and her staff had completed all the end of day tasks around her before making her mindful that it was passed closing time.

"Connie, are you going to choir practice this evening?"

Connie jumped at the sound of Rosie's voice and almost dropped the files on to the floor.

"I am so sorry, Rosie. It was not my intention to keep you. I became engrossed in these files Stephen left for me I was unaware it was so late."

"That's OK. I could see you were busy. I hope you don't mind but we carried on with our end of day cleaning around you and we've had to let the fire die down."

"Oh, I had not noticed." Connie stood, wrapped up warmly, gathered the files together and made her way down the stairs. "Thanks for your kindness."

"You're welcome. See you another day," Rosie called after her cheerfully.

Connie walked briskly to 'Bakers' and apologised to Jennifer for being late for the evening meal.

She made it to choir practice as Adam was about to commence the first piece. Connie closed her eyes and let the music and words wash over her as she sat to catch her breath. *Thank You, Father God, that wherever we are, we are standing, or sitting, in Your presence.*

"Adam always seems to pick songs where music and words marry well together, doesn't he?" Mark commented to Justin and Connie as they walked home together following the choir rehearsal. Threads of conversation circulated around the group of friends as they intermingled.

"Yes, he has a knack for choosing the right song for any given occasion."

"Mmm, and some words linger and are a blessing throughout the week."

"Bye, everyone," Miranda called when they reached the Cooper's front door.

"You working tomorrow?"

"No, day off. Flu jabs this Saturday."

"I must turn here, too," said Justin.

"I'll walk you home," offered Mark. Connie smiled. Others turning off to the right called, "Goodnight."

As they passed Emma's house, she bid everyone farewell and Alex, her sister, joined Connie and Mark till they reached her gate.

"See you again, soon, Connie. Safe trip out, Mark."

"Thanks."

"So, when are you next going fishing?" Connie asked as they neared 'Bakers' gate.

"We sail in the morning."

"Oh, I will pray you have a safe and fruitful trip, and that God will go with you."

Mark stood on the path while Connie unlocked the door. He stayed there till she was safely inside. She turned, waved and smiled. Mark locked that cameo away in his heart. Many times while he was out at sea, he recalled that picture of warmth and loveliness she presented.

The days passed quickly. It was evident that winter was finally here to stay. Shafts of light shimmered through the early morning mist as it hung over the sea and lingered across the common. Connie spent most of her spare time mulling over the contents of the documents Stephen had presented to her. As promised Stephen contacted Lord Edmund and her appointment was due to take place the following week. *My heart turns over at the very thought of it. Whatever will the man have to say when he learns that we are related!*

On this morning she decided to take a break from the archive files. So, warmly wrapped up against the elements she strolled down by the river estuary where it meets the harbour and the sea. Small wooden buildings nestled on the bank near to where Dave Ransome's fishing boat was unloading its catch. Beneath the haze on the banks of the river Connie glimpsed drifts of curling wood smoke languidly ascending from an unusually cone-shaped building. Curiosity got the better of her and she wandered round the structure until she found an entrance but just as her fingers clasped a handle to open the door a voice yelled at her. "Hey, Missy, doan't." Scurrying feet quickly followed the angry shout.

"Oh, I am sorry. I wanted to enquire about this intriguing building and see what is happening inside." Connie stepped back as she addressed the sprightly be-whiskered, arm-waving man coming towards her in such a blazing fury. Clad in brightly coloured orange overalls, donning industrial wellington boots and a green, woolly cap his attire seemed to enhance his aggressive attitude.

"And who might yew be, Miss?" He asked gruffly as he approached her.

Connie thrust out her hand. "Connie Foster, sir, from Barbados."

"Oi've heard o' yew," he said dismissively, ignoring her outstretched hand. "Yew're the new school mistress."

"What is that smell?"

"Thass the fish a'smokin'."

"What does that mean?"

"This be a smoke house where we smokes fish usin' traditional techniques."

"What are they?"

"Fish be suspended over slowly smould'rin' wood shavin's and sawdust."

"Where do you get the wood from?"

"A number o' sources."

"Does it matter what species of tree?"

"Different varieties give off different aromas. When they wuz a clearin' Kezia's Wood we wuz given first option o' the tree trunks as they wuz felled."

"That was good of them."

"The fragrance o' the smoke affects the flavour o' the fish. Oak and apple prove very popular."

"How long do you smoke the fish for?"

"Depends."

"On what?"

"Yew're askin' a lot o' questions," he eyed her suspiciously.

"I want to learn what is going on."

"You thinkin' o' changin' jobs?"

"Why no. I am simply interested in what goes on in the village."

"Thass a diein'. Not much fishin' these days. Juss m'bor Mark in 'Seagull', an' Dave's 'Sunburst', an' ole Sooner goo when the fancy teks 'im."

"Do the school children come to visit?"

"No, oi chases 'em orff, if oi catches 'em a'larkin' around."

"I meant on an official visit."

"What dew yew mean?" he asked snappily.

"The children in my class may know de smokehouse is here but I wonder how many of them know what goes on in here. This is part of their heritage. Would you be willing to tell them about de process and show what you do here?"

"Oi'll see," he replied dubiously.

"I could learn, too." Connie beamed at the sullen face before her.

"Oi've said, oi'll see." He spoke sharply.

"Thank you, Mr...?"

"Bemment, Reggie Bemment."

"I'll be in touch, Mr Bemment. Goodbye."

Connie waved in farewell and continued walking along the quay with a spring in her step. Another possible outdoor activity under her belt! She mulled over her conversation with satisfaction then suddenly pulled up with a start. *Mr Bemment said, "M'bor Mark in 'Seagull'". He must be Mark's dad!*

CHAPTER TEN

Squally storms!

True to his word Stephen accompanied Connie to her appointment with Lord Edmund. Prior to that encounter he had the presence of mind to mention Connie's apprehension about meeting Lord Edmund to Miss Pedwardine one morning when she was on duty in the village library. She listened as he shared Connie's concerns about Lord Edmund's reaction to their common ancestry. Stephen had not always felt at ease with Jennifer Pedwardine. In earlier years he would have approached his formidable headmistress with trepidation but since her retirement they had established a working rapport with one another.

The retired school mistress had badgered Stephen about the value of opening a book-lending service in the village for quite some time. So, when the opportunity arose to supply this facility Stephen approached Jennifer to assist him in setting it up in one of the cottages reclaimed from Kezia's Wood. He believed her enthusiasm for books would encourage villagers of all ages to use the service. Together she and RK Prettyman had established an attractive amenity that appealed to cross sections of the community. Jennifer continued to help-out a few hours a week even though Abigail

Saunders was now qualified as a librarian and officially in charge. If she were honest, Miss Pedwardine still missed the hustle and bustle of school life, contact with staff and pupils, and looked forward to interaction with the users of the well-stocked resource. Stephen was confident that if she could cajole the laziest of readers to open a book, she could smooth a pathway for an amicable discussion to take place about a potentially tricky topic between Connie and Lord Edmund.

So, Miss Pedwardine engineered an informal introduction between the two over coffee, after church on Sunday morning, so that they would not be complete strangers when they met up at the Manor to discuss Connie's forebears and a possible connection to the de Vessey family.

"He seemed quite pleasant," Connie commented to Stephen as they battled against the wind and rain on their way up the lane towards the Manor just after lunch. "Though, I was a little wary when he greeted me gruffly with, "Well, young lady, you have certainly opened a can of worms." I thought he was going to refuse to see me, but Jennifer put a hand on his arm. He turned and smiled at her, looked back at me and told me there was a bundle of yellowing correspondence that had not been opened in years and I was welcome to plough through it if I had the inclination."

"That's good news. Let's get up there out of this storm as quickly as we can so you can make a start."

"I am glad the vicar's wife loaned me this raincoat with a hood."

"It is very becoming," Stephen teased as the squally weather buffeted them.

"I would be very wet without it."

"An umbrella would be useless against this onslaught. The wind is too strong."

"It is hard work walking against it."

"Walking back will be easier," Stephen encouraged "because it will be blowing in the opposite direction so will propel us down the lane."

They approached the entrance porch to Newton Manor via the driveway but as Stephen reached out to ring the doorbell a deafening claxon sounded down by the harbour. Simultaneously his mobile phone beeped.

"What is that?" Connie looked at Stephen quizzically.

Lord Edmund, himself, opened the door to his guests and stood looking at the pair somewhat bemused as they appeared unaware of his presence.

"Good afternoon! Are you coming in or are we holding our tete-a-tete outside? If so, I'll need an overcoat."

"Sorry, sir, a shout, I'm afraid. Sorry, Connie, I must dash." He called over his shoulder as he tore down the drive.

Connie looked bewildered.

"Wait, young man, the car is in the drive. Quicker if I take you down to the station." His Lordship grabbed his coat from off a hook behind him and felt in his pocket for keys. "Come on. Go in young lady," he called to Connie as he sprinted to the car. "Jennifer will look after you."

"Sorry, Connie," Stephen shouted again as he clambered aboard the vehicle. "Thank you, sir."

Feeling abandoned in an unfamiliar place Connie thought, "What do I do now?" She was soon left in no doubt about her next steps as a voice called out from within, "Do be quick and close the door. It is blowing a gale in here and you are letting all the warm air out."

A voice she recognised stirred her to action. Connie stepped inside the porch and pushed with all her might to close the solid oak front door. The wind fought against her, determined to win the battle, but eventually she succeeded. She walked into the spacious hall and called a tentative, "Hello."

"In here," directed Miss Pedwardine.

Connie entered the chintz drawing room.

"What a lovely room." It was reminiscent of pictures she had seen of sitting rooms in the former English garrison at Bridgetown.

As soon as she spotted the soaked, windblown young woman Miss Pedwardine jumped up and admonished her. "Take off your wet things, girl. You will catch your death let alone ruin the carpet." She rapidly ushered Connie into the kitchen. "Towel, please, Lettie," she demanded of Lord Edmund's housekeeper.

"Where are the men?"

Perplexed Connie replied, "I do not know. They rushed off in a car."

In unison Jennifer and Lettie asked, "Is something wrong?"

"I am not sure. There was a loud clanging noise from the direction of the harbour as we arrived, closely followed by a call on Stephen's cell phone. He said to Lord Edmund, "It's a shout," who replied, "I will take you to the station," and ordered him to get into the car. What does it mean?"

"Oh, no!" Lettie put her hands up to her face. "Doug has gone out with Mark on 'The Seagull'."

Connie looked at them both, very confused.

"It means a boat is in distress out at sea and the lifeboat has been called out. Stephen is part of the crew.

Edmund is patron. Doug Ransome is Lettie's brother acting as first mate for Mark Bemment because Sam injured his leg last trip out." Whilst talking she helped strip Connie of her outer clothing. "They won't be back for some time. Could we have coffee now, please, Lettie. Warm this girl up. Come, let us get you thawed out." She briskly led Connie back into the drawing room where a blazing fire lit up the hearth and seated her in the chair closest to its warmth.

"We'll pray for a successful launch and that all will be well for those involved."

Connie was stunned by this sudden and unexpected turn of events.

"We can then chat about some of the topics you wished to discuss with Lord Edmund. I may not have all the answers…"

Connie waived her words aside.

"But…" *Mumma would say de Greats do not matter de present is more important than de past.* "…isn't there anything we can do?"

"Such as?"

"Support the fishermen's families."

"How?"

"At home, this situation does not happen often but, when it does, we take pots of food and drink down to the beach and meet up with the relatives there. We sing and pray them safely home."

The door opened. "Thanks, Lettie, so kind." The housekeeper placed a tray on the coffee table. "Oh, you have on your coat."

"I must go to Christina."

"Drink your coffee first while I ring Hugh Darnell."

The Vicar answered immediately. "Organized, as usual, Hugh?" Jennifer said.

"Aah, Jennifer, I guess you're ringing about the distress call. It has been confirmed it is the 'Seagull'. I believe Jansy is shepherding the families of the crew to Green Pastures where they will be mothered and prayed for by Bernice and Roy. Their sunroom, as you know, gives an excellent view of the harbour mouth."

"I presume Dave will be going out with the lifeboat as his Dad is aboard the 'Seagull' with Mark?"

"You're correct. We have no further details at present other than it is a gale force 9, high seas and visibility is greatly reduced.

"Ben is organizing a prayer vigil in the Church and my wife is getting a W.I. team together to arrange sustenance in the church hall, if needed.

"I understand one of the Doctors is planning to go to the harbour master's lookout on the quay to stay with Wills and be on hand as needed. Dan Prettyman hasn't gone with the crew, having given up his place to Dave so, he and Sergeant Catchpole are preparing to keep the inevitable sightseers at bay so that nothing hinders the rescue."

"Is anyone taking drinks to those on the quay and in the harbour office?"

"Not sure."

"I have Connie Foster and Lettie with me. We will attend to that need. The temperature seems to be plummeting as the day wears on. We do not want additional hypothermia casualties. We will take down flasks of coffee and soup, as well as, hot water bottles, and rustle up extra scarves and blankets."

"Thanks, Jenni..." she almost dropped the phone as she barked out orders to Lettie and Connie. She had them organized and moving so rapidly that within minutes they were propelled into the small car Lord Edmund put at her disposal and on their way to the quay, Connie wrapped in a borrowed, oversized but dry anorak. All happy thoughts of discovering further news about her forebears dissolving under the black cloud that had descended upon Newton Westerby.

CHAPTER ELEVEN

Plummeting temperature!

The little car inched its way through a crowd gathered along the lane that led to the quayside. "How does bad news travel so fast?"

"And why do strangers want to gawp so avidly at the tragedy of others?"

"No," said Miss Pedwardine emphatically, "despite the prolific village grapevine, word concerning the 'Seagull' would not have spread around that quickly. I think these are the usual Saturday afternoon visitors. But I cannot see why they are congregated across the lane in such a fashion blocking vehicle access."

The car crawled to a standstill.

"It is amazing that this many people are out in such awful weather," commented Connie from her huddled position on the back seat. "It is so wet and cold."

"For some it is habit, for others it is a whim, a change to the confines of town, an opportunity to savour the bracing sea air before returning to the comforts of home."

"Look," called out Lettie, "there is Nicky Andaman. Perhaps he can help us."

Jennifer honked the horn and opened the car window. Nicky strode over.

"Nicholas, what is going on?"

"One of the Beckingsdale horses got out of Top Field and bolted directly in front of a delivery van on its way to the Ship Inn."

"Oh, noo," gasped Lettie.

"I'm afraid the lane is blocked."

"Could you assist us to carry supplies to the Harbour Master's lookout?"

"Yes, Miss Pedwardine."

"How is the horse?"

"Doesn't look too good. Doc Roger is attending to things till the vet arrives but he's not too hopeful."

"How could something like that happen?" Connie asked.

"Either the horse was spooked, could be the stormy weather and it jumped the hedge and bolted, or someone carelessly left the field gate open."

"I will leave the car here. Nicholas, can you help Miss Foster carry these flasks and hot water bottles? Lettie and I will manage the woollen scarves and blankets. It is only a few steps to the harbour master's office."

"But we'll never get through this lot!" exclaimed Lettie. The narrow lane leading to the harbour seemed to be teeming with people hampering their progress.

Miss Pedwardine scanned the crowd. "You are right," she commented. "Oh, there's Dan Prettyman. Nicholas, call him over." PC Daniel Prettyman was soon outside the car.

"How can I assist, ladies?"

"Dan, we have brought supplies for Wills and others who are helping but need an escort through this throng."

The constable's height, long legs and uniform soon paved a way through the crowd, so they were able to distribute the offerings of warmth to the waiting rescuers. Jennifer spied Lord Edmund inside the lookout with Wills, the harbour master, and marched inside. "Can you ensure the men keep well wrapped up and drink the coffee and soup. Give a call and we will replenish when the need arises."

Back in the car Jennifer turned to Lettie, "I understand your sister-in-law, Christina, is at the Durrant's. I can drop you off there unless you would prefer to come with us to the church."

"No, Bernice's will be fine. If Ben be at the church where be Rachel and the children?"

"I didn't ask but I expect she will be with her mother."

Connie was well acquainted with the younger Durrants. "I could look after Mark and Rhoda. They know me from school, and we have also met at church."

"Good thinking, girl. Take them away from a highly charged situation and keep them occupied. Go to 'Bakers' if need be."

Miss Pedwardine drove to 'Green Pastures' without further hindrance. Lettie was out of the car in a flash and through the front door that was opened by Jansy Ransome the moment she put a foot on the front step. She rushed in to hug her sister-in-law. "I'm so very sorry, Christina."

"Doug should never have gone but it was calm when they set sail yesterday morning."

A sombre group was congregated in the 'Green Pastures' sun lounge that was ironically named, as it was shrouded in gloom this Saturday afternoon.

When she saw Rosalie, the Village Stores manager, alongside her sister Christina, Miss Pedwardine demanded "Who is taking care of the shop?"

"Rosie and young Maxine Cook are manning the Tea Rooms and shop between them. Emma and Alex are on call should the need arise."

"Billy has closed the butcher's as no one is expecting many customers, in the circumstances."

"Don't be too sure of that. The Quay seems to be heaving with people."

"No!" chorused a number present in disbelief.

"It's true. There appears to have been an incident with a Beckingsdale horse and delivery van. I had to request an escort from the Ship car park to the harbour master's office."

"Is that roite?"

"Yes, Dan and Nicky kindly obliged."

While conversation was going on around her Connie located the Durrant children. She crouched down by the side of Rhoda. Mark was hovering protectively nearby. "Would you like to come with me to the coffee shop for hot chocolate and cookies?" Childish eyes lit up at her suggestion.

"Get your coats while I let your Mum know where we are going." Together they nodded. The solemn atmosphere was beyond their understanding. A struggling boat was outside of their experience. They only knew that their Grandad was in danger and family and friends were doing all they could to help him, and Mark Bemment, bring the 'Seagull' back to harbour safely. "Dad said it's proving difficult because of the stormy weather," young Mark whispered to Connie. "Then we must pray that de Good Lord will take care of them."

When Miss Pedwardine offered to drive them the short distance to the Tea Rooms, Connie shook her head. "Be best for them to be active. We will wrap up warmly." True to her word she had the children skipping and running along the lane, at times joining in with them. She instigated games that involved looking out for everything beginning with the letter S. Instead of taking the lift, up to the Tea Rooms, they jumped up the stairs amidst much giggling when Connie could not manage some of the steps.

Despite the small number of customers Rosie still had a good fire burning in the stove.

"Hi, you lovely people, what can I get for you?" Rosie greeted Connie and the children cheerfully.

"Hot chocolate with all the works," Mark ordered boldly.

Rhoda looked shyly at Connie, who nodded. "Hot chocolate, please. Is Pansy here today?"

"No, Poppet, she's at home helping Mum with the baking and looking after the animals. They don't like this wild wind." While her hands were busy Rosie's eyes rested on Connie, her eyebrows raised.

"Yes please, three hot chocolates. All the works, as Mark requested and some cookies, if you have any."

"I like your fire, Rosie," Mark complimented.

"Most people head to this table. You're lucky to find it vacant."

She turned back to Connie and whispered, "Any news?"

Connie shook her head. "But the quay is busy with people, so you might soon get more customers. It's very cold out there."

"During the lull after lunch I've been getting prepared. Doc Rog has been in touch with Emma and she's coming in if we get an influx so, we're going to stay open as long as necessary."

"If you need an extra pair of hands, I am available."

"Thanks, I'll bear that in mind."

"I can wash dishes or clear the tables," Connie spread out her arms, "or anything at all that will be helpful."

Rosie patted Connie's shoulder, "You're a star!"

"Right, kiddos, three hot chocolates with cookies coming up." She flashed the children a smile and bounced jauntily back to the preparation area.

"I like Rosie. Her sister, Pansy, is my bestest friend," Rhoda confided."

"Yeah, she's pretty cool and good fun." Mark acknowledged. "I sometimes go up to the Mill to play with Keir."

"That is real nice."

As Connie predicted the Tea Rooms began to fill with customers and in no time at all Rosie was hard pushed to keep up with orders. Some customers grumbled and became impatient. The children also began to get restless with waiting so Connie took out a pen and began to make marks on a serviette.

"Do you know how to play hangman?"

Mark nodded.

"You do this together, Rhoda's standard." Connie looked at Mark knowingly.

He shrugged. "OK."

She stood up, clapped her hands and beamed at the customers crowded round the counter.

"Good afternoon. Thank you for coming to de Tea Rooms but you all came at once. So, please be patient.

You will be served as soon as possible. Kindly sit at a table. I will wash my hands then take your orders."

Surprised, the jostling group quickly dispersed, and calm was created out of the chaos.

"Bossy madam," someone grumbled.

"Proper school ma'am," commented another unaware of Connie's occupation.

In no time at all Connie reappeared from the preparation kitchen clad in the signatory apron, pad and pen dangling from the pocket. She clapped her hands.

"Excuse me! The special this afternoon is home-made soup with roll, or cheese toastie, and we have a selection of scones, cakes and pastries available. As I do not know who came in first, I am going to work systematically along de tables, starting here." She indicated the table nearest to where she was standing then looked across the room. "You, sir, as you are the closest, I am putting in charge of the fire. Logs are in de basket. Everyone needs to keep warm. I know you are all here to pray and support the people of the village. Have a pleasant afternoon."

Connie glanced towards Mark and Rhoda. Rosie had served their drinks and cookies and a couple Connie recognised from church had joined the children. She expressed her thanks with a nod and a smile then commenced her self-appointed task.

"My word, she's a natural," Rosie observed to Emma who arrived as Connie was organizing the customers.

"You can see why she is such an excellent teacher. By the way, I've closed the shop and asked Maxine to put a notice on the door suggesting that if shopping is urgent folks come up here and we'll arrange to serve what they require. She's coming shortly to give us a hand. Do we have sufficient food to meet the demands of such an influx?"

"I have enough soup for 20 servings, not many people came in at lunch time today. I can make as many toasties as necessary. There are a fair selection of cakes and pastries. Scones are almost gone."

"I think with this cold weather we are going to need more soup."

"I'm sure Jilly will come in, if we give her a call."

"I'll do that."

Rosie served out four soups and called "table 3". Emma replaced the receiver and took them out to the customers. "No reply from Jilly," she called over her shoulder. As she turned back from serving table 3, she almost bumped into RK, Dan Prettyman's wife.

"Sorry, RK."

"Hi, Emma, I've come to help. Dan called to say he thought you might be busy. I can take the money. Free you up to see to people or food."

"Bless you, RK, I'd appreciate that." Emma quickly drew up a chair and seated RK by the till. RK, PC Prettyman's wife, blinded in a road accident two years previously, worked in the library and helped in Stephen Cooper's bookshop. She was adept at dealing with customers and handling money.

"What dew yew want me to dew?" Emma turned to greet Maxine Cook. "Thanks for your willingness to give us a hand. Will you serve as Rosie prepares? Connie Foster has devised an order system, so we'll go with the flow, for the time being."

Connie kept half an eye on Mark and Rhoda, in between fulfilling her self-appointed task, but her mind eased when she saw that the church couple were keeping the children engrossed in some sort of activity. *How these people pull together in adversity! Dear God, I pray for Mark and Doug caught up in this storm out at sea and those who are involved in the rescue. Keep them safe and in your care.* She prayed in her heart as she moved on to the next table.

Emma, with a practised eye, kept close watch on the flow of customers as she cleared tables and re-stacked the dishwasher. She broke off as the intercom which linked the Tea Room preparation area with the main kitchen downstairs buzzed.

"Hello?"

"Hi, Emma."

"Oh, Jilly, I'm so pleased to hear you. I've been trying to contact you."

"When I heard the news, I thought you might need more food. I have a batch of scones in the oven and prepared some fresh carrot and coriander soup. Do you need anything else?"

"Could you send up, on the dumb waiter, any rolls and bread still in the shop and, also bacon. We'll put bacon butties on the menu, they're usually acceptable when the weather's cold. Thanks, my dear friend."

She conveyed this news to her stand-in staff. And began to re-write the 'available' menu on the Specials Board.

Connie reacted immediately. She clapped her hands. "Excuse me, dear customers. For those newly come in there will soon be carrot and coriander soup, bacon butties and freshly made scones available. Thank you all for your patience."

She darted quickly to the children's table. "All OK?"

The lady smiled. "Yes, we're getting on famously."

"Being well entertained," responded the man.

"This is my Dad's friend, Mr Piper, he lives at Newton Lokesby and has lots of boats."

"Well, that is great. Thanks, Mr and Mrs Piper."

"Yew're a'doin' a grand job m'girl. It's the least we can dew in the circumstances."

Down on the quay light was fading fast, but the storm was not abating nor the crowd diminishing. Flasks had been replenished for those manning the harbour master's look-out and controlling the inquisitive crowds. Repeatedly Constable Prettyman and Sergeant Catchpole requested people to leave the scene and go home but still many lingered or visited the church hall or Tea Rooms then returned to stand and watch. Most were reluctant to go. Anxious eyes peered across the gloom as contact was maintained with the lifeboat. Still no sighting of the 'Seagull'.

Sadness hovered over the village, heightened when the vet arrived on the scene and unfortunately, the injured horse had to be put down and dealt with appropriately. The curious spectators dispersed to the quay or in search of warmth offered in the Tea Rooms.

In the church Ben Durrant and Adam Catton led prayers of intercession interspersed by interludes of appropriate organ music played by Stuart Jenner, Rosie's father. Those gathered sang hymns of faith and trust, intermingled with words of encouragement by Hugh Darnell, the vicar, and readings from the Bible.

On seeing lights through the stained-glass windows and hearing music across the gathering dusk several visitors to the village drifted into the church. Those who did not find their way to the Tea Rooms ended up in the church hall to warm up with tea, coffee or soup. At the insistence of some of their customers a collection plate had been placed at the end of the serving table. "For the lifeboat or some such." People experienced helplessness against the elements but felt they wanted to do something practical towards the effort and show their appreciation of the work done by the rescue crew.

Jilly did not find any rolls or bread in the Village Stores because Pauline and Trixie had taken the entire stock as soon as the emergency was known, along with as many tins of soup, ham, cheese and tomatoes as they could carry, for the vicar's wife and her team at the church hall to make quickly prepared snacks. She did find two dozen rolls in the main kitchen freezer as well as four medium sliced loaves. "Ideal for toasted sandwiches." And commenced to make another batch of bread and baps straight away.

At 5.50pm came the news that all had been waiting for. "We've got a sighting."

CHAPTER TWELVE

Gale force 9!

A week the following Sunday the sun shone, and a calm sea gently lapped against the shore. A south westerly breeze edged its way lazily up the coast. Words from Psalm 107, much beloved by Tina Morehouse, dipped into Hugh Darnell's thoughts as he donned his vestments before walking out to face a packed church, 'He maketh the storm a calm so that the waves thereof are still'. The sceptics would have argued, 'Why didn't He do that last week?' With anguish of heart Hugh had spent much time in prayer before the Lord during the week in preparation for this service of worship and thankfulness. In the stillness of the vestry his mind revisited the chronology of the dramatic rescue that so many of the congregation had participated in either at sea or on land.

"I give thanks, Father God, for the manner in which the villagers, as well as those from further afield, pulled together and supported one another in this crisis."

After the initial May Day call had come in Wills, the harbour master, lost contact with the 'Seagull' so, although the life-boat crew were aware of the possible position they were having to rely on a homing device

Mark Bemment had installed on his boat. The turbulence of the stormy seas coupled with the force of the wind made the signal indistinct at times. The search and rescue helicopter had been on stand-by since the first shout, but weather conditions were so treacherous it was deemed too dangerous to take to the air. The controller prohibited take-off. "We don't want to risk other lives needlessly."

However, Andy Rawlins was duty pilot and Pete Boggis his co-pilot. Between them they had many hours of rescue flying experience under their belts. After hours of inactivity, hoping weather conditions would abate, when the lifeboat had been out a considerable length of time without a sighting, there appeared to be a lull in the gale. Andy turned to his crew and said, "I'm going up. I can't sit here twiddling my thumbs any longer when good men are fighting the elements for their lives."

"Don't be a fool," shouted Flt Lt Ward, manager of the unit. "You'll be putting your own lives at risk as well as the possible loss of a costly machine."

Pete turned to Andy as he picked up his gear, "I'm with you mate, let's make the best of this break in the storm," he uttered softly.

"If you're going up, you'll need me," Suzy Watkins, duty doctor, gathered her medics bag. "Me too," agreed one of the specialist paramedic winchmen.

"I'm not so sure this is a good idea," said the other winchman who recognized how precarious the wind made his task. Reluctantly he rose and picked up his gear and followed his colleagues.

"This is madness," the Flt Lt's face turned purple with rage. "Be this on your head, Rawlins."

"Sir, don't rail at me. Pray! Pray the lull will last long enough for us to locate them."

Andy marched firmly towards the waiting machine, his crew following closely in his footsteps. He punched in the satnav data he had been given. After thorough checks he turned on the controls. He spoke with air traffic control. Then, waited. After a short while they were cleared to go. The helicopter rose in an unorthodox manner into the air. It rocked unsteadily. Andy fought for control of his aircraft as it was buffeted by the wind. However, within 25 minutes of take-off they had located the stricken vessel and passed on its position to the lifeboat crew. With considerable skill a paramedic was winched down to the 'Seagull' where he found two unconscious men aboard. By the time the lifeboat reached the stricken vessel they had winched Doug aboard the helicopter and Suzy was using her expertise to assess his condition and administer necessary medical care.

"We don't really have room for another patient," Andy relayed to the coxswain on the lifeboat, "but these are exceptional circumstances. If you can get crew on board to steady the stricken vessel and assist with the manoeuvre, we think the other casualty will have a better chance if we can winch him up. We can get him to hospital quicker than you and a land ambulance could."

Hugh paused in his recollections, straightened his collar and smoothed his hair. "Thank you, Father God, for the skill and courage of those men."

Once the unconscious men were safely aboard the search and rescue helicopter the coxswain relayed the information to the harbour master's office. Wills suggested someone transport the immediate family to the Norwich hospital. "The search and rescue helicopter will probably land on the helipad at the hospital ahead of them." Ben Durrant left Adam to lead the prayer vigil in the church and persuaded Doug's wife, daughter and daughter-in-law into his car and drove to them hospital. Doctor Roger turned to his father, Doctor John, "I know I should be on call but if you will hold the fort, I'll take Doug's sister, Lettie and Mark's Dad to the hospital."

"Might be best if I go," John said quietly.

"You privy to insider information?"

John nodded. "I'll collect Lettie and Reggie from 'Green Pastures' and pick up Mum from the church hall. We may both be needed in the circumstances." On arrival at the hospital he accompanied Reg to the side room where his still unconscious son, Mark, had been placed then shepherded Lettie to the ward where the family were gathered round the bedside of her brother.

Dave desperately wanted to go with his father in the helicopter but recognised the impossibility of fulfilling that need. He knew his wife, his sister and Ben Durrant, his brother-in-law, would take care of their mother so he concentrated on rescuing Mark's struggling vessel and steering it safely into harbour. Hands were looking out for the arrival of the wrecked craft as they reached harbour to help salvage the boat and land the catch. Hugh Darnell was waiting with a car and change of clothing to drive him to the hospital. Not until he realised PC Prettyman was also on hand with his police motor bike to escort them to the hospital was Dave made aware of the seriousness of his father's condition.

Dave put his arms around his wife and sister as soon as he walked through the door of the side ward where his father lay. Christina was holding her husband's hand and bent low to hear the barely audible words that Doug was gasping to spurt out.

"Are you OK, Mum?"

When he heard Dave's voice, Doug reached out his free hand. "M'bor," he gasped, "Oi'm a 'goin' hum."

"You are, Dad?" Dave held tightly the hand extended to him.

"Oi, see Him, m'bor. He's a'reachin' out to me."

Tears coursed unbidden down Dave's cheeks.

"I'm so glad, Dad." He returned the squeeze that Doug gave him.

"Mek sure yew're Mam knows the way, m'bor. Oi'll see yew there."

"I will, Dad."

Doug's eyes sought Christina's, "Foller the rud, m'gal, foller the rud..." then he seemed to look beyond her, intently focussed on something or someone directly behind her. A smile broadened his lips, and his hands gradually relaxed their hold. He entered Heaven.

As tears flowed Hugh stretched out his hands in blessing.

"Behold, I see a new heaven and a new earth... I see the Holy city, the new Jerusalem, coming down out of heaven from God, prepared as a bride beautifully dressed for her husband. And I heard a loud voice from the throne saying, "Now the dwelling of God is with men, and He will live with them. They will be His people, and God Himself will be with them and be their God. He will wipe every tear from their eyes. There will be no more death or mourning or crying or pain, for the old order of things has passed away.

"He who was seated on the throne said, "I am making everything new!" Then He said, "Write this down, for these words are trustworthy and true."

"He said to me: "It is done, I am the Alpha and the Omega, the Beginning and the End. To him who is thirsty I will give to drink without cost from the spring of the water of life. He who overcomes will inherit all this, and I will be his God and he will be my son."

"Father God, thank you that we have been privileged to see our brother enter into eternal life. May the arms of love that reached down to receive him home now embrace those who are left behind with divine comfort and compassion in the name of Jesus, the risen one, who intercedes before Your throne on our behalf. Amen."

After a quiet word with Christina, Doctor John whispered to his wife, "I'll go along to sit with Reggie." Trixie nodded and moved towards the grieving women and ministered to them with her heart of compassion as he knew she would. *How blest I am to have such a wife who can get alongside people and be who they need her to be without being intrusive.* Trixie certainly had a gift to say and do the right thing even if often it meant remaining silent.

In those moments of quietude in the vestry before stepping out to address the congregation Hugh reflected how the jigsaw of events surrounding the tragedy fitted into place as different people subsequently shared their stories of that day.

Not until he recovered consciousness almost twenty-four hours after the rescue was Mark able to recount what happened aboard the 'Seagull' prior to losing contact with Wills, the harbour master.

"We'd had a good night's fishing, were on the return journey when a squall turned into a gale force storm, and we were caught broad side on. Wind and 20foot waves buffeted the boat till at times the deck was almost vertical. I lost my footing. Doug reached out to grab me to stop me going overboard but instantly another wave knocked us both into the turbulent sea. Thankfully, we were both wearing life jackets and were attached to the safety harnesses. With the swell I was able to snatch at a rail as another big wave seemed to spue me out and I could haul myself back aboard. Doug was less able to do that.

"I sent out the May Day signal then set about getting him back on board. Conditions were mighty difficult, and he seemed too weak to offer any assistance. The deck was still tilted, unbelievably slippery, so that I was unable to get a stable footing, but I persevered until I managed to attach myself to the spare safety line. I was determined to get Doug back on board. With each swell I could just about see the floating life jacket and he was still in it.

"I prayed for added strength to haul him in. It seemed to take forever. By this time, my hands were bleeding where the line had cut into them through my gloves with the constant effort of pulling on his safety harness. By God's help I eventually got him aboard and pushed him down by the hatch. "Leave me be, bor, oi'm a'goin' home. Yew git back." He kept saying repeatedly, "Oi'm a'goin' home". Almost as though he knew."

Doctor John nodded. "Yes, he knew. Terminal cancer, but he didn't want anyone else to know."

Christina knew. "He wanted to go out one last time which is why he offered to go with Mark when Sam was injured."

"I didn't know," said Dave quietly, "but Dad asked if he could come to the Wednesday house group a few weeks ago."

"He changed," Christina sniffed. "He was at peace about his illness and the future. Which is more than oi was. One day he said, "Come wi' me, m'gal." Oi went a couple of times to please him but this Christian squit ent for me," said Christina emphatically.

"But it made a difference to Dad?"

"Yes, it did, and he definitely saw something behind me just a'fore he died, didn't he?"

"Meks yew think, doan't it?" murmured Lettie.

"Mmm," murmured Christina dubiously.

"What happened to Mark?"

"Doesn't remember a thing after he tried to push Doug towards the hatch. Thinks a wave may have caught him unawares as he tried to get to the wheelhouse which thrust his head against something hard and caused him to lose consciousness."

Connie marvelled at the way the villagers supported the family during the following days. Numerous people passed her in the street carrying full pots and pans making their way to Christina's cottage. And daily, many friends made the trip to Norwich with Reggie, ensuring he had meals, and his son, Mark, was not left alone.

Although Christina agreed to a thanksgiving service in the church, for Dave and Rachel's sake, she was still adamant she was remaining an atheist. "Managed pretty well to be self-sufficient all my life this far so, oi'm sure oi can cope for the rest o' my life wi'out any heavenly prop. If yew're Dad felt the need to tek on board a Bible brace to see him through his final days, thass his choice, juss doan't come a'preachin' at me."

Doug's sister Lettie was of a different mind. "That Connie gal doan't goo around preachin' but she sure dew bounce with a joy that ent put on. Oi'd like a bit o' what she's got. An' his Lordship, he's a'bin different for some whiles."

"Why doan't you come to the Wednesday house group, Aunt Lettie? Try it for yourself. I'll pick you up at 6.45pm."

"Oi'll have to ask his Lordship's permission."

"Why?"

"'Cos oi'll hev to change the time o' his meal that day. Who else goes to it?"

"Well me, obviously, and Rachel, Michelle Cook, Connie, Mark, when he's ashore, Mrs Jenner, when she remembers, Uncle Billy and Aunt Pauline, RK and Dan, when he's off duty."

"Not yew, Dave?"

"Jansy and I go to the one at the Castleton's on Tuesdays."

"No strangers, then?"

"All people you know."

"Oi'll give it a goo, then."

Rachel put her arms around her, "Oh Aunt Lettie," and kissed her cheek. Ben smiled at her and in his heart breathed a prayer, "Thank you, Lord."

Chapter Thirteen

Icicles!

Winter came on apace and Stephen managed to rearrange the meeting with Lord Edmund before Connie became engulfed in copious preparations for an English Christmas both at school and church. Adam introduced the score for the Hallelujah Chorus in choir practice, as well as a John Rutter piece he was quite taken with. Connie's memory took flight to Christmas in Barbados the previous year when she had sung with the choir at the annual Royal Barbados Police Band New Year's concert held in the Prince Cave Hall when the combined voices had almost lifted the roof. How could the English choir match that?

She did enjoy the challenge of singing it again albeit in a different setting with different people. It was the sort of music that lifted one's spirit to heavenly realms and reminded one of the ultimate joys of singing praises around the eternal throne. She caught Mark's eye and smiled. *How good to see him back, singing in the choir after his ordeal.* "And He shall reign for ever and ever," the notes rang out. *What a great day that will be!*

Following the epilogue at the end of the practice the choir members left the church in an exhilarated huddle. Connie was alongside Alex and Emma.

"Wow! That was a powerful rehearsal!"

"I agree. Exacting but stimulating."

Miranda, Jackie and Mark joined them.

"Good to see you today, Mark," said Emma.

"Have you completely recovered from your ordeal in the sea?" Connie asked.

Mark turned towards her. In the light of an open doorway, as one of the members reached home, Connie caught his smile. "It's kind of you to ask. I have occasional lapses of memory, but Doc says that's not surprising considering the knock to the head I suffered but otherwise I am fine."

"De Good Lord be praised!"

"More like thanks to good nursing care," muttered Jackie sourly.

"That is encouraging news," Alex commented more positively.

Emma reached her gate. "I'll say 'good night' but so glad you're feeling better, Mark."

"Have you been back out to sea?" Connie asked as they continued down the lane.

"Yes, just last week. Repairs to the 'Seagull' took longer than anticipated but Doc said that was a good thing, gave me more time to recuperate and Dad a bit of respite in the smoke house."

"Best not to rush things."

"Yes, that's what I discovered which is why we only stayed out for a short trip. Next time we'll remain out fishing for a longer period."

Alex and Jackie bid them farewell and went their separate ways home.

"How did your conversation with Lord Edmund go?" asked Mark as they neared 'Bakers'.

Connie stopped by the gate and for a moment did not reply.

"Connie?" Mark could see she was struggling with her emotions.

Eventually, with a break in her voice, Connie said quietly, "Lord Edmund is a really sensitive man. I think the bluff persona he presents is a cover up for his natural gentle disposition."

"No!" Mark ejaculated.

Connie slowly nodded. "I am telling you the truth. The evidence that points to our families being related because of the actions of one of his ancestors obviously tore at his heart."

"I think those in the village who have been at the receiving end of his curtness over the years would find it hard to believe that was true."

But Connie recalled the graciousness and compassion of a man in tears as they shared precious moments together. "He was anxious to make reparation, but I made it clear that was not what I was looking for. I simply wanted to know our family's beginnings."

Jackie had requested Connie work with Kerry Stafford on the singing aspect of the Nativity production while other members of staff were allocated further areas of responsibility.

Emma with her artistic flair designed an amazing back drop, very simple but effective. Class 6 had great fun painting within the outline that she had drawn.

"Look, Mrs Cooper, oi've med the star gold."

"That's great Katy, When James and Gracie have finished painting the sky, I'll show you how to make the rays from the star shine over the stable."

"Wow! Really?"

Emma nodded. "Stay inside the lines."

Tina Morehouse was making costumes with her class.

"Nothing too elaborate," reminded Jackie. "Simple is most appealing and it must be within the children's capabilities. It's a reflection of their skills not those of the costumiers of the Dramatic Society," she concluded, referring to a previous year when Tina involved the seamstresses from the amateur dramatic society to which she belonged, who produced creations far too elaborate for a school nativity production.

When the day for the first performance dawned spirits were high and excitement was infectious. Some were confident, others nervous, necessitating more frequent trips to the toilets than was usual.

"Can't remember ma loines, Miss."

"You will be fine. You were word perfect at the rehearsal."

"Miss, where be ma head dress?" asked Rich frantically tipping props all over the floor.

"It should be in the red box on the shelf by your table if you put it away yesterday."

"Yew be roite, Miss."

"Put these back, please," Connie instructed indicating the mess on the floor.

"Yus, Miss," he said sheepishly.

The school hall could only accommodate a limited number of people in an audience so three performances were planned to allow as many parents and family members as possible to see their children's efforts. They were spread over three days, morning, afternoon and early evening to fit in with all work patterns.

The culmination of all the hard work was the presentation at the Church Carol Service on the last Sunday evening prior to Christmas Day.

Excitement was at fever pitch. School had broken up for the Christmas holidays and Connie had been warned that some of the performers might well not turn up.

"Some of the parents are lax in supporting their offspring's activities at school let alone a nativity performance in the church," Jackie explained. "I send repeated notices home with all the pupils reminding them of dates and times. Stuart Jenner and Stephen Cooper take out the minibus after lunch to pick up those who live too far away to walk back home from the village in the dark, unaccompanied. The men go early because they often must wait since children are not ready or parents have forgotten. One year we didn't have a Joseph, but thankfully because the children are so good at learning each other's lines we were able to find a stand in."

"I trust we do not have that problem this year," Connie remarked hopefully.

"It happens all the time. We get used to it," Jackie said resignedly. "Someone always falls ill, generally from nerves or stage fright or overindulgence."

"At one time the nativity performance was the finale of the Carol Service, by which time the children were fidgety and fed up, but Hugh Darnell has changed the format drastically. It works remarkably well. The children are now part of the service from the start," Emma explained to Connie.

"They actually sit in church all through the service?"

"Oh, yes, no standing in the vestry or draughty porch waiting for cues and trying to keep them quiet during proceedings."

"That must have been hard work."

"Mmm. There is now a rehearsal in the afternoon, so you will see how it all flows and comes together as a whole. The vicar's wife and her team of ladies from the W.I. provide tea in the church hall for everyone involved."

"But we also have choir practice that Sunday afternoon!"

"That is usual, but it all fits nicely as a glove. You'll see."

Connie raised her eyebrows and shrugged in disbelief but still beamed her signature smile at Emma showing her willingness to accept her word that all would go well.

The day after school had broken up for the holidays Connie met up with Miranda during her lunch break at the Tea Rooms. As previously arranged RK was already there to greet them.

"I hear the school nativity performances were superb and went without a hitch."

"The children did exceptionally well. I loved the way they encouraged one another. If anyone faltered with their words someone close by was able to prompt them."

"I'm looking forward to seeing it on Sunday."

Connie was somewhat nonplussed at RK's turn of phrase considering she was totally blind.

"Morning, ladies," Rosie approached their table with a bright grin. "I understand these two are introducing you to an English Christmas delicacy, Connie."

Connie looked at her companions with a bemused smile on her face.

"Mince pies," explained Miranda.

"Ooh," said Connie slowly unsure what was going to be set before her to sample.

"And to drink?"

"Coffee, please," said RK.

"Usual, Rosie," said Miranda.

"Connie?" Rosie enquired.

"No, don't answer. I know, 'Hot chocolate and all the works,' to quote Mark Durrant."

Connie's rich laughter reverberated around the Tea Rooms causing other customers to look in their direction and break into smiles and grins.

"How do you remember all the preferences of all your customers?"

"Practise and experience."

"But you have so many!"

Rosie went away to prepare their order, laughter sitting on her shoulders.

After she had left them RK leaned forwards and placed a hand on Connie's arm and asked quietly, "How's the romance going?"

Connie gasped and looked up astonished.

RK sensed a negative reaction. Since her accident RK had learned to read silences and noises and as her hand was still on Connie's arm, the tension at her question.

"I'm sorry, Connie, have I spoken out of turn? I understood that you and Mark Bemment have been walking out together."

"That is right. He walks me home after choir practice and house group when he is home from sea, and we have met up once or twice in here for lunch and afternoon tea."

"But what do you think of him?" Miranda enquired probingly.

"He is a gentle giant. I enjoy spending time with him. We find much to talk about. But romance does not come into it."

"I wouldn't be too sure. Mark is not known to walk out with young ladies. He is a very eligible bachelor. Many have tried to catch his eye, unsuccessfully I might add."

"I value his friendship. Please, do not spoil it by suggesting anything else. I return home to Barbados at the end of the school year. I did not come to England seeking a young man. I shall be so embarrassed when I next see him in case that is what he thinks."

"Sorry, Connie, I didn't plan to upset you. When I heard you were keeping company with one another I simply thought you were two lovely people who were so well suited and was pleased for you both. I won't mention it again."

"Bless you, RK. I assure you we are simply friends who like talking together. When de Good Lord wishes me to have a mate, He will make it clear to me."

Sunday afternoon rehearsal was quite a revelation. Year 5 knew the routine well and kept Connie abreast of proceedings.

"We 'ave t'look fer our names on the seats, Miss, an' the vicar will tell us what to dew."

"Your name will be on two seats, Miss Foster, because you're our teacher and also in the choir," Daniel explained.

"I see," replied Connie.

"Here's yew'res, Miss," yelled Jess.

"Thank you, Jessica, but don't shout so loudly in church."

The children are right. The rehearsal is going like clockwork under the direction of the vicar, Connie mused as the afternoon wore on without a hitch.

She had panicked at the commencement of the rehearsal because Gracie and Keir, who were Mary and Joseph, were nowhere to be seen.

Daniel allayed her fears and kept her informed. "Don't worry, Miss Foster, they'll come in when it's their turn."

"Sit back and enjoy," quoted Archie in a grown-up voice. She smiled.

"It's good. Real good."

Once again, the children were spot on with their assessment. Hugh Darnell did indeed pilot everything through with panache and dignity, as well as sensitivity.

At the conclusion of the dummy run the children were instructed to place their costumes under their seats then, class by class, escorted to the church hall where a sumptuous tea was served to them. Individual cardboard plates had been filled with goodies that most children like and covered with cling film. Connie noticed that amongst her pupils there was a little swapping of food stuffs going on, but nothing was wasted. After a little while ladies came round offering drinks of blackcurrant and orange squash.

After visits to the toilets, the classes were shepherded back into the church at 5:30pm. As her class walked down the nave, mostly in an orderly fashion, an excited buzz greeted them. The church was already three-quarters full.

"By the time the service starts, Miss, it will be standing room only."

"No one wants to stand so they get here early."

"We needs to put on our costumes."

By the time Hugh Darnell ascended the pulpit steps the atmosphere was electric. As the church choir rose to sing, 'Angels from the realms of Glory', angels of various sizes and ages 'flew' down the aisles to sit on suitably placed chairs on either side of the altar. Then the voice of Ricky Saunders broke the silence that followed singing the opening verse of 'Once in Royal David's City'. The school choir stood and joined him in verse two, the church choir swelling the volume when they reached verse three. The organ crescendo-ed before verse four and the congregation rose as one and joined in singing the remainder of the carol.

The Christmas story unfolded before their eyes in verses of scripture and carols interspersed by the children's enactment of the nativity narrative.

Connie felt a tug on her sleeve.

"See, Miss, oi told yew they'd be here," whispered Archie, as Gracie, dressed as Mary, and Keir as Joseph leading the donkey ambled down the nave.

"You were so right."

The service culminated with the Hallelujah chorus. The atmosphere was stirringly charged. Not a few eyes were puddled with tears. Connie was proud of her pupils. They stood when everyone else stood as is the custom when the Hallelujah Chorus is performed. But this was not a performance. It was an act of worship. She kept half an eye on the children as well as, on Adam who was conducting the choir and those in the congregation who wished to join in. As far as she could see all were well behaved. *Must congratulate them.*

At its conclusion, the congregation sat down. Hugh spoke from the pulpit. "My sermon this evening is taken from John chapter 3 verse 16." Groans rippled across the church.

Hugh smiled across his congregation. "One sentence, so listen carefully.

God loved and gave

We believe and live.

I will say it again and then I want you to repeat some words after me.

God loved and gave

We believe and live.

God loves me and gave Jesus for me.

I am the reason He was born, died and rose again.

If I believe I will live with Him in eternity.

Do not forget it! The most important message of the Christmas story.

Let us stand and sing in conclusion 'Silent Night', as our benediction.

Have a blessed and God filled Christmas. Don't forget the Christingle service on Christmas Eve at four-thirty."

Chapter Fourteen

Mists all around!

By her place setting on Christmas morning Connie found a Christmas stocking filled with lumps and bumps.

"Happy Christmas, Connie," Miss Pedwardine greeted warmly as she completed preparations for their breakfast.

"Happy Christmas and de Good Lord's blessings be on you," Connie beamed as she placed a beautifully wrapped parcel at the far end of the kitchen table. Since this Caribbean young lady had come to share her home Jennifer Pedwardine's face broke into smiles far more readily than before. She found that Connie's natural ebullience and genuine joy was infectious. One could not fail to respond.

"Please, open this now," Connie pleaded excitedly. "I so want to know if it pleases you. I asked Clyde to send it specially for you."

"First, let us eat breakfast while it is still hot." They had agreed that Jennifer would prepare a traditional English breakfast Christmas morning and Connie would do the honours Boxing Day with a typical Barbadian breakfast. "If I can find the ingredients," Connie added with a chuckle.

As Jennifer placed the full plates on the table then poured coffee from the coffee pot Connie peaked into her stocking.

"Wow! As Joss would say." Jennifer smiled at Connie's reaction then gave thanks.

After one mouthful Connie could not resist drawing something out of the stocking – a clementine, some almonds and walnuts in their shells. Her eyes opened wide. She put down her cutlery. Next, she took out a Mars Bar, followed by a Kit Kat, a bar of soap, hand cream, hat, gloves and scarf to match and in the toe, she found a tiny coin.

"Eat up, girl, before it gets cold." Connie positioned the coin carefully on the table and did as she was told.

"A silver threepenny piece," explained her companion. "I used to receive the many-sided threepenny bit in my stocking each year as a child, but I wanted you to have this silver one because it is part of your English heritage and would have been in circulation during the time of your ancestors."

"Really? Oh, how lovely." Connie picked it up and looked at it more closely.

"The first silver 3d was issued in 1551 in the reign of Edward V1. This particular one doesn't go that far back but I would like to take you to the jewellers in Norwich to have this put into a filigree setting of your choice and made into a necklace or a brooch so that you have a permanent reminder of your English roots."

Connie clapped her hands gleefully. "Oh, thank you, thank you. That is such a generous and kind gift." She rose spontaneously from her seat, flung her arms around the seated Jennifer, bent forward and hugged her.

"You are so caring. You pretend to be so stiff and stern, but de Good Lord has blessed you with a heart of overflowing love." Miss Pedwardine, so unused to such a demonstration of affection, coloured-up with embarrassment.

Connie darted back to her place. Ate a few more mouthfuls of food unaware of the emotion she had stirred in Jennifer. She had simply behaved in a manner that was normal to her.

"Now undo your present," she instructed.

Jennifer took a moment to blow her nose. Slowly sipped some of her coffee, giving herself time to recover from Connie's display of warmth and friendliness. She replaced her coffee cup and began to undo the elaborate wrapping enveloping the large oblong-shaped parcel Connie pushed in front of her.

Connie fidgeted excitedly in her seat, more reminiscent of her restless pupils than a sedate young lady of mature years. She watched intently as Jennifer cautiously withdrew the contents out of the box.

"My word, girl, what have we here?"

"It is all official." Connie assured her. "There is a certificate of authentication, and it has been scrutinized by customs. My brother, Clyde, went through the botanical society to ensure that it was all done correctly."

Gingerly, Jennifer unwrapped the plants so carefully snuggled within the packaging and laid them on the end of the kitchen table they were not using and perused the paperwork attached to the parcel.

"Bougainvillea?" She counted the plants. "So many!"

"They will grow in your sunroom all through the year or the greenhouse in Summer. I know how you like to experiment with your plants. At home we grow them in the garden."

"Too cold here." Jennifer continued to delve inside the box.

"What have we here?" she asked again.

"Orchids. In Barbados they appear to be parasitic but, in fact, they attach themselves to a host tree and air grow. I'm not sure how they will grow in an English climate."

"What a thoughtful gesture, Connie. Thank you so much. I will get tremendous pleasure from learning about these plants and hopefully growing them successfully too. I will contact the local horticultural society or perhaps the British orchid society will be the better option and seek their advice."

Jennifer placed her new plants back on the table and glanced at the kitchen clock.

"We need to get a move on, or we'll be late. More coffee?"

In no time at all they finished their meal, washed up and prepared for the Christmas morning service.

They walked companionably to the church each thrilled that their choice of gift had been so favourably received.

Following the service of praise and worship Jennifer met up with Lord Edmund and arm in arm they strolled to 'Green Pastures' to celebrate Christmas with his sister Bernice, Roy and Justin. Lettie, Lord Edmund's housekeeper had been given the day off. So, she, along with her sister-in–law, Christina, were having Christmas dinner with Ben, Rachel and the children, Mark and Rhoda. As it was the first Christmas without Doug Rachel thought it best if they did something different this year. Christmas Day had always been Christina's day. She revelled in entertaining all her family at home under one roof. Rachel felt they would all cope better if they broke with tradition.

Rhoda held on to Aunt Lettie's hand as they walked across the Green chatting about the doll she had received as a present and the friends she had seen at church. Lettie had been attending the house group held in the Tea Rooms on Wednesday evenings ever since Doug's funeral and in more recent weeks travelled with Lord Edmund down to the Sunday morning 11o'clock service. The vicar's words about God's love being displayed in a baby born to die had moved her heart. She was pleased to have a few moments to ponder on those thoughts as she walked along with her chatty, great niece. Christina was still very anti-Christianity but made the effort to go on Christmas morning to please her children. Mark spoke to her about the new kitten who had recently joined their family.

"She's a tortoiseshell, Nan, and likes playing with pieces of string or Mum's rollers if they fall on the floor. I'll let you stroke her when we get home. She is very soft and cuddly."

"Thass a lot o' extra work," muttered Christina disapprovingly.

"I look after her all by myself," he said boastfully.

"I wonder how long that will last!" she remarked disparagingly.

"I feed her and sort out her litter tray before and after school."

"Won't be long a'fore yew get fed-up."

Undeterred the young lad remained cheerful. He had a compassionate heart, knew his Nan was still sad about losing his grandad, but he loved his little cat and knew he would never tire of her.

"Oh look, there's Miss Foster," he pointed across the Green where Connie was walking with Emma and Doctor Roger Cooper.

"Happy Christmas, Miss Foster," he shouted merrily.

Connie waved. "Happy Christmas Mark. Have a great day. De Good Lord be with you."

"Much hope of that," Christina grumbled.

"He is with us, Nan. Dad says it tells us that in the Bible."

"Load o' ole squit."

Mark skipped to walk with Rhoda and Aunt Lettie. Rachel stepped back to keep company with her mother. She slipped her arm through Christina's. "Come on, Mum, no sour faces today."

Across the Green the young people entered the home of Doctor John and Trixie Cooper where Connie had been invited for Christmas lunch.

"Make yourself at home, Connie," Trixie welcomed. "I know it's not at all like home, but I want you to relax and feel comfortable."

"That is so good of you, Mrs Cooper."

"Trixie, please."

"Coffee and mince pies coming up," Jansy walked in carrying a full tray. She and Dave had arrived at the house first and prepared the drinks.

"Christmas dinner is usually served a little later than on a normal day, but we try and be finished by 3 o'clock so that we can listen to the Queen's message," Trixie explained.

"Then, if the weather's favourable, we all go for a brief walk before it gets dark. Not compulsory, but generally good fun." Emma grinned.

"That all sounds excellent to me. No sea bath, then?" teased Connie.

"Well, some people in Lowestoft will have been for a charity swim though usually it's nothing more than a toe-dip into the water and out again as it is so cold."

"Don't you believe them, Miss Foster," Stephen quipped. "When I took part a few years ago I got thoroughly soaked."

"Yeah, yeah, yeah," Roger joked.

"In Barbados we have a sea bath after the service and a picnic lunch at Folkstone beach then Mumma prepares a meal for all the family in the early evening of Christmas Day."

"Is Christmas very different?"

"Christmas is a beautiful time to visit the island as it is pleasantly hot but not blisteringly so. Most homes and businesses are decorated with Christmas lights. Bridgetown is lit up in red and green and the roundabouts portray different themes. A Christmas drive is a must for most families. We usually do that after our meal. We exchange gifts and it is a day of celebrating de birth of our Lord Jesus. Everyone goes to church.

"Mumma makes Great Cake and baked ham. Music is important to Bajan people, so the radio station blares out Christmas music all day and there are numerous Christmas concerts across the island.

"We always attend the one held in Prince Cave Hall given by the Royal Barbados Police Band which is accompanied by one of the many choirs we have in Barbados."

"I didn't know about the baked ham, but I asked Jilly Briggs to instruct me in some of the recipes you have spoken about. I hope they are to your taste."

Connie jumped up and flung her arms enthusiastically around Trixie almost knocking her off balance.

"You are too kind and thoughtful. I shall enjoy whatever you have prepared as long as it is not roast beef and Yorkshire pudding." She pulled a face. Everybody laughed.

"It's a good job you are not coming tomorrow then," said Stephen still curled up with merriment.

"Why is that?"

"We always have roast beef and Yorkshire pudding on Boxing Day."

"Good. That is not to my taste!"

After a very enjoyable meal, excellent food interspersed with interesting conversation, the family watched the Christmas message from the Queen."

"As usual a distinctive Christian message from her Majesty. Very thought provoking." Doctor John rose. "Trixie and I are going to visit Reggie and Mark Bemment."

"When we've loaded up the dish washer Dave and I are walking over to see Rachel and Ben."

"We'll give you a hand, then Emma and I are going for a stroll by the river. What are you planning to do, Stephen?"

"Just popping down the lane to meet up with Nicky. Thanks for a delicious meal, Mum. First class as always."

"You are most welcome. You have a choice, Connie. Tag on to any of the strolling walkers or stay in by the fire."

"May I come along with you and Doctor John?"

"Sure."

When they arrived at the Bemment's house Mark invited Connie to walk with him down by the quay. "Before the dusk falls."

"It's a'goin' to be foggy tonoite, bor," warned Reggie.

"We won't be long, Dad."

"We'll keep company with Reggie till you return, Mark. Enjoy your walk while it's fine and still daylight."

Chapter Fifteen

Foggy patches!

Connie pulled her new hat down over her ears, muffled her scarf tighter around her neck then snuggled her gloved hands into the deep pockets of the winter coat she was grateful Penny Darnell had given to her. She walked companionably alongside Mark occasionally taking a skip between steps to keep up with his long strides.

"You are very quiet, today."

"I am just thinking of what my family may be doing?"

"I trust they are well?"

"My brother Clyde wrote this week to say Mumma had a fall which required hospital treatment. He doesn't go into details, but they are spending Christmas day at my Aunt's house."

"I am so sorry your mother has been injured."

"Mmm! For Mumma not to prepare for a family Christmas I fear she must be more seriously hurt than he is telling me."

"Perhaps you could Facetime them later today. Speaking with her might put your fears to rest."

Thoughtfully, Connie put her head to one side. "I will need help to make that connection."

"We could do that when we return to the house."

"Thank you, that would be good."

"How are you finding Christmas celebrations in England?"

"Somewhat different!"

"In what way?"

"The weather, for one, which obviously contributes to closed doors."

"Oh?"

"Yes, we would have doors and windows wide open so that everyone's noise and festivities blend into one, whether at home or in church."

"One continuous party, then?"

"Sort of," she replied, then kept him entertained with colourful descriptions of Christmas activities in Barbados including some of the antics her siblings had indulged in.

"One Christmas Daddy was on call at the hospital. He was poised to carve the baked ham Mumma had prepared when the phone rang. 'Sorry, Mumma Madge.' He put the carving implements down on the table and prepared to leave.

'Don't you worry, Daddy, I will take your place.' My brother Garfield was about 7 or 8 at the time. He climbed on to Daddy's chair at the table, picked up the carving knife and fork and commenced to carve.

"Mumma's eyes were nearly popping out of her head at his audacity. Daddy grinned and nodded as he exited through the door. Garry stabbed the carving fork into the ham and pulled back the knife with a flourish to make the first cut. Unfortunately, he took his eyes off what he was supposed to be doing to look at his audience and the ham moved as though it had a will of its own. The knife hit the ham at an awkward angle, cut off a chunk instead of a slice that bounced on to the table. Mumma let him continue but all the time he was chasing the ham around the platter. 'It will not stay still,' he moaned. In fact, it almost ended up on the floor, but Clyde reacted quickly enough to catch it. At one point Garry threw the carving knife and fork on to the table in disgust. 'Daddy makes it look so easy. I cannot do this.' He slammed his hand on to the table crossly.

"'Practise and perseverance. Pick up de knife and fork, Garfield, and finish de job.' Mumma instructed firmly. 'We are waiting. You never leave a job unfinished that you have started.' Garry grimaced and reluctantly continued.

"We had chunks of ham, all sizes, that Christmas Day dinner and Mumma made sure we all learnt a valuable lesson."

Mark chuckled at the vision of a ham rolling all around a well-set Christmas table.

"Daddy is a surgeon so is used to cutting accurately with a knife."

Mark erupted into laughter.

Connie realised her gaff. "I did not mean to suggest he treats his patients like a baked ham."

"I'm sure you didn't, but obviously he has quite a skill at wielding knives. Nothing so dramatic happened in our family but Mum and Dad always ensured my sister, and I had a happy day. This is our first Christmas without Mum. I think Dad is finding it hard. He doesn't speak about his feelings, but he really misses her, so I'm glad Doc John and Mrs Cooper have called in to visit him."

"I am so sorry about your Mumma."

"Her heart just gave out. Dad blames himself. Thinks he worked her too hard in the smoke house and fish stall. But it was our livelihood, and we all did our bit even when we were children. My sister, Helen, couldn't stand it so when her husband Simon was offered a transfer to New Zealand with his firm, she was delighted to be free from the tie of all the work associated with fish. They emigrated three years ago. They now have two children. Mum and Dad were saving up to go and visit them this coming year so that they could spend time with their grandchildren. I've told Dad he should still go for a holiday but he's adamant he's not going on his own."

"Afraid of the unknown, I suppose."

"You're right. He's very much a home-loving person. It was Mum who wanted to travel. He's spent all his working life at sea, so he's used to its hardship and accustomed to all that the elements throw up but doesn't trust flying."

"Mumma is the same. 'You not get me in dem flying machines,' she said when I suggested she come to England to see me. 'Dat ocean is too big for a sea bath,' was her reason."

"I guess your parents, like mine, struggled to make ends meet in the early years of their married life and wanted better for their children."

Connie nodded. "As well as working hard at their careers and building a home Mumma and Daddy, in particular, had to contend with racial prejudice amongst other things and insisted we work hard to become the best we can be on whatever pathway de Good Lord sends us on."

"You were obviously brought up in a family where Christian values were an important part of daily life."

"Yes, but we also had to learn that our parents' experience was not ours."

"Same here."

"Mumma always said, 'You must trust de Good Lord for your own salvation. Mine is mine and yours is yours.' I made my own decision when I was 11 after an invitation given by our Pastor."

"I also made a decision as a child but during my teenage years at college I was plagued with doubts. I started to indulge in pursuits other lads on my course engaged in over weekends. Also, about that time, I stopped going to church. I came to my senses one Saturday night. I had been drinking with my so-called mates but unbeknown to me someone slipped something into my drink. I understand I became out of my mind. I can't remember anything about it other than what others have subsequently told me. I didn't arrive home that night. Mum and Dad were beside themselves with worry so called the vicar who organized a prayer circle on my behalf and friends went out to look for me.

"The town pastors found me on Lowestoft seafront semi-unconscious, covered in vomit. As I was in no condition to respond to their questions, they asked those who were hanging around me if they knew who I was then got Mum and Dad's number from my mobile.

"Apparently I kept repeating, 'I can't go home, I can't go home like this.'

"They also called paramedics who took me to the local hospital to be checked over.

"In the early hours of the morning, Justin and Dave collected me from the hospital and took me directly to

Aunt Bernice's. Godly woman that she is, dear Aunt Bernice soon got me sorted out and back on the straight and narrow. She loved me and prayed me back into the fold. I no longer had the desire to be doing those things that messed up my life and displeased God. I stayed at 'Green Pastures' for about a week and returned home a new man, truly reborn, rejuvenated. I thank the Lord for second chances, for His ever-abounding grace and mercy, which I certainly don't deserve.

"Ever since that time I have been on the town pastors' team in the town, serving one weekend each month when I am home from sea. Having been there I know what temptations and unknown pitfalls these young people face."

Connie reached out and touched Mark's arm. "De Good Lord is so gracious to love and strengthen us even when we fail Him."

"More than we can imagine."

"Don't we learn, through the wilderness experiences of life, the truth about trust and righteousness?"

"And the measure of His grace."

"Yes, it is only God's grace that keeps us from falling apart at times."

Mark nodded in agreement. "How glad I am that in His providential care He holds on to us in all circumstances of life. I am particularly conscious of His presence when I am out at sea."

"Look at Nelson Mandella." Mark stopped and turned towards Connie, titled his head and raised his eyebrows at her. Connie proceeded to elaborate. "Archbishop Tutu said of Mandella's 27 years in jail, 'They mellowed him,' yet, he was stronger when he was released than when he went in. Look at what was achieved in that country."

"The situation is still far from perfect."

"True, but it was a start. We never know who or what de Good Lord plans through our trust and obedience."

"He certainly rescued me through the ministrations of Dave and Justin, who are only a year or so older than me but have become such supportive mates on my Christian journey. I am especially grateful for the love and prayers of Aunt Bernice."

"And look at how the community prayed and pulled together on the night of the storm."

"Yes, I was amazed when I learned of all that went on during that night yet when we know Jesus as Lord there are unseen bonds that hold believers together and prompts them to offer support to one another."

"From sinking sand, He lifted me," Connie began to sing. Mark smiled and took hold of her hand as they continued to walk.

"Bless you, Constance Joy Foster."

Immediately, she stopped singing. "You know my name?"

"Of course, you are rightly named. Every day you live out your name. You are constantly full of joy and an inspiration to so many. I thank the Good Lord that you ever came to Newton Westerby."

"You do?"

"You may not know it, but you have touched many lives with your constant joy, your ready smile, gentle words and willing hands."

Connie shook her head. "I simply live for Him."

"And it shows."

Mark turned and looked directly into her eyes, his weathered face wreathed in smiles, and he squeezed her hand tightly.

Her heart took an unexpected leap.

Constance Joy you have not come here to find an English young man! You came to teach the children and find out about your Greats, she admonished.

But in that moment as the sea mist descended and fog began to engulf them her heart said otherwise.

CHAPTER SIXTEEN

Warm with a gentle breeze!

Memories of Christmas festivities faded as Connie immersed herself in teaching preparation for class 5 at the commencement of the new spring term. In her free time she continued the research of her English ancestors. Some days she sat in the Tea Rooms wading through the copious files Stephen Cooper had unearthed for her out of the de Vessey archives making notes of dates and names. On others she ploughed through information that was displayed in the museum. Some she found pertinent whilst other material was interesting but far from relevant. The yellowing letters Lord Edmund had unearthed she fitted into plastic sleeves in order to protect them, placed them in chronological order, and painstakingly transcribed the barely legible handwriting.

One day she chatted with Tina Morehouse, whom she thought as a local girl would have had some in-depth knowledge of the history of the area and could point her in the right direction, but Tina impatiently brushed her aside. "Not interested in all that outdated bosh. Suggest you ask Tim Draycott."

When Connie learned that Tim also had a degree and interest in history, she endeavoured to catch him one afternoon at the end of the school day. "Mr Draycott, can you spare me a moment of your time." He looked briefly at his watch. "Of course, but it will need to be quick as I do need to escort Jack and Leonie home."

Connie acknowledged his concern about collecting his son and daughter to ensure they reached home safely. "If you meet the children, perhaps I could join you at the school gate and accompany you down the lane and speak with you as we walk."

"Certainly, I'll see you in a few moments." He cast his eyes around his immaculate classroom to ensure that all was spick and span, picked up his briefcase and walked briskly towards Leonie's classroom exit.

Connie dashed back to year 5's classroom put on her coat and collected her bags. She checked that nothing was out of place, turned off the lights and made her way to the main school gate where Tim and the children were waiting for her.

She smiled at Jack and Leonie, "Hi, you two, have you had a good day?" Leonie looked at her sheepishly pulling behind her father, but Jack proceeded to fill her in on all the activities he had been up to with his classmates.

"It sounds as though you've had an interesting day," Tim commented, "But now, Miss Foster and I would like to have a little talk." He glanced enquiringly at Connie.

"Mr Draycott, what do you know about the history of this place we live in, particularly from the early 1800's onwards?" If Tim Draycott was surprised at Connie's question, he did not show it but proceeded to mention specific volumes in the library that covered the topic she was interested in. "I'm sure Mrs Prettyman or

Abigail Saunders could point you in the right direction. For a village library they have an excellent local history section. I have also acquired some old maps depicting the area before the sea claimed Newton Easterby which I can loan to you. They make fascinating reading. I'll bring them along to school tomorrow."

Connie gaily clapped her hands together. "Oh, thank you, that may help me to piece together some of the missing pieces in the jigsaw surrounding my family tree."

Whilst Connie had much to occupy her working and leisure time Mark too was actively engaged having returned to his regular fishing schedule following the 'Seagull's' repair and overhaul. To Reggie's delight a couple of lads showed an interest in the Smoke House so he employed them as part-time apprentices on the student day release scheme from the college. Now that she was no longer running Ransome's fish stall on the quay because Dave was diversifying by taking people on sea-angling trips Christina worked part-time for Reggie and Mark. She was currently training one of the village girls to fillet fish, man the stall on Tuesday and Friday mornings and pack smoked fish into boxes devised by Stephen and Mark and made up by the apprentices. "In ma grandmother's day smoked herrin's an' kippers were sent by post all uvver the country. But this practice declined dramatically as supermarkets opened wi' inhouse fish counters but Lizzie Bemment saw a niche an' established an online service. It's really tek'n off, but we only send out orders once a fortnoite."

Since both Connie and Mark were thus involved in the day-to-day routine of their busy lives, their paths rarely crossed. Only when Mark was ashore did they occasionally meet at Sunday services, Wednesday Bible Study group or choir practice on a Thursday. They smiled and spoke, but the intimacy of the Christmas afternoon walk was not repeated, circumstances and Connie's resolve, to ensure her head rule her heart, determined that. Yet, her eyes always looked for him.

Sometimes an English Spring gambolled in gently like a lamb, at other times it roared in like a lion, thrusting doors open and sending washing billowing across the gardens, looking like sails on a ship, fastened to ships masts as they were. The wind playfully teased the housewives by tugging at the many pegs they used to anchor clothes to the line then sending them scurrying after garments that were whisked away by sudden gusts into the mud of a neighbour's garden.

This year it started out like the first but was soon taken over by fierce winds and rough seas making Connie fearful she was going to have to revert to extra layers of clothing during the day and hot water bottles at night. Then, with the changing of the clocks to British Summer Time, the wind died down, the sun shone with a pleasant warmth and the sea became a gentle calm.

Easter was well behind them and now they found themselves nearly to mid-April.

"Spring is passing all too quickly," Rosie commented to Lyndsay and Tracy, as she instructed them to change the drooping flowers displayed on the windowsills. They were students from the College on work placement at the Tea Rooms for the latter half of the spring term,

"Fresh flowers are on the table by the door. Please attend to them there and not by the food preparation area." She turned to check the fresh salad supplies which had been delivered by her brother Nathan earlier that morning from the market garden he ran with his mother at Jenner's Mill.

A buzzer sounded on the wall to her left. She placed the lettuce on the bench as she picked up the intercom speaker between the tea rooms and the Village Stores kitchen.

"Hi, Jilly."

"Morning, Rosie, have we received an order from the school about their requirements for Sports Day?" Jilly asked. "I need to place the order for requisitions with our suppliers in the next day or so. I must ensure we have sufficient ingredients for all the extra baking required for the combined Sports Day and Village Fete."

"No, I'm not aware of a call. It's unlike them to be behind in notifying us. Mrs Scholes usually sends a letter of confirmation as well. I'll check the file."

"Thanks, Rosie. The day is drawing closer, and I want to make sure I have sufficient students available for the baking and preparation beforehand as well as the many necessary tasks on the day. Be good 'hands on' experience for them."

"Emma will be in today, so I'll ask her if they've been in touch."

"Thanks, sorry to put this extra work on you but it will reflect badly on the business if we run out of food or are short staffed."

"No worries. I'll get back to you shortly."

Rosie glanced up at the clock. Twenty-five minutes before opening time. She walked briskly through the

Tea Rooms towards the office. With a practised eye she checked that chairs and tables were in place, clean and laid out correctly, cloths and curtains hanging straight, and all condiments had been replenished as she passed by. Emma and Jilly had instilled in her the importance of detail and appearance when they were training her when she first came to work in the Village Stores kitchen and then the Tea Rooms. This mindset had never left her. She replaced a curtain tie-back and straightened a lopsided picture. As she reached the door she turned and looked back. At the commencement of every day all should be in its rightful place, pleasing to the eye, so that we offer our customers a welcoming experience, they had instructed. She was satisfied with what she saw.

When Emma and Roger moved out of the little flat on the opposite side of the stairs to the tearoom, the bedroom had been converted into an office and the lounge became the rest room for the kitchen, shop and tearoom staff. The space downstairs, occupied by the former office that had been used by Emma's parents, was now partially incorporated into the current baking kitchen managed by Jilly and a small portion, along with the original storeroom, had been used for the lift space to give access to the Tea Rooms for the less able, wheelchairs and baby buggies.

Rosie unlocked the door to the office, stepped up to the filing cabinet and quickly located the orders file.

"Umm, nothing pending," she noted.

She locked up and made her way back to the Tea Rooms, notified Jilly then rang the school.

As she dialled, she heard the dumb waiter ascending from the kitchen below. "Lyndsay," she called gesticulating to the corner of the room and mouthed, "Collect the scones. Set them out on the tray in the display cabinet. Put domes over them."

"Oh, good morning, Mrs Scholes, it's Rosie from the Tea Rooms. We were wondering about the school order for the Fete and Sports day.'

"I sent it some weeks ago."

"Well, we don't seem to have received it."

"I'll email another copy right away."

"Thank you. 'Bye."

"Thanks for doing that, Lyndsay. Have you taken the butters out of the fridge and placed them in the cool cabinet?"

"Not yet."

"Always look around you and check that all is in place before we open the doors to customers."

"Yes, Rosie." Lyndsay was the newest catering student from the college to be assigned to the Tea Rooms.

Rosie pressed the intercom and conveyed Mrs Scholes's message to Jilly who suggested they ask Emma to check that it had arrived as soon as she came in. Rosie balanced the handset between her shoulder and chin as she carefully lifted the gateaux from the dumb waiter into the cabinet.

"Have you heard Connie has requested we provide some Barbadian food in the refreshment tent?" Jilly commented

"No! That will be different. I wonder how popular it will prove to be?"

"Well, it will go one of two ways. Either it will be a complete flop and a waste of money and food, or else people will rave over it, and we won't be able to keep up with demand."

"You're right. We'll have to wait and see." She replaced the mouthpiece in its holder.

"Have you put the cutlery containers onto the counter, Tracy?"

"Not yet."

"Are they full? Put the plates and napkins on the shelf below so that you can easily reach them."

"I've done that."

"Good. Are the kettles full? In case we need them. Is the coffee machine on? Are the jam pots replenished? Today's choice is strawberry and blackcurrant."

"You don't have the same every day?"

"No. We like to ring the changes."

"But some people like the same all the time."

"I know, but Emma doesn't want every day to be predictable. The same reason we have different gateaux each day and frequently introduce something new."

At the school, each class was busy in last minute preparations for the great day. It was an important event in the village and school calendar. For many years both events competed, unsuccessfully, with one another and somehow ended up defeating the object of the exercise. With dwindling resources and less people willing to help both struggled to raise interest or funds. Unwilling to continue pouring time and effort into a failing enterprise, Jennifer Pedwardine, during her headship, instigated an amalgamation of village and school resources working for the common good. It had been a success ever since; the proceeds of the venture being divided equally between village schemes and the school.

Following discussion with Jackie and Emma year 5 planned a stall for the Village Fete centred around a theme about the island of Barbados. Ben Durrant had blown up, then printed a photograph Connie had taken on her mobile phone of the Caribbean beach where she frequently went swimming. This was to form the backdrop to the stall.

The pictures, drawings and essays the children produced in history and geography projects earlier in the year concerning Barbados were being attached to screens which were to stand along one side of their stall. They depicted houses, turtle boats, coconut palms, mango trees, the sugar plantations and many other aspects of Bajan life. Using other photographs Connie had taken, which Ben had printed for her, Jade, alongside Jessica and Esme were creating a collage to hang from the table at the front of the stall.

In their neatest and most careful handwriting Daniel, Gracie and Keir were copying out some Bajan recipes that were favourite meals in Miss Foster's family. These were the recipes Connie was hoping Jilly and her team would be able to produce for tasting at the Village Fete. They, too, were going to be displayed together with relevant pictures on a stand-up display board and instructions to try the tasters on offer in the church hall.

Following on from the success of the 'outside' visits to places of interest in and around the village Connie had asked Stephen Cooper to give her more practical students, like Ricky, Archie and Joss, a taste of woodwork and carpentry in his workshop. The boys produced some interesting items with a Barbados theme which were going to be displayed for sale on the table nestled on a Barbados flag.

The day before the fete three of the girls had been chosen, because of good behaviour, to help bake some Bajan sour dough rolls and coconut sweetbread in the village bakery with Jilly Briggs. Connie wanted these to be available on year 5's stall but it had been decided that all food, apart from ice cream, would only be served from the refreshment stalls in the church hall. Michelle Cook and Laura Catton offered to look after the stall assisted by the pupils chosen for this task.

Some students were also going to demonstrate marble cricket which was played extensively on the less busy roads in Barbados. Ever since Connie introduced the game to the boys, and some of the girls, they had been hooked. It was planned to hold a tournament between the classes in between various races and other sports activities during the afternoon on the roadway in front of the church hall. They hoped to catch the attention of all those going to or coming from the refreshment stalls. The winning team would then challenge a parents' team to a match.

Other classes were equally engaged in presenting stalls that reflected some aspect of learning during the previous school terms. Some involved competitions and games, while others had items to sell that the children had made.

Quite some time before Mrs Beckingsdale was scheduled to officially open the fete Harry Saunders was directing traffic into the village car park. A stream of visitors began to form a queue in the lane where a ribbon barrier had been erected next to the podium. While Jackie Cooper was collecting entrance fees Tim Draycott stamped wrists with an ink pad to show who had paid. Sergeant Catchpole was in attendance early to ensure crowds did not get unruly.

Since so many of the village and hamlet families had children at school the event impacted on the whole community. Most of the businesses shut and posted closed notices on their doors. Emma helped Mrs Beckett shepherd and encourage year 6, while Rosalie operated the till in the refreshment hall. The other members of staff from the Village Stores and Tea Rooms also helped in some capacity in the church hall, Jilly Briggs and Rosie ensuring there was a continuous supply of freshly made sandwiches and buttered scones.

Billy Cooper, the butcher, supervised a hog roast while his wife, Pauline, served the customers this traditional savoury treat.

Stephen Cooper and Graeme Castleton marked out the pitch for the marble cricket tournament then, in conjunction with other lads from the cricket team, supervised the matches and gave oversight to the races.

The Library and Museum doors were shut for the day so RK, Abigail and Miss Pedwardine gave their support and encouragement wherever it was required.

The W.I. presided over the cake and jam making competition and supervised the home-made produce stall. Reggie Bemment along with other keen gardeners and allotmenteers manned the plant stall.

"Miss, Miss, Rich 'as ripped the recipe chart."

"Noo, oi Nivver!"

"Miss Foster, oi can't find the flag to put the wood carvings on."

"I expect it is still in the box we put it into when we were packing up at school, Archie."

"Where's the drawing pins, Miss?"

"Here," Connie handed the box to Daniel so that he and Keir could attach the recipe poster to the display board. "And here is a reel of Sellotape to fix the tear, Jade."

"Thanks, Miss."

One thing Connie knew for sure. These children certainly kept her on her toes. She smiled at them as they busily displayed everything in its rightful place on the stall.

"This alroite, Miss?"

She nodded encouragement.

"It looks very colourful and attractive. I am sure all the visitors will stop and admire your handiwork." Jade and Keir beamed back at her.

Each stall had its own little last-minute preparation scenarios taking place. A horn sounded and over the loudspeaker system that had been erected across the village from the lane to and around the Village Green, as well as inside the church hall, Lord Edmund's voice boomed out. As Lord of the Manor and Chair of Governors at Newton Westerby Primary School he introduced Mrs Beckingsdale. She smiled at her brother as she stepped up onto the podium then spoke into the microphone.

"I welcome you all on this glorious day to this auspicious occasion. Isn't it good to have the sun shining on us? Many people, young and old, have been involved in the preparations for today. We want you all to enjoy the day and may I ask that you make it a happy day for someone else, too. May the sun continue to shine its benevolence on all that takes place today including the emptying of your pockets and the filling of your bags and baskets for the benefit of our school and village.

Support the stall holders and competitors with generosity of spirit and enthusiastic fairness. I declare the Newton Westerby School and Village Fete open."

Joss stepped up to Mrs Beckingsdale and handed her the ceremonial scissors after which Kirsten Catton came forward to present a delightful bouquet to Mrs Beckingsdale which had been designed by Lily Jenner. As was the custom no one could cross the cut ribbon until Mrs Beckingsdale walked along the lane to the first stall.

"She's a'comin'." Excited voices echoed the news up the lane and across The Green.

Chapter Seventeen

Icy waters!

At the beginning of the Summer term Jackie approached Connie about staying on at the school for another year.

"As a colleague I truly value your input. You get on so well with the other members of staff, too. Your cheeriness and quirky sense of humour are infectious, and you create a delightful atmosphere in the classroom, as well as the staffroom, which has done wonders for some of our more disruptive pupils. The children love you." Jackie smiled encouragingly but Connie slowly shook her head and started to utter a rejection of Jackie's request. However, before she could speak, Jackie promptly reminded her that once she had got into the swing of the English curriculum and adjusted to the Suffolk dialect, she had built an incredible rapport with the children.

"You have exhibited a knack for getting even the slackest of pupils to knuckle down and produce work to a reasonable standard which is reflected in the recent communication from Ofsted. Their extra monitoring visits acknowledge that the school is moving in the right direction."

Jackie attributed this improvement to the skill of all her staff for pulling together after the Mr Brankscome debacle, drawing out the best work from the children in their classes. However, she believed Connie's influence to be a major contributing factor. She could not put her finger on what it was exactly, but her presence certainly had a remarkable effect on both staff and children.

The corners of Connie's smiling mouth drooped momentarily as she screwed up her eyes. *My dear friend you do not know what a hard question you ask of me.*

"Aah! Miss Cooper, I promised Mumma I would return to Barbados when my year was up. I cannot disappoint Mumma. It cost her a lot to allow me to come here with her blessing."

Jackie knew Connie was not referring to any monetary outlay.

"Please give it some thought, Connie. Your involvement has been invaluable to the children's wellbeing and a vital contribution to the school's improved interim Ofsted report."

"I said I would only stay a year."

"Yes, I know, but you have had such an impact on the slow learners and that small band of 'difficult' children. Somehow you gel with them, and they respond to your method of teaching, even the most belligerent ones, like Joss and Jessica. You've done wonders there."

Connie beamed and clapped her hands together in a wide sweeping movement. "It has been a joy to see their faces light up when they learn something new."

"That's the miracle, getting them to realise they have the ability to learn. You have such a gift, Connie. I know it's selfish of me, but I want to harness your skill for my children here in Newton Westerby for a little bit longer before you journey back to Barbados permanently. Wouldn't you like to see that particular group through their final primary school year?"

"I really must go home at the end of the summer term. Mumma is fretting at having one of her chicks so far across de ocean."

"You've been a great team member to work with and some of your enthusiasm has rubbed off onto other members of staff, for which I'm thankful, not only in the classroom but extracurricular activities, such as the out-of-doors experiences, your involvement with the school choir and cricket club. How do we follow that if you go?"

Connie sighed. "I do not feel I have done anything special, simply loved and taught the children as I would have done at home in Barbados. I have enjoyed my time here and am thankful de Good Lord has given me this marvellous opportunity. They are good children and I love them even though they are a challenge. There is a lot I set out to do that I have not been able to achieve, yet. So... maybe another year ... I do not promise but I will give your request some thought but I must go home in the summer."

For the time being Jackie had to be content with Connie's answer. Sharing her home for a spell with Connie meant they had spent much time together. Connie's effervescent personality stemmed from her faith and trust in God, there was no side to her. Open, honest, cheerful and zealous dealings were her hallmarks. Jackie was more guarded and reserved in her associations with people and whilst they developed a friendship of sorts, she veered to keeping their relationship on a professional level. She admitted she liked Connie as a person. She was pleased with the efficiency of her work and the thorough manner with which she prepared for class each day. The changes in attitude and development of some of the 'awkward' year 5 children was remarkable and clearly down to Connie's handling of difficult situations and her direct approach to issues of behaviour and tolerance. She never raised her voice nor was she overheard telling the children off for misbehaviour but the change in year 5 was incredible.

"What you've already achieved in 2 terms is amazing. I haven't been able to get through to some of those children in 6 years."

Three days later they were sat at home following the evening meal which it had been Connie's turn to prepare and cook, an arrangement they had reached when Connie came to share Jackie's home while Miss Pedwardine was away on her long-awaited tour of the Holy Land. They each agreed to at least try one another's preferences and waive those things that were a definite 'no, no.'

"I really can't stand Bajan hot sauce, it's too spicy!"

"And I really do not like your roast beef and Yorkshire puddings!" The girls chuckled at their own idiosyncrasies.

They had been invited on several occasions to Sunday lunch at the home of Jackie's parents and each time Pauline cooked a traditional English roast, until Connie felt she knew them well enough to voice her aversion without causing offence. They all laughed and agreed to honour each other's tastes and preferences. Thereafter, Connie and Pauline swapped culinary skills and recipes so that there was always something on the table that they all enjoyed.

"I'm already cooking a selection of meals because of Hilary's vegetarian preferences. Another dish adds to the variety of choice on offer."

Connie looked across to Jackie and began to make conversation when they sat down with a cup of tea. "I have considered the offer to renew my contract for another year."

"Ye...es?" Jackie leaned forward in expectation.

"I will stay on for another year, but I must go home for the holiday. I promised Mumma I would return home, but I want you to come with me so that you can see my beautiful country and meet my family. Your family have been so kind to me."

Jackie sat bold upright, pursed her lips and vehemently shook her head. "No, no, no, I cannot do that."

"Why ever not? Have you made other plans for the holiday?" Knowing full well that she had not.

Again, Jackie shook her head. "I haven't got a passport."

"Well, apply for one, and soon. Come and enjoy the aqua-blue sea, the perpetual sunshine and warm Barbados hospitality."

"No!" Jackie replied emphatically. "I can't do that. I can't go so far from home. I need to be here to prepare for the next school year."

"You need a break from work. De Good Lord does not intend us to work every waking moment."

"Don't bring Him into the equation. He is the reason I work morning, noon and night. He took away any other purpose I might have had for living..." she spat out bitterly, "and I don't..."

"What about the plans He might have for living?"

"...intend to lose what I've achieved by sneaking off somewhere then having to contend with sloppy work schedules because I'm pushed for time. No, I am not going away!" She practically shouted at Connie. The bitterness in her voice was almost tangible. She got up with a start and spilled her tea in her lap and on to the carpet.

Connie was equally quick to get up from her chair and offered to assist.

Irritably, Jackie pushed her away. "Don't fuss. Leave me alone. It is only tea. It will probably stain but what does it matter."

Connie, undeterred, darted swiftly into the kitchen for a bowl of water and a J cloth. She returned and began mopping up the spillage from the sofa and the carpet. She did not dare offer to sponge down Jackie's trousers but quietly said, "If you go and change, we can soak those while still damp and they won't stain."

Jackie stomped off. She knew she was behaving badly but Connie had unwittingly brought to mind the reason she was such a workaholic. Connie's words had rekindled memories long since hidden and feelings she did not want to resurrect. She was Miss Jacqueline Cooper, the efficient, hardworking head teacher of Newton Westerby Primary School. Emotion and pleasure went out of her life many years ago along with faith and trust. They had died along with the love of her life. But she had no intention of sharing that information with anyone.

Connie was somewhat perplexed at Jackie's reaction to the invitation to spend some of her holiday in the Foster home in Barbados. Never had she seen Jackie in such a mood even when dealing with the most trying situation, difficult child or belligerent parent at school.

Jackie clomped back down the stairs and noisily flung her trousers into the washing machine. "Well, that's that!" she declared snappily and struck her palms together in scissor-like motion as if to wash her hands of the incident.

"They will be less likely to stain if they're soaked first." Connie spoke gently as she stood at the sink and finished washing up the mugs then proceeded to refill the bowl with cold water. However, Jackie made no attempt to remove the trousers. She stood sullenly by the wall, arms folded, watching her houseguest. Connie calmly walked over to the machine to retrieve the article. She rinsed them through, put them into the bowl to soak, dried her hands and then reached out to place one on Jackie's arm. "Light, life and love are in the healing fountain that flows from Calvary, and they are available for you." She spoke quietly. "I am off to bed. Good night. God be with you."

Jackie stood as though rooted to the spot. No wonder Connie had success with recalcitrant children. Nothing seemed to phase her. There was no hint of anger or censure in her voice. She just dealt with the situation calmly. Did not blow her top at carelessness or criticise the culprit, in this instance, herself, but suggested ways the problem could be resolved and lent a hand to rectify matters. Despite the rawness the incident had evoked for Jackie's heart, Connie's handling of it raised respect for her colleague even higher.

The morning came all too soon, and Jackie felt anything but rested following a sleepless night. The silly incident the previous evening sparked by Connie's innocent invitation to holiday in Barbados played on her mind or at least her reaction to it. Her stubbornness hung over her like a thundercloud. She recalled her vehement denial of venturing further afield than her own beach and relived their conversation over and over again.

'*You live in a bubble.*'

'*Don't talk such rubbish.*'

'*It is true, Miss Cooper. You are constantly seeking to broaden your pupils' experience and horizons, but you adamantly refuse to do the same for yourself.*'

'*Nonsense.*'

'*Your life would be so much richer if you burst the bubble so that you could see what was on the outside.*'

'*You are rather fanciful!*'

'*Not at all! I think you are afraid - afraid to fly? No, afraid to leave your comfort zone!*'

'*You have no idea!*'

'*I think I do. You do not want your current existence to be shaken. If you venture further afield you might meet new people, cope with unfamiliar situations, deal with new emotions and different experiences. If you stay here everyone knows you, Miss stick-in-the-mud, stay-at-home Cooper. All is familiar. Despite your desire to be always in control you refuse to acknowledge that in fact de Good Lord is in all and over all. You continue to uphold the pretence that all is well.*'

'*Miss Foster, you are over-stepping the mark!*'

'*Am I? You may deny yourself the pleasure of developing new horizons but just think what a project you could make of it for your pupils when you return. History, Geography for certain, even Maths and English, as well as Art and Science. No aspect of the curriculum need be left out. Some of these children will never have the opportunity to travel, just think what you can add to their education. What a difference you can make to their understanding of the world they live in. De Good Lord has given us a beautiful world which has sadly been spoiled by selfish and greedy people. Let Him open your heart to the loveliness He wants you to enjoy."*

Such a gentle admonition but a perfectly reasoned argument.

"Oh, I treated her horribly last evening."

Jackie's obstinacy hung over her ominously following Connie's invitation to travel with her to Barbados. Her rude response and forceful denial of venturing further afield than the Newton Westerby beach plagued her.

"How ever am I going to put things right?"

<hr />

There were no after school clubs the following day so immediately her responsibilities at school were completed Connie walked briskly down the lane to the Post Office.

"Good afternoon, Alex, please may I have a passport application form."

Alex did not query the unusual request but turned to the shelf behind her and picked out the appropriate form.

"And also, an airmail letter for Barbados, please."

"Here is the passport form and this is a stamp and airmail sticker for an ordinary envelope to Barbados. You won't be restricted in the amount you can write."

Connie beamed. "Oh, thank you, so much."

From the Post Office she walked quickly across the road to the butcher's shop, but Billy was pulling down the window blind. Connie pushed open the shop door and stepped inside. "Are you closed?"

"Yes, we are." Pauline said without looking up as she continued to wipe down the serving counter.

Billy saw Connie's crest fallen face.

"What can I do for you, Miss Foster?" he enquired kindly.

Pauline's head jerked up. "Hello, Connie, I didn't realise it was you."

"I..." Connie hesitated. "I am sorry," she turned to leave the shop.

"Don't go. What did you need?"

"I wanted to know what Jackie's favourite meal is," she said diffidently.

Billy burst into raucous laughter. "Oh, that's easy to answer. Anything that's got meat in it."

Pauline chuckled. "True, but she is particularly partial to chicken-based dishes like chicken supreme."

"How do you make that?" Connie asked eagerly.

Within minutes Connie was furnished with a package of chicken breast and a list of other ingredients available from the Village Stores plus a written detailed recipe.

With Rosalie's help she purchased the necessary groceries and walked back to Jackie's cottage with a spring in her step. With her mind very much on the method of cooking the dish Pauline had described she bumped into Mark who was returning home from the quay. He steadied her by the arm so that she did not trip over.

"Hi, there, stranger, you were miles away."

"Sorry, Mark. Yes, I am engaged on a mission. Please pray for Jackie. She is in great conflict. Also my brother, Joel. Will you help me Facetime home again?"

Mark waited for further explanation but knowing Connie was not a gossip and she must have good reason for saying what she did he replied, "Sure! Will I see you at choir practise this evening?"

"Oh my, that had slipped my mind. I must hurry, I have much to do, you know, and so short a time to do it in but I will see you at de church later."

In a flash she was gone. Mark stood staring after her. *A serious, thoughtful Connie is something new. No smile?* He mused. *Dear Lord, You know what is going on even though I am in the dark. May Your blessing, mercy and grace be on Connie and Jackie and Joel in this moment. Surround them each in Your love.*"

Jackie was astounded when she arrived home an hour later. Connie was singing along to a CD she had put into the CD player and a delicious aroma emanated from the kitchen which tantalised her taste buds. But it's my turn to cook tea, she thought peevishly, even though she had only remembered on her way home and decided tea would have to be something quick from the freezer. She was further taken aback when she saw the table so delightfully laid with candles and flowers from the garden as the centre piece, napkins artistically arranged and a sheaf of paper, a pen and stamped envelope at her place setting.

"What is..." she started, flabbergasted.

Connie stopped stirring the pot on the stove and looked round at Jackie with a beaming face.

"Come, sit, and enjoy your favourite meal."

"But it's supposed to be my turn to cook."

"I know, but you've had a stressful day, come and relax," Connie cajoled.

"I'll go wash and get changed." Jackie dumped down her bags and dashed upstairs.

Whoa! How can she be so kind when I treated her so horribly last evening?

She truly lives out what she believes. There's no side to her. She's as open as the day is long as Dad would say. She shows Christian love in everything she says and does. Where has that thought come from? Jackie fought to suppress it and then admonished herself. *Be gracious enough to accept a gift of kindness.* She gulped down the lump that had risen in her throat.

God, You dealt me a very raw deal, don't You dare think You can weasel Your way back into my life through Connie Foster.

Jackie quickly washed, threw her clothes on the floor and grabbed her jump suit.

My grace is sufficient.

No, No, No.

Yes! Sufficient for you.

She brushed aside the tears that threatened to tumble down her cheeks. Get a grip girl! She undid her hair, pulled a brush through it and raced down the stairs.

The meal Connie prepared was delicious and before she left for choir practice, she had persuaded her housemate to fill in the passport application.

"You will then have options."

Chapter Eighteen

Billowing clouds!

Connie ignored the cheeky retort, decidedly turned her back on the class, took up a black pen and commenced writing figures on the white board.

"Aw, Miss, not Maths!"

The Summer term was moving along at quite a rapid pace. Miss Pedwardine had returned from her extended trip to the Holy Land, so Connie had moved back into 'Bakers'. It would soon be time for Connie to pack her bags and return home to Barbados. Whether she would have company on the flight was another matter, an issue Jackie Cooper still had to deal with. In the meantime, there was much to keep her occupied at school and in the community.

Stephen and his mates from the cricket club had kept to their end of the bargain that had been struck the week Connie Foster arrived in Newton Westerby. They had given time since the commencement of the cricket season to coach a group of pupils from year 5 into an enthusiastic kwik cricket team. Progress had been so good they were participating in an inter-school's competition.

There were also several youngsters showing promise in the more usual form of the game who had developed into a passable under 11's cricket team augmented by some from year 6. A few had been invited for trials into the village Colts team. Little did Miss Foster realise when she introduced cricket to her pupils that their enthusiasm for the game would become a passion. She used that passion to encourage even the most reluctant of learners to apply their interest to Maths and English lessons. Sometimes it was a successful ploy but at other times it was hard work.

Today, it was the quarter finals of the inter-schools kwik cricket tournament.

Most minds were anywhere but on the maths lesson.

An audible groan rippled across the classroom. Soon it was accompanied by a rhythmic beating of fists upon the tables. This reverberated to a crescendo as each child joined in the protest to show their displeasure at Connie's change in tactics.

"We wants tew dew cricket! We wants tew dew CRICKET! We wants tew dew…"

Connie swivelled round and faced her rowdy pupils. In a quiet but firm voice she said, "All good cricketers need maths." Recalling with gratitude her mother's words to her brothers.

The strumming stopped. Heads shook in disbelief.

"Noo!"

"Rubbish!"

"Squit!"

Connie ignored the shouts.

"Get out your maths books. England are playing a 50 over match against South Africa. Root scored 43 runs, Bairstow 17 and Morgan 39. Buttler was out for a duck…"

"Noo! He's tew good fer that, Miss."

"In this match he did not score. At this stage of the game what is England's total score and how many batsmen are out?"

The talking subsided. Heads bent down in concentration. Connie waited till, one by one, eyes looked up at her.

"Number two: - Lowestoft seconds scored 89 in their first innings and 114 in their second innings. Newton Westerby scored 97 in their first innings and now have 27 in their second innings. How many runs does Newton Westerby need to win de match?"

When she saw several with perplexed brows and others sucking on their pencil ends Connie repeated the question.

"Number three: - At de, sorry, the match on Saturday Mrs Cooper and Jilly Briggs are responsible for the catering. Newton Westerby have 11 players, as do the visiting team. There are 2 umpires with 2 scorers and 1 groundsman. How many will be eating tea?

"'Ow many more, Miss?"

"Aw, Miss, ma fingers be achin'."

"There are 3 more to complete before break. We cannot go out to play until you are all finished, then afterwards we will chat about our team."

Joss banged down his pencil in protest and started to complain, loudly.

"Stop yew're squit, Joss, we wants to goo out to play."

"The next one is about attendance at a cricket match. I want to know the percentage of children at the match. Our whole class, including me, is at the match. Altogether there are 90 watching the game – 50 men, 25 ladies, as well as children. What is the percentage of children watching the game?"

"Is Mr Castleton playing, Miss?'

"Mr Castleton?"

"Yus, if he's in the team Bethany will be there cos Mrs Castleton allus comes."

"I see. We'll assume Bethany is at the match, then."

"Please, Miss, if oi go Mum will insist oi tek our Lewis."

Other hands waved and tongues wagged in agreement about having to drag along younger siblings.

With a broad smile across her face Connie clapped her hands for silence.

"In order to solve this maths problem we will only count those in our class plus Bethany, Lewis and Tyler. Is that understood?" Heads nodded then swivelled to the left, then right, behind and in front as each child endeavoured to count their peers. The lesson continued without further interruption until the bell was heard for the start of play time.

"Phew!" exclaimed Ricky and Archie simultaneously. "Thank gawd thass all uvver."

"Boys," Connie admonished gently. "What must we not do?"

With a resigned shrug of their shoulders they replied as one, "Tek the name o' the Lord in vain."

"Thank you. Please remember."

"Yus Miss," they chorused as they dashed out of the classroom into the freedom of the playground.

The tournament quarterfinals were being held at Newton Westerby cricket club. Stephen Cooper, Len Armes, the groundsman, and a number from the cricket team worked together to ensure the ground was prepared to receive the expected hordes of enthusiastic youngsters from visiting primary schools as well as the local pupils.

"Thankfully, we've had fine weather for the last week, so the outfield is dry."

"The children have all been told to bring something to sit on,

"Jilly and Rosie have organized a refreshment stall so that should satisfy the most insatiable of appetites.

The pupils from years 5 and 6 who were not in the team were going as spectators to encourage their team along.

Mark Bemment was ashore and accompanied Graeme Castleton to escort them to the ground. He greeted Connie warmly and enquired about Joel.

"He is doing nicely, thank you," she replied, pleased he had remembered the snippet she had shared about an attack on Joel and his friend, Fruendel, Mumma had mentioned in a letter.

Mark laughed. "You're picking up the local twang. I'm glad to hear your brother is recovering from his ordeal." Connie's heart did a flip at the smile he gave her before he turned to organize his group to walk the ½ mile to the ground. *Get a grip, girl,* she admonished, *concentrate on the task in hand.*

Excitement was tangible and the 34 or so from Newton Westerby Primary shouted and cheered till they were hoarse. Whether it was their enthusiastic encouragement or the skill of the participants, Newton Westerby Primary got through to the semi-finals. These, along with the finals, were being held on the same day at the Denes, the Lowestoft Town cricket club ground the following week.

When the team returned from that event with the cup it was presented before the whole school in Assembly. Year 5's joy knew no bounds. Connie beamed at her pupils. "I am proud of your achievement. You have worked so hard. Not only those of you in the playing team but also those of you who encouraged your friends to do their best. It has been a real team effort. You have all played a part. Thank you." She clapped her hands together as she looked across the classroom a broad smile for every one of her pupils. They all cheered.

"Whom else should we thank?"

Names came out like bullets, "Mr Cooper." "Mr Castleton." "Nicky Andaman." "Mr Bemment…"

She clapped her hands again.

"How can we thank them?"

"Send a card."

"Write a letter."

"Have a party."

Connie gave Joss a wad of white paper.

"Please give one of these to everyone." She proceeded to write on the blackboard, Dear Mr Cooper and cricket team…

"I would like some of you to write thank you notes and the rest of you to invite them to a party which we will hold here next week instead of going to the cricket ground."

As many as were able to, from the cricket team, graciously accepted the invitation. The children enjoyed playing host to the men who had contributed so much to their achievement.

Jackie Cooper's passport duly arrived. Initially it was relegated to the back of a drawer in the kitchen. However, after much cajoling from her family and encouragement from friends she finally agreed to accompany Connie to Barbados. It was with trepidation that she made preparation to embark on, what was for her, a tremendous undertaking. She was reluctant to admit it, but she was also feeling a stomach-churning thrill of anticipation at venturing into the unknown. It was as if the adventurous spirit of the free roaming child, she had once been, was resurrected from enforced slumber. In company with her mother and sister, Miranda, she went on a shopping spree to Norwich where she purchased a suitcase, and clothes suitable for a climate hotter than she was used to.

"You'll need a swimsuit," said Miranda.

Jackie's response was a frown, but she acquiesced at her sister's insistence. "You can't travel all the way to the Caribbean and not go into the sea!"

She even allowed Rachel Durrant to restyle her hair.

The day before they were due to leave for the airport Pauline invited Jackie and Connie for a meal. "Get your cases packed and I'll fix an evening meal, allow you time to check your documents and ensure you have all you need without having to think about mundane things such as food preparation. Just come and eat."

Connie was strolling up the lane from 'Bakers' when she saw Jackie enter the front door of her parent's home. The village seemed curiously quiet. There was not even a customer in the Village Stores as she glanced in.

"Hi, Miss Foster," a familiar youthful voice called out as she reached up to press the bell at the Cooper's house. Connie turned and waved to Daniel Catton who was stood, with Kirsten and Poppy, at the garden gate of their home opposite the butcher's shop.

"Come in, come in," Billy opened the door and ushered Connie along the hallway. "Almost ready!" She had barely walked two steps when the doorbell rang again. The door opened and Stephen Cooper and Mark Bemment breezed in.

"Escorts present to chaperone two young ladies," Stephen teased and ceremoniously bowed. As laughter erupted at his antics Connie's eyes locked with Mark's. His warm smile caused her heart to somersault. He moved close and drew her arm through his. "Are you ready?" Totally unsure what she was expected to be ready for Connie simply returned his smile and nodded. Stephen stood upright and yelled, "You ready, Jack?"

"Of course," Jackie responded in her best school ma'am voice. "What took you so long?" Then her lips curled into the grimace of a smile at her cousin. "Stop dithering! I'm starving!" She dug her father playfully in the ribs as she passed by him. "What's going on, Dad?"

"You'll soon see," was all Billy would say. But instead of leading them into the dining room the young women were ushered out of the front door.

The cluster of friends processed up the lane, across the Green and into the open door of the church hall. Spontaneous cheering, clapping and laughter embraced them. The greeting took Jackie's breath away.

The girl's looked at one another.

"The whole village is here," Connie gasped.

"Of course, can't have you sneaking away without a good send-off," Stephen joked. "You might not come back!" He pulled a face. "We can't offer you the perennial warmth of sun and sea of Barbados, but we can show you the love of family and friends of Newton Westerby." The hall grew quiet.

Both teachers felt their eyes begin to tear up at the genuineness of Stephen's words.

Hugh Darnell took opportunity in the silence to welcome everyone. "This is a celebration of two special people who day in and day out contribute so much to our community."

"Yeah! Yeah! Yeah! Hip, Hip, Hooray!" A voiced yelled out.

Joss Brady! Connie nodded and beamed across at the young man. A boy, for so long, the bane of her life, but her persistence had uncovered hidden depths to the wayward boy's character. He was just one of the many children she had encouraged to discover the thrill of learning about words and numbers, the world around them and areas further afield. Her patience and praise unlocked skills and abilities they did not know they possessed which may have remained dormant for always but for her nudging.

Connie in her own inimitable way had taught year 5 in a manner that was different, but which had eventually brought out the best in each child.

Her influence had not remained solely in the classroom but as she interacted with the residents of the village and beyond, her positive, joyful spirit had impacted, in some measure, on them all from Lord Edmund, at the Manor to Lucy Sands in Marsh Newton.

This is what the village wanted to acknowledge and celebrate.

"We knows a good thing when we sees one," said Mrs Saunders sagely to those around her.

Jackie Cooper was known as the staid, head schoolteacher whom most saw as the clever, capable, unflappable organized daughter of Billy Cooper, the butcher, who ensured the school ran smoothly despite many setbacks and difficulties.

She had steered them through the disastrous debacle of the Mr Brankscome episode and turned the school fortunes around so that they were no longer regarded as requiring improvement. Most held to their own version of what that incident was all about. Only a few were party to what truly transpired.

The man the villagers knew as Mr Brankscome had been sitting begging on the street of a town some distance away when the real Mr Brankscome offered to buy him a meal in the nearby McDonald's restaurant. He accepted. During conversation, the genuine Mr Brankscome learned that his companion had need of accommodation. He kindly made a few phone calls and through his contacts was able to secure the man a place for the night. He offered to drive him there. During the car journey it transpired that Mr Brankscome was a teacher en route to an interview for a new post. Passing a wooded area the imposter pleaded for a toilet stop. He used the moment to knock the benevolent driver unconscious and swiftly dragged him into the scrubland. In the seclusion, out of sight of passing vehicles, behind the bushes and trees he stripped his victim and changed clothes with him. He proceeded to relieve him of his wallet, keys, documents, and watch. On his return to the car he opened Mr Brankscome's briefcase to find papers pertinent to the interview at Newton Westerby Primary school. The rest of his deception was well known. Following his attack on

Jackie he was ultimately charged, tried and sentenced for his crimes.

'God moves in a mysterious way' many would concur for, had the Brankscome affair not occurred, Connie Foster would never have come to Newton Westerby. There was much to rejoice and be thankful for.

After Hugh Darnell's words of welcome, he gave thanks. There followed a happy time of enjoyment composed of food, fun, fellowship and friendship. So many clamoured to speak with Connie and Jackie they were in danger of missing out on the food prepared in their honour but their escorts, true to their word, ensured they had sufficient to sustain them.

Not a few hearts were heavy at the conclusion of the evening. Some were fearful that once Connie was back in her beloved Barbados she would not return.

The following morning dawn crept in as the darkness rolled away streaking the sky with feathery red strands. As Jackie opened the curtains the old saying her Grannie Cooper used to frequently quote came to mind, 'Red sky at night, Shepherd's delight, Red sky in the morning, Shepherd's warning.' Foreboding sank like lead to the pit of her stomach.

Connie looked out at the same patterns in the sky that nature was weaving and prayed, "Father, God, I know that the creation You formed is still in Your hands, under Your control, so I will not fear but trust You for this day."

The road out of the village was lined with groups of friends, many wearing tearful faces, waving to wish Godspeed and a safe journey to the girls as Mark and Stephen continued as escorts, co-driving them to Heathrow Central Travelodge. The roads were quite busy. "So glad you changed your minds about leaving at the crack of dawn tomorrow," commented Stephen, "we might not have made your flight in time. Arriving at the airport this evening means you won't be rushed in the morning."

The hotel was not too far from the airport terminal but under the flight path of the aeroplanes so consequently rather noisy. After Mark and Stephen dropped them off, carried their cases into the hotel then departed for home, Connie and Jackie settled down for the night. "Enjoy your adventure, but don't lose your return ticket," Stephen quipped to the girls as he waved in farewell. But Mark tenderly gripped Connie's hand and said quietly, "Savour with delight the time with your family. I shall eagerly await your return," and smiled into her eyes. The hand he held tingled, and her face beamed. Excitement bubbled up inside her at the thought of returning home and seeing her family again, but Jackie was overwhelmed by the thought that she was really going on this journey. *Eddie would never believe I was doing this.*

CHAPTER NINETEEN

Unexpected turbulence!

They woke to the sound of rain splattering on the hotel window.

"What a dismal start to a holiday," Jackie grumbled and snuggled deeper under her duvet.

"I am sure de Good Lord will turn the downpour into showers of blessing."

"Sure," retorted her roommate, sarcastically, "I really look forward to being soaked before we even board the airport bus."

"I think after the recent spell of dry weather the gardens and fields will be glad of the rain. The land will be refreshed, the crops will swell, and we will relish eating the produce."

"Why are you always so cheerful?" came the muffled response from Jackie.

"De Bible teaches us to be thankful for all things and I find it is rewarding to look for the best in people and circumstances. It is also God honouring."

"I don't know about the God thing but," Jackie paused as she pushed up onto her elbows, "I have noticed throughout your stay in the village you always have a positive outlook on every situation, which has had a marked effect. That's the reason the most awkward and disruptive pupils have flourished under your care and guidance."

"De Good Lord blesses us in order that we might be a blessing to others and that is reflected in ways that it is impossible for us to imagine and certainly cannot determine."

"Here endeth the Gospel according to Connie Foster!"

Connie brushed aside Jackie's derision.

"Are you getting up today? I have finished in de bathroom so, I will leave you to it and meet you in the restaurant for breakfast."

"Ugh!" Jackie pulled a face then turned back into her pillow.

Playfully Connie yanked back the bed covers. "We will have a good day. You are going to enjoy lots of new experiences de Good Lord has in store for you."

Connie gathered her shoulder bag, Bible and devotional, but when Jackie made no attempt to move, she bent down, picked up a pillow and threw it at her with a chuckle. When it struck her Jackie shot up, "You're quite a kid at heart, aren't you, Miss Foster?"

Connie shook her head. "No, No, No," she protested, "I am not Miss Foster, today. I am Constance Joy excited to be travelling home to see Mumma and my family with my friend, Jacqueline. You, too, have left Miss Prim and Proper Cooper behind at de school. You are on an adventure! Come on let us get started."

"You've already reverted to Barbados lingo."

Connie chuckled. "Not deliberately, I assure you." She opened the door and called back over her shoulder, "See you in twenty minutes."

Punctual Miss Cooper entered the dining area right on time and the girls ate a full English breakfast together in a pleasant restaurant space surrounded by luscious greenery displayed in large blue ceramic pots.

Forty minutes later they boarded the hotel hopper bound for terminus 3 at Heathrow airport. The rain had not abated but Jackie barely noticed it as she trundled her case aboard the bus.

They booked in their baggage. Connie breathed a sigh of relief when their cases weighed in a fraction below the weight limit and passed through customs without a hitch, apart from the face recognition machine at first not accepting Jackie's passport. A friendly airport official stepped up to offer his assistance and eventually she was allowed through. Knowing her plan was to return for the Autumn term Connie left some of her belongings behind at 'Bakers' where she lodged with Miss Pedwardine and filled up her case with items of clothing for her family, particularly those things which were expensive or unobtainable in Barbados.

As they sat in the departure lounge waiting for their flight to be called Jackie was surprised at the number of texts and messages they received from family and friends, all wishing them safe travelling and a happy time in the Caribbean.

"Flight 248 proceed to gate 19," the instruction over the tannoy caught their attention.

The young women swiftly joined the procession of people who responded to the unseen voice.

"I see it's still raining," Jackie remarked indicating the vista through a window to the side of the walkway they were traversing.

"But we are in the dry and we are on the way," Connie beamed.

After following the route for 15 minutes, turning to the left, then the right and down a seemingly endless corridor Jackie stopped to catch her breath.

"What a trek! Do they expect us to walk to Barbados?"

Connie's laughter erupted and echoed along the spacious causeway causing many within earshot to grin or chuckle.

"Each step is one step closer to our destination." She paused then continued in a wavery, theatrical voice, "If it is too much for you, my dear, you could take the moving pathway." She pointed to the horizontal, mechanical walkway on her right conveying people and luggage.

Jackie rolled her eyes, Joss Brady-like, producing in Connie even more hilarity.

"Decorum, Miss Foster," Jackie admonished in her best school ma'am voice.

"Noo!" Connie responded in the manner of Jessica Saunders, "I am a little girl on de way home." She added a jaunty skip to her step which initiated even more laughter.

They boarded the plane. The cabin crew helped them find their seats in the centre towards the rear of the plane and, in no time at all, they were belted up. Jackie's heart pounded as the engine accelerated. Connie handed her a boiled sweet. She shook her head to refuse it, but Connie insisted. "You need it. Suck it slowly, it will help your ear pressure on take-off," she instructed.

Soon they were in the air soaring beyond the rain and clouds towards blue sky and the sunlight.

"Wow! What a sight!" Jackie was mesmerised and craned her neck to absorb the view through her nearest porthole.

"Incredible, is it not?"

"Mmm. How long is our flight?"

"About 8 hours. I plan to divide the time up into ½ hour sections and keep changing what I am doing so the time seems to pass more quickly."

"That sounds a good idea, but doing what?"

"Read, write, eat, drink, watch a film, close my eyes for a nap and on this screen, you can track our flight." Jackie watched as Connie pressed a few buttons. "Look, we are now travelling at just under 36,000 feet." She encouraged Jackie to experiment.

For the most part the flight was smooth and uneventful until they met the jet stream and turbulence.

"Fasten your seat belts!" came the instruction.

Jackie looked alarmed at the sudden buffeting.

"It's OK, just do as he says." The pilot announced he was going to gradually take the plane down to 32,000 feet to try to avoid the rocking but unfortunately it was present for some while.

To Jackie's astonishment they landed smoothly.

Wide eyed she looked at Connie. "We're here." Connie nodded as she collected her hand luggage.

Heat hit them as they disembarked causing Jackie to gasp for breath. They walked alongside the runway to the arrival hall following the side of a building which was resplendently decked in magenta coloured bougainvillea.

"We'll be here for ever," grumbled Jackie wearily, when she saw the long queue of tourists at the customs gate.

"No, we will not. Follow me." Connie walked boldly, passed the line of travellers, to a booth where no one was waiting and handed in their ticket.

"Afternoon, Jeshua," she greeted.

"Welcome home, Miss Connie, how's you?"

"Fine, Jeshua, just mighty fine."

"You's glad to be home?"

"Oh, yes," she replied enthusiastically.

When they were outside the Grantley Adams International Airport building, accompanied by a porter Connie addressed as Seth who willingly loaded their luggage on to a trolley, Jackie asked, "How did you manage that? Familial connections?"

Connie laughed. "No, although it does help when you know everyone, and they know you. There were two channels, one for tourists, the other for nationals. I am a national. We have a joint ticket, so you got through quickly because you were with me! If you did not know me, you would still be inside waiting to pass through customs!" As she spoke her roving eyes scanned across the concourse of vehicles entering and leaving the airport.

"There he is, Seth." She pointed and waved vigorously. "He is in the far lane, 30 metres or so away." A figure raised an arm in acknowledgement.

Connie ran across the road and flung her arms around an erect, young man, with a well-proportioned frame who was hurrying towards her. Jackie, still struggling with the overwhelming heat walked more sedately by the side of the trolley-pushing Seth, watched the uninhibited reunion. Belatedly, remembering her manners Connie stepped back to meet them, grabbed her friend's arm. "Jackie, please meet my twin, Clyde. Clyde, this is my friend Miss Jacqueline Cooper." With a firm hand clasp the tall, fine-looking man sporting bronzed features not dissimilar to Connie's welcomed her on to Bajan soil but when she looked into his eyes, they appeared to hold a sadness and distinct lack of lustre. "Welcome to our island. I trust you will treasure all that you see and lock away in your heart precious memories to take out and revisit when you are no longer here." *My word, what a handsome man!*

"What a special welcome, thank you. I will do just that," but her smile was returned with a wan grin as Clyde swiftly reverted to the business in hand. Introductions over, luggage stowed as best as it could be in the car, he squeezed his passengers into available gaps and headed towards their parents' home along the ABC highway. While Connie and Clyde chatted away and caught up on news, making up for the year's separation, Jackie watched the, oh so different, scenery they were driving passed. She did not want to miss a thing but for some unaccountable reason she felt incredibly tired, and her body sagged into the back seat in sheer exhaustion. Although Clyde had turned up the air-conditioning Jackie found the heat overbearing.

Within a few minutes Clyde turned off the highway, drove up a narrow road without paths and pulled up at gates outside a delightful Barbados home on a raised elevation giving a view of the airport and the, not too distant, sea enhanced by the setting sun. In between the edge of the property and the house were shrubs covered in flowers of pink, blue and yellow. *How colourful against that background of bright green and purple.* Colour was everywhere. Not a brick could be seen. Every house in sight, well to Jackie's eye they all looked like bungalows, was painted a different colour, some in two or three different colours.

As they approached the steps up to the veranda dogs barked and cats came running out.

"You have a colourful home, Connie."

"Oh, we do not live here. This is the home of Aunt Myrtle and Uncle Peter."

Once inside the house Jackie experienced warmth of a different kind as Connie's relatives extended friendship, hospitality and acceptance to her as though she too was family. She soon had in her hand an iced glass of homemade sorrel. Unsure of the taste on her palate she drank it because the heat had made her thirsty.

After about 30 minutes they left with promises to visit again. When they stepped outside it was pitch black. Jackie looked at her watch. *Only 6.15. Must have stopped. Dark this early in summer? Impossible!* They re-joined the ABC highway and a never-ending stream of traffic.

On arrival at Connie's home they were greeted with doting enthusiasm by all the family. "Oh, Mumma, Mumma," tears flowed down Connie's cheeks as she was hugged and held in love by her parents and siblings. Jackie was not left out but also embraced affectionately and made to feel that she was one of them.

After a brief tour of their home, Jackie sat with Connie and her family on the veranda as they caught up with all the family news, another refreshing drink in her hand. Light refreshments were offered to her before she was introduced to a mosquito net which Mumma Madge and Jacinth had erected over her bed. It was now midnight by English time, and she had been up since 6am. She felt shattered.

"Why don't you's have a quick shower to cool down then slip into bed," Madge suggested. Jackie happily complied, too exhausted almost to converse, fell asleep to the chorus of crickets heard through the netted open window thinking, "This is going to be more of a challenge than I anticipated."

God, thankfully I have arrived here in one piece fluttered across her mind as she sank into sleep. Had anyone mentioned it, she would not have admitted to conversing with the Almighty.

Heavy rain woke Jackie at 4.15am. Her first thought was, "Oh, not another wet day!" For a few moments she was disorientated. *Rain in Barbados!* It took her a while to locate the zip to extricate herself from the mosquito net but when she was free, she peered out of the mesh covered open window. Outside it was still pitch black but she could hear heavy raindrops bouncing off the decking below the window and a cacophony of croaking sounds. She clambered back under the net and laid down. The air was still and very hot. She partially pulled up the sheet and dozed until 'cock-a-doodling' cockerels broke into her subconscious. Day light streamed through the window. The rain had stopped. The sun was shining.

"Oh, gosh, I've overslept." She rushed her morning ablutions, as much as the heat would allow, pleased she had the luxury of an en-suite attached to her room.

When she stepped into the living area Mumma Madge was busy in the kitchen.

"I'm sorry to be so late."

"God bless you. You's not late. You sleep well?"

"Yes, very well, thank you." Jackie glanced at the clock on the wall above her hostess's head. The hands indicated 6.15am.

"Constance," Madge called, her hands hovering over a pan on the stove.

"You's like coffee?"

"Yes, please."

Connie came in through the doors open onto the veranda terrace her face radiant.

"Morning, I thought you might sleep-in late," she tucked an arm through Jackie's. Unused to such familiarity Jackie stiffened.

"Relax," whispered Connie, "you are on holiday." She proceeded to lead her to a chair under the canopy on the veranda overlooking an abundance of luscious foliage and colourful flowers. The brightness was almost blinding. Jackie was astonished that there was no evidence of the night-time downpour. Connie observed her puzzlement with amusement. "Different to English weather?" She grinned.

Jackie returned her mirth and nodded.

"Coffee," Jacinth placed a tray of full mugs on a table.

"Thanks."

Sudden movement by her elbow made Jackie jump up, knock the table and spill the coffees.

"Oh, I'm sorry."

The girls immediately mopped up the spillage, but Joel could not stop laughing at the incident.

Connie pushed his shoulder playfully. "You tease! It is only a lizard, Jackie."

"A lizard," she stammered.

"Quite normal. You'll see lots," the boy explained and almost to prove his words correct a couple more slithered up a palm tree to the left of them. Jackie shuddered.

"It was a surprise, so unexpected."

"No damage done. Have your drink, at least, what is left of it."

Jackie complied but kept a wary eye on the unpredictable movement of the amphibians much to Joel's amusement.

"We usually go for a walk on de beach before breakfast. You want to come?" Connie invited.

Jackie gulped down the remainder of her coffee and nodded.

"No hurry. You will need to smother on sun-screen, and I suggest you wear sunglasses and sunhat as you are unused to our heat."

Jackie scurried to her room to get ready, but she was to discover during her stay that Bajan timekeeping was somewhat different to what she was accustomed to in England and found she was the one waiting on the terrace for the others to leave. It gave her opportunity to savour the quietness and the richness of colour exhibited by the abundance of flowers displayed in the garden. *How Miss Pedwardine would enjoy this garden. I must capture it to share with her on my return home. Camera!* She rushed to collect it.

"Slow down, ma girl, or de heat will take you's energy." Mumma Madge wafted a spatula as she passed by her.

CHAPTER TWENTY

Stifling heat!

It was a lively group that made its way to the beach, the boys teasing their eldest sister for being lethargic and out of form as she kept pace with Jackie rather than with them. They walked along potholed roads with no paths avoiding vehicles that drove by them at incredible speeds. The architecture of the houses along the route intrigued Jackie.

"Different?" Garry asked when he caught her gaping at one particular property.

"Very! So vibrant! Uniquely diverse! All painted in various colours, no two alike. No wonder Connie found our village houses boring and lifeless, brick or stone, terraced, semi or detached."

"Only a couple painted in Suffolk pink!" Connie commented.

"Everyone has a balcony!"

"Well, we do spend more time out-of-doors, so we need an outside space, preferably covered to offer shade from the sun."

The sky was the richest blue Jackie had ever seen, mirrored in the sea, as a clear, aqua blue palette that stretched as far as the eye could see. When they reached the beach, they all slipped off their footwear. Jackie followed suit. The sand was warm, silver in colour and as soft as icing sugar trickling over her toes.

"This is not a safe swimming beach, but we can paddle," Connie warned. "On another day, when the waves are higher, this area will be full of kite surfers."

Jackie was prepared for a chill as she tentatively stepped into the final flow of the rolling waves that pounded against the shoreline. "Ooo, it's warm."

"What did you expect?" Jacinth asked.

"At home, the sea usually feels cold even at this time of year. Only the hardiest, and generally the children, would consider swimming. The rest of us are content to simply dabble our toes in the water."

"Even in the winter months it is still possible to enjoy a sea bath. The old people say it is too cold, but I find it pleasantly comfortable."

"I can't believe how warm it feels. Almost as if someone has tipped a million kettles full of boiling water in to heat it up. Even our local indoor swimming pool isn't ever this warm."

"Your winters are unbearably cold, even de chill of the damp, half frozen earth seeped through de soles of de boots Mrs Darnell gave to me and every day my toes would ache with numbness because of de cold. I would not have dreamt of going for a swim in the North Sea at any time. It is grey, cold and completely uninviting."

"You're right. There's no comparison."

"Time to retrace our steps," Connie called. "Must not keep Daddy waiting. You got training, Garry?"

"Yes, I have been picked for a match tomorrow."

"What are you doing, today, Joel?"

"Meeting up with Frue."

"Jacinth?"

"Swimming at Miami Beach with Esther and Becca. Will be home later as Sonja is coming with her Mum Jo who is delivering cousin Benji's car for Aunt May and Uncle Al to use when they arrive back from Grenada." Connie seemed able to digest the convoluting message without any explanation, so Jackie decided to let it wash over her. The complex family relationships of people on the island seemed too baffling to unravel. She decided she would greet all whom she met with a smile regardless of their connection.

"Has your brother Clyde already left for work?"

"Clyde opens his Doctor's office at 8am."

"Oh, I see." It was evident she did not see at all.

"He doesn't live with us," Jacinth explained. "He has his own house near to his office."

"Race you to the tap," Joel commenced running even as he spoke.

The others picked up their pace but as Garry and Jacinth chased after Joel, Connie followed with Jackie at a more sedate gait walking through a palm grove. Jackie stopped, bent down and picked up a tiny, hard oval ball.

"What is this?" she held it up for Connie to see.

"A baby coconut. It must have blown off in last night's storm."

"Please hold it in front of the palm tree." She focussed her camera and pressed the button to capture the fruit.

"What are these?" Jackie pointed to shrubs rooted in the sand on the perimeter of the beach.

Connie followed her finger then touched the foliage of one.

"This is fat pork and de one on that side is sea grape."

"And the red flower by the tap?"

"The 'Pride of Barbados'. You will find it depicted on many things. It is the national flower of Barbados."

"And the name?"

"That is the name, 'Pride of Barbados', and the blotchy plant with many colours beside it is named 'match me not'."

"No!"

"The botanical name is 'Acalypha'."

Jackie continued to capture these gems on her camera amazed that such attractive plants were growing so resplendently in the wild. "I must write these names down when we get back to the house before I forget them."

They rinsed their sandy feet under the public foot tap when the boys had finished and slipped their feet into open sandals. In minutes they were dry.

"Is it always this hot?" Jackie wiped her brow with a handkerchief. They all nodded.

"This is normal for this time of year. Early mornings are the coolest part of the day which is why we walk before breakfast. Later it will be even hotter."

Strolling back along the road it became necessary to press close to the chain-link fences bordering the properties they were walking beside as cars and ZRs raced by them at speed. Joel pointed out painted lines criss-crossing the road. "That's a street cricket pitch. I'm in our local league but Garry's given it up now he's in the Barbados Pride under 19's team."

"So, that's what the boys were doing at the fete? It really does take place, then. I must photograph this to show the boys in my school. Connie introduced it to them."

As they continued their return to the house, they walked next to a patch of grass where black bellied sheep were grazing.

"They resemble English goats," Jackie commented, snapping away with her camera. The boys laughed.

Jacinth darted into a wooden fronted house-looking building.

"Just calling in for extra sourdough rolls for Mumma."

"Come on," Connie pulled on Jackie's arm. "I can see you're fascinated." She dragged her through the open door.

"Different, uh?"

Jackie nodded as she cast her eyes around the dim interior. Unrecognisable fruit, vegetables, bakery and household goods were openly displayed. "Like a higgle-di-piggle-di market stall."

Connie beamed and nodded. "I'll just help Jacinth carry the rolls." She made her way to the till by the door.

Jackie discovered breakfast was freshly pressed orange juice followed by fluffy egg and fried plantain on the toasted sourdough rolls. She thought the plantain looked like a banana. "No, dis is a vegetable and you's cook it," explained Mumma Madge.

"No Bajan seasoning in yours," Connie whispered. Jackie started to pick up her juice but when she lifted her eyes around the table, she noticed that everyone seemed to be sitting quietly...waiting. As soon as they were all served and Mumma Madge was seated Wilson lifted his hands and gave thanks. Jackie quickly removed her hand from her glass and jerked her head downwards. *Forgot how religious Connie is. Obviously, a family thing!*

Conversation revolved around everyone's planned activities for the day. Partway through the meal Connie's cell phone pinged. Her face screwed up in consternation. "Daddy, please excuse me. That is the WhatsApp signal. It must be important." Wilson nodded. Connie retrieved her phone and looked at the screen. "Oh, Jackie, it's Miranda. Your family are concerned because they haven't heard from you."

"Haven't they received my text messages?"

"No."

"Constance, take your friend to Digicel at Sheraton this morning and get her cell phone sorted out."

"Yes, Daddy."

At the conclusion of the meal they all helped with the clean-up so that they were soon ready to leave for the various pursuits arranged for the day.

"We will take a ZR to Sheraton..." Connie began but Joel butted in, "Be prepared for quite an experience." The boy laughed as he leapt out of the house and down the steps.

He was not joking, Jackie discovered, as she clung for her life to the split, unfixed foam seat at the back of a ZR minibus, where passengers were packed in like sardines. It was like no other minibus she had ever travelled on. *Larger than a taxi but smaller than a minibus at home. Clearly, no health and safety ruling in operation here!* Her heart was in her mouth as the driver careened at high speed to the blaring of loud music along the potholed roads, constantly braking suddenly to pick up ever more passengers. *3.50B$ to end my life!* She began to feel she would not survive this ride. Never had she felt so scared in all her days. It was more frightening than the plane take-off at the airport and the buffeting when they encountered the Jet Stream, and that was bad enough!

Connie was chatting above the clamour of noise to the other passengers as though nothing life threatening was taking place. Jackie tried closing her eyes but the continuous jerking and swaying, jolting and braking churned her stomach. Her breakfast did not like the experience. At one point they almost crashed into an oncoming vehicle as the ZR took a bend too wide and too fast. The main road was at a nose to tail 'stand-still' so, the driver turned up his music even louder, turned right and then left on to a one-way street. Jackie gripped the seat harder. "We're going the wrong way down a no-entry road!"

"He is trying to circumnavigate de traffic jam," someone explained.

"Hold-ups means loss of money. They used to pay de first 250$ of their daily takings to de PSV owner for de lease but they's now demanding 500$ to 1000$. Makes it impossible to earn a living wage," the conductor clarified between his constant swinging on and off the vehicle, when it stopped, to push more passengers in.

"I ain't get no more money than I does get. All drivers at square one. De owners wicked," cut in the driver, keen to make his point, and air his grievances against the exploiting owners of the ZRs before accelerating excessively from the spot.

Arrival at Sheraton Mall came as a relief. Jackie extricated herself from incarceration with difficulty. Her legs seemed to have turned to jelly, her stomach anxious to relieve itself of the contents and her head pounded with dizziness as though it did not belong to the rest of her body. Connie firmly held her arm and guided her across the road. As her legs were reluctant to move forward, when they reached the steps up to the entrance of the Mall, the girls stood still.

"Take a deep breath. You will make it. There are benches inside."

Never had Jackie felt so thankful for a firm, static seat. Connie disappeared but returned within minutes carrying a glass of iced water and a plain sour dough roll in her hand.

"Sip slowly, then, take a small bite. You will soon feel OK. Sorry about that. He was a bad driver. They are not all like that."

Crowds milled around them.

"Hi, Connie."

"Hello, Squib. You here alone?"

"Mum and Dad are getting coffees over there."

"JoJo and Clay," Connie squealed as she rushed forwards to hug the couple walking towards her.

"So good to see you, Constance, how's you?"

Introductions and explanations followed but were only a forerunner of the many reunions of the morning.

"Are you related to everyone on this island?"

Connie beamed. "Not quite!"

They eventually walked into Digicel at 12.24pm.

'*I am discovering that life in Barbados is one of constant contrasts,*' Jackie wrote in the next letter to her family. '*One moment it is pouring with rain and the next the sun is shining evaporating the rain with its heat. Washing dries in minutes of being hung out.*

The pace of life may be much slower, but they seem to pack a lot of activity into a day. However, you can depend on it that if the arranged departure is one time it will be at least ½ hour later before we eventually leave. Plans are changed on the spur of the moment so that frequently I think we have left the house to visit or meet up with someone at a certain venue only to discover we are travelling to somewhere totally different. On one occasion the midday meal was already planned, but on our way home it was decided to turn right instead of left and we ended up at Pom Marine, the catering college where students prepare and serve meals. It was very nice, and I chose king fish with a medley of Bajan vegetables. Connie's siblings insisted I taste mauby and coconut drinks but after sips of both I decided to stick to iced water. It is the most delicious water I have ever tasted. Half-way through the meal, Clyde, Connie's twin, joined us. Apparently, his Doctor's office is not too far away, and he frequently calls into Pom Marine for lunch. He explained the reason for the purity and flavour of Bajan water is because Barbados is a coral island, the only one of the Caribbean islands to be so. The others are volcanic. Rain passes through the soil then filters through the coral into an aquifer before it is piped to people's homes and businesses. Everyone keeps water in the fridge so that iced water is always available.' She continued to regale them with the many things she had seen and done since her arrival on the island.

'It has taken quite a while to adjust to the climate here. I am constantly tired, probably jet lag coupled with the excessive heat may have much to do with that. The family insist I have a siesta each afternoon!

I still cannot believe I am in this place, but I am determined to make the most of this visit and learn from it.

Love to you all
Jackie'

Chapter Twenty-One

32 degrees and soaring!

'No one warned me that monkeys roam freely around the island. Rain, which seems to fall daily, had eased and I was hanging the washing out on the line when monkeys suddenly appeared in the garden and made me jump. They came tripping along the chain-link fence that denotes garden boundaries between properties, with tremendous agility, a mother and two young ones, saucily pinching pomegranates from a neighbour's tree as if it were their right. I began to wonder what other creatures would appear unexpectedly because they have complete freedom on the island. I did not have long to wait to find out.*

Today, Connie borrowed Mumma Madge's car to drive us to Miami Beach for what the Barbados people call a sea bath but is really a swim. Along one road we had to stop and wait while a man fed some chickens in the middle of the road. "Maybe he's fattening them for some future meal," I joked but Connie explained they roam wild around the island and if you want one for lunch you nab it, kill it, pluck it, cook it, then eat it!!!'

Jackie wrote a continuous letter to her family as a journal to keep them abreast of all that she was experiencing on her Barbados adventure and posted the pages whenever they travelled in the vicinity of the post office in Oistins, which appeared to have limited opening times.

On the way to Miami Beach they drove by palm trees loaded with coconuts as well as heavily laden bread fruit and mango trees. "I'll make sure you sample all of those before you leave. They'll taste vastly different to anything you buy in the UK."

After parking the car, Connie and Jackie climbed down the wooden steps that led on to the beach. They were already clad in swimsuits over which they wore beach dresses They swiftly de-robed and hung their swim bags on natural pegs jutting out from the branches of trees growing on the beach. Jackie's breath caught in her throat as she witnessed again the bluest sea one can imagine. She stepped over the foam that was leisurely breaking onto the soft silver sand expecting to feel a chilly sensation on her skin, but the water was pleasantly warm and incredibly clear. "No wonder they call this experience a sea bath." Connie laughed and plunged beneath the water emerging quite some feet away from where Jackie was still standing. Jackie followed amazed to find the water as still as a mill pond. When she caught up with her friend, Connie pointed along the coast and advised, "Don't go beyond that promontory, there are life threatening currents at that point."

"This is exceedingly delicious!"

"Worth coming all this way for?" Connie teased and swam away. Jackie followed suit, her whole-body revelling in the experience. There was an indescribable freedom, being able to move uninhibited. She suddenly felt something brush close by her knee, stopped, turned and looked through the clear water to see a busy shoal of small fish. "Unbelievable!"

After some while Connie called, "We've been in for about an hour, I think it's time we went out."

"How do you know the length of time we've been swimming. You're not wearing a watch."

"I look at de position of de sun."

Jackie eyed her quizzically, but Connie swam towards the shore to a depth where she was able to stand up and made her way across the sand to the tree hooks. She towelled her hair, dried her face and hands and slipped on her colourful beach dress over her swimsuit. Jackie soon followed her friend.

"Carry your sandals and we'll go and rinse our feet."

At the top of the steps, to the right, were public showers and a tap to rinse sand off one's feet.

"We are meeting Mumma at Aunt Fran's so we will shower and get dressed at her house."

"But I'm wet," Jackie began.

"That is OK, sit on your towel. You will soon dry."

Within 15 minutes Connie was parking on the road in front of an attractive house painted pink and green. Mumma Madge and Aunt Fran sat on the veranda. Connie greeted them and introduced her friend to her aunt then proceeded to walk through the house. She led Jackie to the bathroom picking up a clean towel laid out on the kitchen table.

"Here, you go shower first. You will find all you need on a shelf to your left."

It seemed most unusual to Jackie to walk into someone else's home to have a shower after swimming in the sea, but obviously it was accepted as the norm in Barbados.

When the girls were dressed and had enjoyed a refreshing iced drink, they waved good-bye to Fran. Mumma Madge drove while the friends sat together in the back of the car, Connie pointing out and naming many places of interest until they left residential areas behind and appeared to be driving through wild countryside.

"We seem to be travelling higher."

"This is a hillier part of de island."

"We haven't been on this road before, have we?"

"No, this area was once sugar plantations. Only one or two remain in existence because Barbados can no longer compete in de international commercial market when larger countries can commit such vast acreages to sugar cane production."

"So, sugar no longer contributes to Barbados economy?"

Connie hesitated for a moment and then said, "We will take a bus to de museum in Speightstown…"

"You's tell her about you's ancestors." Madge called over her shoulder.

"Yes, Mumma," Connie turned back to Jackie. "It has an in-depth display of de former sugar industry."

"Right, that will be interesting," replied Jackie

As Jackie puzzled their reluctance to discuss the decline of the sugar industry Connie pondered on the information she had gleaned from the de Vessey archives concerning her mother's forebears and was anxious to refresh her memory about the data held at the Speightstown (pronounced Spikestown) Museum to see how the two linked together. She had not yet shared anything about her research with her family. She wanted to be certain of all the facts before enlightening them with her findings.

After a 30-minute drive along narrow, windy, pot-holed roads, whose gradient seemed to increase with each bend, the character of the country changed. Madge turned into what appeared to be an entry into a former plantation. Connie explained, "This was built as an entrance to a gated community but as only a few of the plots have been sold just the sides are in place and the envisaged security is not yet operational."

"Surely it is a good thing to use the land rather than leave it to grow wild."

"Maybe, in some instances," Connie replied dubiously.

Before Jackie could question her further, on what seemed to be a touchy subject, Madge drove into a driveway alongside a beautifully spacious house painted cream and gold trimmed with brown and orange surrounded by trees.

"This house is built on one of de highest ridges in Barbados and is over 900ft above sea level."

"It's very impressive."

"It has been built at a higher elevation than originally planned because when they commenced digging de foundations de builders found a cave."

"Oh, my goodness, that must have been a shock. Did it scupper their plans?"

"Not at all. Tilda and Lennie were not deterred. They simply prayed about de problem and what could have been a disaster turned in to a blessing."

"How's that?"

"The cave became a basement room, and de rest of de house was built above it. I am sure Tilda will show you what they do with that space. Shall we get out?"

The moment they alighted from the car the front door opened and a large, buxom lady, with a beam almost as wide as she was long, embraced them in turn.

"Dear girl, so good to see you. How is that brother of yours? Any progress on the heart front?" Connie gave an almost unnoticeable shake of the head. "Humph! We will have to do something about that. Come in. Lennie is making drinks."

"This is Tilda, my godmother. She and Lennie have lived and worked all over de world but come home to Barbados to retire. Here in St. Thomas is the highest point of de island. On a good, clear day it is possible to see the deep-water harbour in Bridgetown in de parish of St. Michael, and right along de coast south to Christchurch, from their balcony."

"Don't stand gossiping on the doorstep, come in, come in and share your news with us all." She ushered the girls into her home. Madge had already made her way to the kitchen and was sat chatting to Lennie as he poured out coffee that had been percolating.

"We'll take this on to the terrace while it is still dry. I fear a storm is forecast. Look out at ten-past-the-hour and you will see sea mist already gathering down by the harbour in Bridgetown."

The view took Jackie's breath away. The terraced balcony wrapped partially around three sides of the house and gave an amazing 180degree panoramic view of the garden across the parish of St. Thomas to St. James and beyond. Its sides were open giving an uninhibited aspect of the vista. They were so high up they were able to look down over the canopy of trees that stretched out below them to the left. A profusion of tulip trees in full bloom splattered the amazing view with red.

"The birds also like to fly in and out at will. Watch your cake or they will relieve you of it."

While Lennie and Madge discussed the overabundance of fruit from their trees and what to do with the surplus of bananas, limes and passion fruit, Tilda took Jackie on a tour of her home when they had finished their coffee and cakes.

"We'll leave the cooks to swap recipes and concoct new ones. Lennie loves to experiment. He's trying different combinations for marmalade and I'm sure your Mumma will bolster his imagination further. They are two of a kind."

"Mumma does love to cook. De passion fruit curd in de meringues was delicious."

"Lennie, I'm sure, will give Madge the recipe plus the fruit to make it. The Good Lord has blessed us with an abundance!"

The magnificence of Tilda and Lennie's home was such a contrast to the Foster home, which though nice and homely was modestly furnished, however, she showed them round with such humility and graciousness, constantly giving thanks for the rich blessings of the Good Lord to them over the years, that Jackie was quite taken aback.

"We have always been blessed with a roof over our heads, clothes on our backs, food in our bellies and a place to sleep. We now give thanks by always having a bed and food for anyone who needs them."

When they reached the cave basement Jackie's breath was taken away. Three of the white painted walls were barely visible because they bore shelves stacked full of food from floor to ceiling. On the fourth side was a table holding about a dozen large cardboard boxes packed to overflowing with a variety of tinned and packeted goods. Placed on the top of each one Jackie identified mangoes and bananas mingled with Bajan vegetables.

"These are ready for this week's distribution. You want to come?" Tilda looked at the young women expectantly. "I think Clyde is on the rota this week, you know."

Jackie looked confused unsure what she was letting herself in for.

"I think, Tilda, you had better explain."

Tilda nodded. "You ever go hungry, girl?"

Jackie shook her head. "No. My parents run the butcher's shop in the village. Mum is a good cook so they both ensure we always have wholesome meals and sufficient to eat."

"If you haven't discovered already, you soon will, you know, that Barbados is an island of many contrasts. On the one hand, there are the very rich who live in such grandeur they waste more than you or I will ever see. On the other hand, there is such poverty and hardship it would break your heart, you know. Children are so hungry they go scavenging for what they can find around the rubbish bins of places like KFC down by the Boardwalk before rats or seagulls claim the thrown away food or the bins of the wealthy along the Platinum coast and up to Port St. Charles, but if they are caught get whipped for it or reported to the authorities for stealing."

"Oh, how cruel!"

"Fact of life here, you know. You seen the wild chickens in the streets?"

"Yes, we had to wait one day while a man was feeding some."

"You thought it quaint?" Jackie looked shame-faced and nodded.

"Well, in the poverty-stricken areas of Bridgetown people are so hungry they have been driven to brawls over the chickens in the street, you know, and the police are called to sort out the fighting."

"No!"

"We are thankful to be so blessed! When we learned what was going on, we wanted to do something positive. Our Bible group at church made it a matter of prayer then Lennie contacted the Wellington Street Salvation Army in Bridgetown. Now we liaise with them. Each week they give us names and addresses of families in need. Friday morning Lennie bakes a fish or chicken dish that can be placed on top of the food box. In the afternoon, a group of us deliver the parcels. Sometimes we simply hand them over at the door, at other homes we are invited in, and people pour out their troubles. It helps to have a listening ear. We cannot solve their problems but voicing their struggles helps them see their difficulties in a different light, you know. Occasionally, we are able to put them in touch with agencies or departments who might alleviate or help resolve some of the issues."

"That is a tremendous undertaking. It must take some commitment."

"Not at all. It is only fulfilling the Lord's instructions, 'I was hungry and you gave me something to eat, I was thirsty and you gave me something to drink, I was a stranger and you invited me in, I needed clothes and you clothed me, I was sick and you looked after me, I was in prison and you came to visit me...I tell you the truth, whatever you did for one of the least of these brothers of mine, you did for me.'"

"We are simply His hands helping our brothers and sisters in their hour of need."

Jackie looked at Connie in astonishment, "You are also part of this scheme?"

"Oh, yes, when I am at home I go out with de team. Tilda, we will come this week."

She stayed Jackie's arm when Jackie opened her mouth to protest.

"I know you do not want to be shaken out of your cocoon, but you came here to experience life on de island. This is de reality not de artificial world tourist operators present."

"So, you're talking about families similar to those living in Marsh Newton or the Common?"

"No, by comparison they are rich."

CHAPTER TWENTY-TWO

Unsettled conditions!

Friday afternoon, Jackie, clad in borrowed clothing accompanied Connie and Clyde to Lennie and Tilda's home.

"We wear our oldest clothes, and as you do not have any with you, put on these." Connie thrust a bundle of clothing at her friend. Before Jackie could refuse Connie explained, "We do not want to appear too posh, nor would you want to wear your everyday clothing, where we are going."

"Smother yourself with insect repellent," commanded Tilda.

"De houses we are visiting do not have mosquito deterrent barriers," Connie said quietly.

Jackie did as instructed, then helped lift the laden food boxes into the boot of Clyde's car.

"Chicken stew and macaroni pie, today," Lennie called.

"Make sure the lids are tight. Don't want them to spill all over the car," Tilda advised as she gave Connie a list of addresses. "The man at this one is known to be aggressive and violent." She pointed out the address with an asterisk. "Any trouble call this number. Leroy

Corbyn is the policeman on duty and he's aware that we are calling at this address and will send assistance, if necessary, you know."

Connie sat with Clyde in the front of the car but pointed out to Jackie the former British Garrison and the Governor's official residence as they drove by them. They passed the University of the West Indies buildings and soon the area changed from large residences and more modest dwellings to a road track that ran through what appeared to be nothing more than shacks or semi built or derelict houses. "Clyde's office is down that street."

"Barbadians are very good at constructing houses but very poor at maintenance, Daddy always says," commented Connie.

The steps up to the first property were missing treads and the railings were broken. The windows were simply gaps in walls and the door hung off its top hinge so was propped open against the wall, but they were welcomed with open arms and invited in by a heavily pregnant woman. Scantily clad children sat on the floor.

"Oh, bless you, bless you." She burst into tears and put her hands to her face to hide her embarrassment.

"Mumma, don't you's cry," a scrawny boy of about 10 jumped up and put his arms around his mother.

"Can you get some plates?" Connie asked a young girl sitting on the floor amusing a toddler. She came back with an assortment of chipped and cracked dishes and spoons. Connie did a quick head count. "Jackie, hold these, please," then proceeded to serve out the chicken stew.

In the meanwhile, Clyde sat the mother down in the only proper chair in the room and with his doctor's hat on enquired discreetly about her pregnancy.

As they departed, he gave her a piece of paper with the address of his doctor's office and 3.50B$ to cover the fare. "Get a neighbour to keep an eye on the little children when the big ones leave for school. I'll see you Monday morning."

In the car Connie made a note on her list of practical requirements that her practised eye had seen the family had need of.

At the next home, the door was opened barely a fraction by a frail looking woman with scared, suspicious eyes. She was unable to hold the parcel and as she would not let Clyde carry it in-doors he placed it on the cluttered porch by the door. She mumbled something unintelligible then the door was slammed in his face.

The afternoon deliveries proceeded without further incident until they reached the final address on their list.

Before they got out of the car Connie handed Jackie the insect repellent, a hair band and a bandana. "Spray again with this, include your hair, tie it up on top of your head and cover it with the bandana."

Clyde reached into his doctor's case, pulled out face masks and surgical gloves. "Put these on."

The stench emanating through the open doorway caused Jackie to gag.

"Angel, it's Doctor Foster."

They peered through the gloom. It took a while for Jackie's eyes to adjust from the daylight brightness to the unnerving darkness of the room. She stood tentatively on the threshold.

"Is Antonio here?" Clyde appeared to be addressing a bundle of rags in the furthest corner of the wooden and corrugated shack.

Scurrying to the left caught Jackie's attention.

"A rat!" she gasped as the creature foraged around a pile of rags. Involuntarily she let out a cry when she saw it was scavenging all over a small child. She moved forward but Connie stayed her arm, clapped her hands to scare off the rat and said, "Don't touch anything yet, especially the children."

Jackie looked across the room and saw two other bundles laying on the floor.

"We're not sure what we are dealing with. Let Clyde examine them first." She inclined her head towards her brother who, having completed his examination of the woman he had addressed as Angel, was now speaking on his cell phone to emergency services.

"Leroy, Clyde here...I'm at Angel and Tonio's place...No he's not here. I need to get Angel to Queen Elizabeth, ASAP...thanks. Could be lung infection but am suspecting it's TB...Could you get the church cleaning team out here...Yeah, bad, place requires fumigating, rat infestation...also need carpenter...I've yet to examine the children...Hoping it's only malnutrition...Thanks."

"Con, you heard?"

"Yes, Clyde. What shall we do about the children? They seem quite lifeless."

"Carry them carefully to the balcony. I'll be better able to assess them in the daylight," he instructed, his eyes keenly focussed on the very sick mother. He again listened to her rasping chest through his stethoscope.

Between them Connie and Jackie carefully lifted the weak and inert children and placed them where Clyde could examine them more easily.

"They're nothing but skin and bone," said Jackie, horrified.

Clyde knelt on the broken boards and gently examined the emaciated body of the first little girl. As he held her arm, he looked up anguish in his eyes. "Con, ring Mrs Captain and go up the road to the SA kitchen and get some of that chicken stew liquidised into soup so that you can spoon it into these children." Connie nodded her assent and moved swiftly on her errand. She had seen the child's arm.

As she waited for Mrs Captain to liquidise the soup Connie stabbed in numbers on her cell phone. "Leroy Corbyn dis is Connie Foster. You listen to me good. You's get dat Tonio Monks and you's throw de book at him...What for?...Attempted murder...his wife and children...I heard what Clyde said...He's starved them and used their arms like a dart board...Just you's get him!" Mrs Captain raised her eyebrows. Never had she heard Connie raise her voice to anyone.

"Serious?"

"Very!"

"Jackie, come here," Clyde spoke softly. "Simply talk or sing to these children. Keep them awake, register what response you get, finger pressure, flickering eye-lids, breathing movement, anything." Sensing a desperation in the doctor's voice Jackie crouched by the nearest child, picked up her hand and started to sing a nursery rhyme.

With extreme tenderness Clyde moved to the next child and thoroughly examined him. He pulled out his cell phone. "Tilda? Clyde here...We are at Angel and

Tonio's...Not good...Could you take the children in?...
Thanks. They need complete delousing etc and
clothing...lack of nourishment...Yes, Connie's doing
that now at SA...They have been needled...need to go,
ambulance has arrived for Angel...Yes, bye."

In no time at all Angel was stretchered and Clyde
accompanied her to the hospital.

As the ambulance departed Connie returned with
Mrs Captain armed with three lightweight sheets as
well as plastic dishes and teaspoons. The women each
sat on the boards with their backs to the walls of the
shack and held a child in their arms carefully spooning
sips of the warm soup into their mouths. Jackie followed
suit by picking up the little boy who looked about
three years of age but was probably much older. As she
moved him, he opened his eyes and looked at her
petrified, tried to free himself from her hold, but in his
weakened state was barely able to move.

"Shh...shh," she soothed and spoke softly to him as
she tried to spoon soup into his mouth. Thankfully, he
responded by opening his mouth and swallowing the
liquid down.

"Do not let him have too much all at once. He has
probably been denied food for several days, if not
weeks, and his stomach will be unable to cope."

Jackie nodded and continued to talk and sing to him
as she cradled him.

Mrs Captain was not having the same success with
the older girl who was very lethargic and had not
opened her eyes at all. As each drop trickled into her
mouth she gagged.

The younger toddler squirmed in Connie's arms but
when Connie spoke her name and crooned a song, she

was obviously familiar with she calmed down and accepted nourishment from the spoon.

"Why are they in this state?"

"Tonio is not able to hold down a permanent job because of drug addiction, and even when he is in work, pay in Barbados is only 3B\$ an hour and you have seen prices in de supermarket. Families like this cannot afford much of de food on offer let alone bare necessities for living. Most commodities in Barbados must be imported which is why everything is so expensive. There is a big, big, gap between income and cost of living."

"Is there no social service?"

"A government welfare department was recently established to assist impoverished families but many still fall through the net," explained Mrs Captain. "We do our best to keep abreast of those in our neighbourhood who are the neediest and help where we can."

"How does he afford drugs?"

"He doesn't. I guess they are his payment for acting as runner for de drug barons. They are coming here from de South American Continent, infiltrating our country and devastating many lives with their corruption and greed. They are cunningly using innocent citizens, particularly youngsters, in order to avoid detection but also, they are giving back handers to government officials to turn a blind eye. Some of de plantation land has been undersold to them to build so called affordable housing so dat people no longer have to live in shanty districts but prices are way too high for local people, so they are being sold to wealthy Canadians and Americans as holiday homes at considerable profit."

So, that is why Connie, and her mother were reluctant to speak about the sugar plantations, Jackie reflected.

After a short while Lennie and Tilda drew up followed by a van out of which tumbled three women and a couple of men armed with tools and cleaning implements of all sorts. As soon as the children were carefully wrapped in sheets and held securely by the women in Lennie's car the cleaning team set to work. Lennie drove back to St. Thomas followed by Connie driving her brother's car.

Back at Tilda and Lennie's home, in the basement suite attached to the food store, the children were stripped of their soiled and tattered clothing and gently bathed and deloused. Once dressed in clean nightwear and settled side by side on the bed, bolstered by pillows to keep them upright, more chicken broth was spooned into them.

Gradually the children fell into a natural sleep and Tilda prepared to spend the night next to them sitting on a chair by the bed. "You girls get home. Thank you, Mrs Captain, for all your help."

Connie dropped off Mrs Captain at her quarters and went on to the Queen Elizabeth hospital to pick up Clyde.

Tears flooded uncontrollably down Jackie's cheeks. She who was always in control was unable to keep her emotions in check.

"Why? Why? Why?"

"Why, what?" Clyde demanded in his calm way.

"Why does God allow such innocents to suffer so?"

"God? You think it's God's fault?" Connie asked.

"Well, isn't it?" Jackie uttered defiantly.

"Parents have choices," Clyde spoke quietly.

"The family living next to Angel and Tonio also have a young family. Mother and father work, on low wages, but their priorities are paying bills, food and cleanliness. They are very proud and independent, but they are one of the families Mrs Captain keeps an eye on because they do struggle at times but will not ask for help. The children attend youth activities at SA, and she ensures they take something home each time like mangoes, bananas or rice, sweet potato or whatever she has in the food store."

"The decisions we all make affect our lifestyle. Wouldn't you agree?"

"Yes, I suppose so."

"De Good Lord intends good for all people, but we sometimes opt to take ourselves out of His will because we decide we know best."

"That's what makes the difference."

Jackie's tears flowed even more. Connie's words had hit a very raw spot.

Chapter Twenty-Three

Threatening clouds!

Clyde spotted Jackie as she approached the steps of Kensington Oval cricket ground with Connie and waved. He liked what he had seen of his sister's friend. She had certainly proved her worth yesterday at the Monk's place. He found her quite a personable young woman but a hurt from the past made it highly unlikely that he would ever let his guard down and become more than an acquaintance, let alone friends, with any young woman. To his practised eyes she looked somewhat distracted this morning and for a moment he pondered what might be troubling her.

"Hi, Connie, Jackie," he greeted as the girls reached the top of the steps.

He playfully tapped his sister's arm. "I hope you've taken her photo by Garry Sobers statue for posterity."

Connie's laughter burst out and echoed as they stood beneath the entrance to the 3W's stand, named after three eminent Barbados cricketers, Worrell, Walcott and their grandfather's good friend Everton Weekes.

"Clyde, she's not a bit interested in cricket. She's only come today because she is a loyal friend."

"You mean to say you haven't yet initiated her into the wonders of the great game." Clyde teased.

Despite the strain in her eyes Jackie did manage a smile. She had never seen this side of Clyde. He always seemed so remote and quiet. However, she had been impressed by his bedside manner and doctoring skills yesterday afternoon, even though the plight of the people she had engaged with still perturbed her.

"Your sister certainly enthused year 5 pupils in my school, with help from the local cricket captain and his mates."

"Oh, would that be Stephen Cooper mentioned in Connie's letters?"

"Yes, my cousin."

"So, there is interest in the family? There may be hope for you yet." He smiled mischievously.

This really was a Clyde she had not met before. "Only some branches, I don't really understand what all the fuss is about."

"Come, come, Miss Cooper, we must teach you. You can't visit the Caribbean and go home ignorant of its greatest game." Jackie could not fail to respond to his joviality with a broad smile.

"Caribbean cricket is like no other, you know. Oh, the rules are the same for all players the world over but the accompanying razz-ma-tazz here is second to none." He held up his cricket pass to the man in the ticket office.

"Morning Doc Foster, Miss Connie, welcome home. Enjoy de match. Is Garfield playing?"

"Morning, Abe," they chorused together. "Yes, he is."

"Hope he's in better form than last week or de Jaguars will thrash them."

"What happened last week?" Connie asked Clyde as they walked underneath the 3W's stand towards the seats where Clyde knew their father was seated with their youngest brother at the Joel Garner end of the stand.

"He was not at his best. He didn't seem to be concentrating and was out to a stroke a 6-year-old would not have played." Clyde was not criticising his brother but spoke in a matter-of-fact tone about Garry's form.

Connie carried the picnic basket up to where her father and Joel were sitting. Clyde assisted Jackie up the steps.

"Cricket is an entertaining cultural experience and well worth the effort, you know, even if you don't understand the game."

Jackie laughed at his attempt to cajole her into an appreciation of a sport that meant so much to them.

"I truly cannot see the point of 22 men, or women, hitting or bowling a ball for days on end when the entire exercise sometimes ends up without a winner."

"We'll have to do something about that gap in your education, Miss School Teacher, and introduce you to the finer points of the game so that you can watch with enlightenment." Jackie responded to his nonsense with another laugh.

"Today may be a little tame in contrast to the norm as it is only an under 19's 40 over match. The atmosphere would normally be electric, with DJ music, constant whistling, horn-blowing, cheering and banter, our own version of the English 'Barmy Army.' All over the ground, outside as well, everybody has an opinion on the state of the game and is keen to express it.

"Unfortunately, you won't have opportunity to see the West Indies play because they are abroad playing in the World Cup."

It was the most Jackie had ever heard Clyde speak. "You are obviously quite an enthusiast. You would get on well with my cousin Stephen."

"I'd be delighted to meet him."

As they sat down, after greeting Wilson and Joel, a voice came over the loud-speaker system, "Will Miss Connie Foster please make her way to the office."

"Now, what is that all about?" they asked one another.

"Miss Connie, Miss Connie," Abe from the ticket office came flapping his arms and calling up the stairs. "Miss Connie, Jed's had a mishap and can't get here, dey need you to keep score."

"And I planned a quiet day watching cricket with my friend and family, Abe."

"But dem desperate, Miss Connie," he rung his hands.

"Only teasing, Abe, I'll come. Sorry, Jackie, I will have to leave you to the mercy of my father and brothers." She looked around. "And probably my grandfathers as well. I hope they don't bore you too much."

"We'll take good care of her. Won't we, Joel?" Clyde assumed responsibility for his sister's friend.

As Connie rushed away, she called back over her shoulder, "Don't forget to feed her."

"There aren't any score cards today, so I've made up one to give you an idea what is going on in the game." Joel handed Jackie his improvised version of a score card. She was quite touched by his kindness.

"Thank you, Joel, that is most thoughtful of you."

Throughout the morning Wilson and Clyde kept her abreast with what was happening in the game. Joel knew all the players in his brother's team and gave her little potted histories about each of them.

As lunch time approached, he said to his father, "Daddy, I'm hungry. May we eat? I'm sure Jackie is hungry, too." He looked appealingly in her direction, grinned and nodded his head vigorously to encourage her support.

She smiled, and said, "Well, breakfast does seem a long way off, doesn't it? Shall we see what this basket holds?" Together they unfastened the picnic basket and found named packets as well as fruit and crisps and containers of salad, fish, chicken and macaroni pie.

"Quite a feast!"

Joel distributed the food that Madge had thoughtfully prepared, aware of everyone's preferences, particularly Jackie's dislike of Bajan spicy seasoning.

At the end of the 1st innings Connie joined them for her lunch. She had been offered a meal with the players and officials but elected to spend time with her family and Jackie chatting over aspects of the game with her father and Clyde.

"Have the Grands been over?"

"No, we haven't seen them."

"I believe I caught sight of them in the Greenidge and Haynes stand." Wilson nodded in response and picking up the binoculars focussed them in that direction. "I see them. I'll wander over there shortly."

"I thought Garry fielded well, today."

"He certainly seemed more alert and concentrated on what was taking place on the field."

"He took a brilliant catch."

"Mmm, he did. Oh, this is nice," Connie munched on the selection Mumma had prepared for her.

"Hey!" Joel jumped up suddenly, knocking Connie's forkful of fish out of her hand.

"Oops, sorry Connie, but look." He pointed to the right-hand side of the pitch. "On the boundary. Look Daddy! Who's that man pushing Garry around?"

Simultaneously Wilson and Clyde sprang to their feet. They all focussed on the activity surrounding Garry.

"I don't like the look of this." Wilson looked across at Clyde, deep concern etched on his brow.

Clyde pulled his cell phone from his pocket and punched some buttons. "Leroy, Clyde here. Who is on duty at the Oval?... Right...Suspect drug dealing...My brother is being accosted on the edge of the pitch...No sirens...Get them to lock all gates except the main one...Joel has taken pictures on his cell phone...Will do our best to keep them in view."

Clyde turned to Wilson, "Remain here, sir, and keep an eye on them. Stay in touch by phone. Joel, continue taking pictures, but ensure they are in focus. Thanks." He patted Joel affectionately across the shoulders. "Sorry, Jackie. Finish your lunch. Do not let these folks out of your sight." He indicated his father and brother. "Connie, come with me, you know so many people here. Do not want to make any mistakes. The match is going to be late restarting. Hold your phone in your hand in case we need to take pictures or make a sudden call."

They hustled down the steps. At the ticket office window Clyde leaned forwards and spoke quietly to Abe, "You get the message?"

"Yes, doctor, sir. All de gates locked now, and no one can get through this one. Got Jeb on watch till reinforcements come."

"Good man. Must stop these scoundrels."

"Yes, sir."

"Come, Con," he pulled his sister's arm and they rushed down the inner steps that took them to pitch level.

"I will keep look out, Con, you call Daddy to see where the rogues are."

Connie complied. "Still to the right of us on edge of pitch, another man has joined them, has got his arm tight around Garry's shoulders."

"Tell Joel to keep taking pictures and Daddy to pray. I see them. Finish the call, Con, and take pictures at this level. They may be clearer than Joel's as we are now closer to them."

"Oh, my goodness, the teams are coming out! Are you sure it's been delayed? I will have to go. Oh, no, they are going into a huddle around Garry, the men and…" She looked up bewilderment on her face. "Leroy, constables Sam Welch and Josh Alleyn are in de huddle, too, which seems to be moving towards the centre of the field. Oh, dear Lord, keep all de boys safe."

"One, Two, Three, Go," a voice shouted over the sound system.

"Incredible!" Connie clasped her hands across her mouth in amazement. On the word "Go" the team players crouched down to the ground. The three policemen tackled the legs of the two men and Garry who had been left standing. From the boundary other officers came running to support the arresting officers and supervise the players back to the pavilion. Connie, too, ran towards her brother, Clyde close on her heels. Leroy had grounded him but swiftly pulled him up on to his feet and held him firmly by the arm. As she reached them Garry uncharacteristically burst into tears. Connie flung her arms tightly around his shoulders. "Shh... shh...It is OK. It is all going to be OK."

"Connie, they were going to kill Mumma if I did not do what they ordered." He gulped. "And blow-up Daddy's hospital," he explained in between sobs. "And beat up Clyde and Joe and do awful things to you and Jacinth." His body shook with each sob. Never had she seen such emotion in her brother.

"Shh...shh, it is going to be alright." Never had she seen such brokenness in her brother.

"But I will go to prison now," he sobbed. "Sorry, Daddy, please forgive me," his eyes pleaded with Wilson who had joined the group. "I am so very sorry to have brought such disgrace on my family, but I could not bear any of you to get hurt."

Connie kept her arms around Garry, but Clyde looked at Leroy. "You heard?"

Leroy nodded. "Yeah, mitigating circumstances, coercion and provocation I should say."

"You know what, this all makes so much sense now," said Clyde reflectively.

Wilson shook his head slowly in disbelief. "I think you are right, but I never linked those incidents or your poor performance, son, with such horrendous exploits. You should have told us."

"I couldn't. If I gave any indication I had told you or the police their actions would have been so much worse. Daddy, they are ruthless." He broke down again. "They followed me everywhere, always here at the ground. Their hounding was relentless."

Sirens were heard in the distance. The men who earlier had been accosting Garry had been swiftly bundled into police vehicles and taken to police headquarters in Bridgetown.

"We need to get off the pitch. We'll discuss this at the station." Holding on to Garry's arm Leroy and his officers began to escort the group to the edge of the pitch.

"Don't look now but the man and woman seated near the Grands are part of the gang," Garry whispered hoarsely.

Leroy caught the eye of the constable nearest to him. "Keep going, then, softly, softly," he instructed.

Turning back to Garfield Leroy enquired, "Where are you batting?"

"Number 3."

"Did you get lunch?"

Garry shook his head.

"Go have a quick shower. Grab a bite to eat then bat your heart out and win this match for your team. You are not going anywhere so I will take your statement later after close of play."

Connie raised her eyebrows at the policeman as he released her brother to run towards the dressing room.

"Best thing for him to do. Take his pent-up feelings and frustration out on the bat. That will give him release. Must have been hard for him to be under such pressure. No wonder his game has been so poor."

Connie squeezed his hand. "You have extraordinary perception, Leroy. Thanks for your understanding." Leroy quickly extricated his hand from Connie's and brushed aside her remarks. *Keep it professional*, he told himself. He had held a torch for Connie since their teenage years but knew from her viewpoint they would never be anything but good friends.

"I cannot bear to see another innocent's life getting tainted by those Columbian crooks. It makes my blood boil. Doctor Foster, get him a good attorney. Under current Barbados judiciary system Garry is entitled to an attorney, a social worker, a probation officer, church minister plus a few other things. He is not the only young person on the island to be sucked in by malicious threats if they do not comply. Let us pray he is strong enough to speak out and encourage others to be brave enough to spill what is going on."

"But surely such experiences go to make up de rich tapestry of life? We either learn from them or we go under. I, too, pray de Good Lord will bring Garry through, still believing in justice, right and wrong, yet stronger in faith."

"He is fortunate to have a supportive family. Some of the kids pressured into this racket have no one to guide them or speak up for them. They have little choice, either they work for a pittance from these scoundrels or else scavenge the bins in order to survive."

With a furrowed brow Connie wandered back to her seat in the score box extremely concerned. Clyde made his way back to the stand deep in thought. Wilson tapped numbers into his cell phone, left the ground profoundly perturbed, to meet up with the attorney he had just engaged.

CHAPTER TWENTY-FOUR

Troubled waters!

As Sunday morning dawned the portals of heaven opened with cloudless blue sky and scorching sunshine. A sure sign to lift the doldrums that had descended on the family last evening after the incident at the cricket ground despite Garry's magnificent 79 not out contributing to his team's win.

It looked as though breakfast was going to be eaten accompanied by music of praise and worship that was wafting over from the church across the road behind the Foster's home. As it was amplified all around, no one in the vicinity could fail to hear it.

Connie was in the kitchen singing along with the congregation as she prepared breakfast.

"Great things He hath taught us…give Him the glory, great things He hath done." She stopped flicking the fluffy eggs with the spatula for a moment, lost in concentration. "Mmm, thank You, Lord. I will give the praise and glory to You for what You have done for me and my family. Teach us to learn from this experience. Teach us to trust and lean on You. Make Garry strong… ooh!" She turned back to her task and caught the egg just as it was about to burn and sang at the top of her voice, "I will Praise Him…Praise the Lamb for sinners slain…"

Jackie and Jacinth almost collided as they rushed from their rooms.

"You singing to wake the dead?"

Connie shook her head. "Call everyone to come, breakfast is ready." She gave a jug of freshly pressed orange juice to Jackie. "Please put this on the table. It has already been set." She proceeded to serve the egg onto the platter containing cooked bacon and plantain that had been keeping warm in the oven. Once full she replaced it in the oven then took out rolls from the second shelf and put them into the breadbasket and handed that to Jackie to place on the breakfast table. One by one the family gathered at the table.

Wilson prepared to give thanks.

"Excuse me, Daddy." Connie's eyes travelled around the table glancing at each member of her family. "Did you catch the words the church over the way were singing this morning?" Not a few nods replied to her words. "They challenged me. I believe the sin of others should not be allowed to cause us to doubt and be downcast nor to give the devil a foothold in our lives because at this moment in time we feel vulnerable. Our God is great, and He will see us, and Garry, through this experience. He will give us reason to be positive so that we find peace and joy in His presence. He is sovereign and in control. We should praise and give Him glory, trust in what He has done and what He will do."

"Bless you, Constance, we will do as you say and trust de Good Lord to keep His promises to us and also to Garfield," said Mumma, who was distressed that one of her sons was locked in a police cell, out of her care. She looked at Wilson and shared a wifely smile of understanding with her husband.

Wilson raised his hands in blessing and gave thanks. They all sat down and began passing the plates round the table.

Jackie was amazed. It was almost as though a physical barrier had been lifted from all those seated at the table. *The blanket of despondency that descended on them Saturday afternoon has evaporated, been snatched away, tangibly alleviating the gloom.* She felt the atmosphere change. Conversation was neither frivolous nor serious, but meaningful and positive, sparked with genuine joy. There was nothing artificial about their interaction with one another but evidence of their faith in a God they believed in and trusted to keep His promises.

They travelled in two cars to church as there were too many of them to pile into Daddy's 26year old car and were in plenty of time to greet fellow worshipers before the service commenced at 9.45am. They arrived in hot, blazing sunshine having driven through two heavy showers on the way. There were also showers of blessing throughout the service evident in many different guises.

Madge and her daughters went to the robing room. As Jackie walked down the aisle, she fully realised Connie's earlier words, "Dressing well to honour de Lord in His house is important to Barbados people." The women and girls wore beautifully coloured dresses. The men and boys were smartly attired in suits or shirt and tie and when the choir made their appearance, they, too, looked resplendent in their rich maroon gowns trimmed in white.

Wilson and his youngest son escorted Jackie to a row of chairs, where Clyde and his Aunt Myrtle and Uncle

Peter were seated, as well as Tilda and Lennie, three rows back from the altar rail. At the end of the row in front of them sat Leroy accompanied by Garry.

"I will sit here, today," indicated Wilson nodding a greeting to his relatives as he sat down next to his son.

As the service unfolded Jackie thought there must have been collusion between the family and the pastor but knew it was not possible. All that he uttered addressed issues that had occupied their hands and hearts during the last forty-eight hours. For the first time in years she was attentive to the words that were spoken from the pulpit. Her heart had been strangely moved and softened by the incidents she had got caught up in and she marvelled at the prayerful manner her hosts dealt with each one. The Lord Jesus was a very real member of this family. There was nothing artificial about their faith nor pretence concerning their Christian love and service for others.

The theme of the service was 'Revival', with an emphasis on personal renewal. Jackie recognized some of the hymns that she had not sung since she was a girl.

The words of Pastor Desmond resonated with what had been shared at the breakfast table concerning the praise and glory of God. Jackie realised they were not his words, but verses taken from the Bible, Hebrews chapter 1 verse 13, which referred to Jesus being the radiance of God's glory and those who knew it in John chapter 1 verse 14. "In the Old Testament the glory of God filled the temple, and the Israelites were led by it, we are told in Exodus chapter 40 verses 34 and 35." Desmond looked across his congregation. Jackie felt his eyes focussed directly upon her when he said, "In our natural state we fall short of it, we are told in Romans

chapter 3 verse 23, BUT we are promised that at the end
of time, as Revelation chapter 2 verse 23 records,
heaven will shine with it in splendour so great there will
be no need for the sun.

"The glory of the Lord is indescribable. In Psalm 72
verse 19 the Psalmist prayed, 'Let the whole earth be
filled with His glory, Amen and Amen!"

"We get only glimpses here on earth of His
magnificence, but it is all around us if we look for it.
Sometimes we are so intent on our selfish pursuits and
ambitions, we miss it. Yet, one day, those who are the
redeemed of the Lord, will come into His presence
where His radiance will be so powerful, we will only be
able to fall on our knees and worship Him."

The congregation rose to sing "He abides, hallelujah,
He abides with me. I'm rejoicing night and day as I walk
the narrow way for the Comforter abides with me."
Jackie's ears picked out the deep resonating tones of
Wilson's rich bass and the majestic notes of Clyde's
soaring tenor voice. As they reached the chorus a lump
emerged in her throat. *I cannot sing these words
anymore. They are no longer true for me. You do not
abide with me, God. You left me when...I am always
with you.* Tears welled in her eyes. A glimmer of hope
began to emerge in the corner of her mind. She felt
pressure on her hand. Sparks ran along her fingers and
up her arm.

"You alright?" Clyde's voice whispered in her ear. *Be
honest.*

"Not really."

"Talk later?"

She gave a slight nod as the congregation reached the
end of the hymn and sat down.

Towards the end of the service the choir sang Edwin J. Orr's hymn, 'O, Holy Ghost, revival comes from Thee', the chorus being uplifted straight from the final verses of Psalm 139, 'Search me, O God, and know my heart...'

"If there is anything within your heart today that would prevent you enjoying the presence of the Lord now, and in heaven, then put it right. Do not delay! Remember, the first letter of John chapter 1 verse 9 states, 'If we confess our sins, He is faithful and just to forgive us our sins and cleanse us from all unrighteousness.' He always keeps His promises. He will work the miracle of renewal in your life. His blood will never lose its power. The truly repentant will always receive His forgiveness."

A line in the closing hymn echoed Jackie's feeling of what had happened at the breakfast table that morning; 'Then the gloom had all passed...rejoicing at last...' *Wish my gloom was in the past, over and done with,* Jackie bemoaned.

But in Garfield's heart there was a sincere prayer that was endorsed by the next phrases of the hymn.

'I was sure that my heart was made right...
For my Lord I could see in His love died for me,
On the cross...'

At the altar call, he could not stay in his seat. He made his way to the front of the church, tears of remorse streaming down his face. Within seconds, Leroy Corbyn and Jehu, the Pastor's son, were by his side in prayer and support.

Jackie remained in her seat yet knew she ought to be kneeling there, too.

Somehow, through Pastor Desmond's words God's love had penetrated the hardness erected around her heart since Eddie's accident. With eyes closed she prayed as she had not prayed for a very long time. *Search me... forgive me...renew me...lead me in the way everlasting.* And she truly meant it.

When she opened her eyes, Clyde was in prayer beside her, Connie too, along with Madge, Jacinth and Tilda and Lennie. She smiled through her tears, "Thank you." She leapt to her feet and voluntarily hugged Connie. "Thank you, my friend, for your friendship, kindness and love. Your genuine Christianity shines through your life all the time. I am so ashamed of the way I have treated you. Please forgive me."

Connie returned her hug. "De Good Lord teaches us through all of life's experiences if we will but learn from them. Even when you refuse to acknowledge Him." She held her at arms' length and beamed. "Today, your eyes have been opened to see His love, mercy and grace is for you, always."

During her time in England Connie had learned the true state of Jackie's heart but was still unaware of the reason for her anger and bitterness against God.

"The past is settled. I am finally free from the shackles that bound me. Praise God!"

"I'm so glad."

"You still want to talk?" Clyde asked quietly.

Jackie smiled at him shyly. "Yes please."

The hollowness had disappeared from her eyes and her stained face shone with peace and contentment.

"Is that OK?" She glanced at the people around her.

"Of course, ma dear girl," Madge reached forward and embraced her. "De Good Lord be your strength and guide."

"Blessings be on you," Lennie stepped towards her and placed his hand upon her shoulder.

"Amen to that. Lunch is booked for 1:15pm" Tilda explained.

"We'll forego coffee here, then, and meet you there." Clyde took Jackie's elbow and steered her through the clusters of church goers intermingling and sharing fellowship, speaking to this one and that one as they walked by.

"No one seems to want to leave, even though the service has lasted for over two hours."

"They enjoy fellowshipping together."

Meanwhile, Wilson and Garfield still stood by the altar rail deep in conversation with Leroy and Jehu. Pastor Desmond stepped up to place an arm across Garry's shoulders and addressed Wilson and his son. "With your permission I invite Garfield to come for lunch. I believe we have some matters to talk through and pray over."

"Yes, sir," Garry replied.

Wilson nodded gravely. "Of course, Pastor."

"Leroy?"

"I will come and pick him up at 5 o'clock, Pastor. He needs to be in custody for his own safety, for the time being. Interviews are arranged with his attorney and a probation officer in the morning. I have also organized regular patrols in your vicinity, Doctor, for your family's peace of mind and safety."

Once Clyde had seated Jackie in his car he explained, "We are having lunch at the Colony Club Hotel on the

West coast to celebrate Tilda and Lennie's Wedding Anniversary and Mumma's Birthday. It is an annual event for our family. They married on Mumma's birthday, and she was their bridesmaid. The actual day is Wednesday but it is easier for everyone to get together on Sunday."

Clyde has such an easy manner with him, Jackie reflected as she sat quietly in the passenger seat as he negotiated the stream of traffic on Highway 1. *It is no wonder he is a popular doctor.* She felt comfortable and relaxed in his company. He had the ability to draw her out and for the first time she was able to speak freely about Eddie, her heartache, angst against God and distress at the attack by the bogus Dillon Brankscome. Gently Clyde persuaded her to speak of her attempt to protect herself from vulnerability by building a wall of detachment and remoteness about her. His calmness induced her to spill out her need to always be organized and in control denying God and affection an entrance in her heart.

"Till this morning. 'Search me, O God, and know my heart.' Those words brought me up with a start. It was as if everything in the service had been planned with me and my needs in mind. The hymns, the sermon, the choir, even the incident yesterday involving Garry and the plight of the families on Friday, gave me pause to think about my own honesty, or lack of it, before God and my dealings with people. Quite different, I know, but equally applicable and I can see the parallel even if no one else can.

"I guess it's the culmination of a work in progress. I think it started with the arrival of your sister at my school. What a breath of fresh air she has been, so open, so genuine. Her faith shines through everything she undertakes. She is truly God's love personified." Clyde was an excellent listener. As he drove Jackie poured out her heart. He parked the car and conversation continued over coffee in the hotel lounge till the family arrived and they were shown to the table allocated for their meal.

As they stood to join the family Clyde touched her delicately on the arm. "We will find time to continue this conversation. I, too, have learned lessons in recent months about God's goodness and mercy through heartache. I plan to keep my days off free while Connie is at home so I am sure we will have opportunity to catch up again."

The ensuing days began a period of intense joy for Jackie. Each day the presence of the Lord became more real and relevant to her. She saw with fresh awareness the small beauties around her not only in the realm of nature but in the lives of people she met. Everything delighted her. *Dear Lord, thank You for the miracle I experience within my heart and the ability You have given me to recognize the change as Your work of grace.*

CHAPTER TWENTY-FIVE

Rain...Rainbow!

The sun was very hot on the day of Garfield's hearing which was being held in the Lower Court in the District of Oistins, Christchurch. Clyde accompanied Wilson to the courthouse. Mumma Madge struggled to cope with the tension of the occasion, so she rose very early and busied herself with home baking. By the time she and Jacinth were due to depart for the courtroom to give evidence they had prepared food for the family's evening meal and sufficient corn and macaroni pie for days to come as well as mango chutney, coconut bread, sourdough rolls as well as dark cake.

"Mumma, you expecting an army?"

"We's must always be prepared."

"Yes, Mumma." She peeled and chopped the mangos for the chutney, tipped them in a pan. Madge shot in the other ingredients and left them to simmer. They washed their hands.

"You's want to do dark cake or sourdough rolls?"

"Rolls." Jacinth reached for a bowl and measured the flour, added salt and yeast and poured in the warm water.

"Do you think Jackie has romantic notions towards Clyde?" Jacinth asked as she mixed the dough.

"Of course not."

"Then why do they spend so much time talking together?"

"Your brother has de ears that listen well and dat young lady need somebody to talk to."

Connie decided there was little they could do of a practical nature to help either her Mother or her brother so, she declared, "I cannot sit around doing nothing so I will introduce Jackie to the north of the island."

After he had been engaged Garry's lawyer spoke with each member of the family to collate evidence to build the case that would be presented in court. "It seems clear that the pressure tactics used to persuade Garry to do as asked mostly took place during the time you were in England so it will not be necessary to call you as a witness," he told Connie.

"Although I read about some of the incidents in Barbados newspapers and letters from home that I received in the post I never linked them together and had no inkling they were connected to drug activity, or my family," Connie replied." The lawyer argued that as Garfield had first been coerced as a runner when he was 16 his case should be heard in the juvenile court especially as he had only just turned 18, admitted his involvement, been co-operative and given police valuable information to work on. It also transpired that Garfield was neither offered nor received drugs or cash in payment. Threats against the family were the lever used to pressure him into compliance. Following a mandatory probation report by a qualified probation officer required by the Barbados Judiciary a date was set for his hearing. However, the court officials had difficulty finding magistrates who were not acquainted with his father. "They must be seen to be impartial, you know."

Well smothered in factor 50, head covered, and eyes shielded by shades Jackie, accompanied Connie along the road. They stopped a ZR and travelled the short distance to an 'out of city' red circled bus-stop in Bridgetown with a slightly more careful driver than the one on their previous experience. Here they caught a normal ABC bus to Speightstown. While she was anxious about how Garry's case was progressing Connie thought it best to keep busy and a good opportunity to visit the museum in Arlington House to check up on some of the facts she had gleaned from Lord Edmund's family archives. Jackie was keen to learn something of the history of the sugar plantations which she hoped to incorporate into lessons on her return to school in Newton Westerby.

Conversation was impossible in the ear-splitting ZR but on the ABC bus Jackie shared her heart with Connie. Since the service that she subsequently referred to as the 'search me and found me service' she daily gave thanks for the peace she experienced and the lifting of the load that had bound her for so long. Her talk with Clyde had released her pent-up feelings and, as a consequence, she felt compelled to share with her friend the loss of Eddie, the anger she carried against God for taking him away, the way she ploughed all her energy into work, determined to become the perfect head teacher and when things did not go as she planned, the manner with which she brought everything back under her control. She admitted that even her hair style and facial expression became severe and reflected her sour feelings and attitude as Connie had observed.

"I went through the motions of being a Christian because as head of a Church of England school there were expectations of example to be given to the pupils. I displayed no outward signs of affection, not even to my family. I felt I could not afford to let my defences down. I always had to be in control. Oh, I helped the family or anyone else in the village community who had a need, but I would not allow anyone to get close to me emotionally. No matter how kindly the vicar and his wife were to me I kept them at arm's length and when his sermons touched on a raw nerve I switched off and concentrated instead on organizing, in my head, schedules and lessons for forthcoming weeks at school. My remit was the care of my staff and children and their personal achievements. Work was my saviour."

Despite her natural ebullience Connie, like her twin, was a good listener and soon realised her friend needed these moments to unburden all that had been stashed away in her heart for so many years and for a time it stopped her dwelling on Garry's predicament.

"When I look back, I can see I treated so many people abominably. I was incredibly selfish. Other people were hurting but I never once considered them I was too wrapped up in my own misery. Lord Edmund lost not only a son and heir but subsequently, his wife. Lady Phoebe was the sweetest, most gracious lady but she never got over Eddie's death. I never once thought to go and see her even though she was to be my future mother-in-law. I now regret that omission."

"We cannot undo our actions of de past."

"I know, but I could have been more kindly disposed towards Lord Edmund. As Chair of Governors he has worked tirelessly on behalf of the school. I've never once acknowledged his input, simply taken it for granted."

"You can rectify that when you get back."

Jackie's face brightened. "Yes, I can. I will."

A short silence was broken when Jackie suddenly turned towards Connie and blurted, "I owe you an apology, too."

Connie looked taken aback.

"You were never given an explanation as to how your appointment to Newton Westerby Primary School came about. The staff were protective of me and always skirted around the truth concerning the debacle that led Tim Draycott in consultation with Lord Edmund to advertise further afield for a replacement teacher," Jackie's voice quivered.

Compassionately, Connie placed a hand on Jackie's arm. "It is not necessary to cause yourself further distress. I have had a good year in England. I do not need to know what went on before my appointment."

"I feel I owe it to you. I must be honest. If nothing else, my short time here has taught me the importance of truth and honesty. Garry's burden of guilt and deceit could have destroyed his young life if it had continued for much longer. It has marred my own life for too many years. What a waste! I took myself out of God's love. What a lot I have missed. What did the Pastor quote Sunday morning? 'If we confess our sins…He is faithful and just to forgive…' I must confess to you my sin of omission. I want there to be openness and honesty in my dealings with you, and everyone else, from now on."

"Of course, I understand."

Jackie proceeded to tell her all about Dillon Brankscome's deception.

"He is now in prison for the attempted murder of the real Mr Brankscome, whom he impersonated, fraudulently obtaining a position of trust as a teacher, assault on a policeman, Dan Prettyman, sexual harassment and actual bodily harm when he attacked me, broke my arm, cut my head and bruised my ribs. I am so very thankful Miss Pedwardine had the foresight to have the emergency button installed. The outcome could have been so much worse."

"I had no idea. The villagers obviously closed ranks on that information and were certainly very supportive of you."

"I think they were all stunned that something of that nature should happen in our village, especially the school. You came under a cloud because they were initially suspicious of another 'incomer', but you proved to be different. Your faith shone through all that you did. We soon came to know you were genuine, but although I admired you and what you stood for, I could not let you get too close to me. I think I was afraid your transparency would highlight the flaws in my life.

"I now thank God for your constancy and faithful witness. You were well named, Constance Joy. Please forgive my coldness and aloofness towards you during your time in Newton Westerby. Thank you for your persistence. Bless you."

"De Lord's timing is always right."

"I've been surprised at how open people on the island are about their faith."

"Really?"

"Well, as you know, it's not like that in England. Christians are virtually gagged or accused of bigotry or discrimination if they speak the words of truth from the Bible in the public arena, so they clam up.

"Whereas in Barbados, the gospel message is proclaimed unashamedly in conversation and even on lamp posts. It is reported in the newspapers, you pray openly in public places like the restaurant on Sunday and amazingly, in the poshest store in Bridgetown, Christian books and plaques are prominently displayed. There are well attended churches on almost every street corner..."

"But, as you witnessed with Garry's episode, crime is subtly infiltrating Bajan society. Our core values are being undermined."

"It is very distressing that cunning schemers from overseas are being allowed to wreak such havoc."

"While de principles of de Christian faith are still important to many Barbadian people there are those on the island who are tempted by de promise of extra dollars in their pocket no matter what de consequences may entail."

"No!"

"I am afraid it is true. Backhanders in high places are not unheard of and as a result, lives further down de chain are being destroyed, as you saw de other day. However, sadly, corruption in Barbados is not a new phenomenon. History shows this to be a fact as you will see depicted in de museum. Our ancestors were treated abominably by deceit and deception because of man's craving for wealth and power."

Raindrops trickled down the bus window as another shower ceased. Bodies and noise clamoured for space all around them.

"I hadn't realised the bus was so full," Jackie commented.

Connie grinned. "Too busy in our own little world," she suggested.

"I guess so."

"A rainbow," a child's voice cried out causing conversations to stop and heads to turn.

"De sign of God's promise," said Connie quietly. "In spite of de devil's ploys, God continues to bless us, day after day."

Jackie focussed on the rainbow and in the quietness of her heart prayed. *Father God, the promise of your presence and protection gives me hope. You not only created me but in Jesus you have given me new life. You know me so well. Please, release me from this obsession that I must always be in control. Hold me and lead me by your almighty power in the direction you want me to go.*

The bus jerked to another stop.

"How do you think Garry's case is progressing?"

"Clyde is going to call me with news when he gets opportunity." Connie grabbed Jackie's arm. "This is where we get off."

Jackie glanced at her watch and was surprised to note they had been on the bus for almost an hour.

"How far is it between Bridgetown and Speightstown?"

"About 13 miles." Connie hurried her friend along the bus aisle.

"Slow going!"

Chapter Twenty-Six

Brighter skies ahead!

As Connie and Jackie alighted from the bus another heavy squall fell. "I don't believe this," Jackie called as she pulled up her collar and drew her jacket more closely around her, not that it afforded much protection from the downpour.

"This is Barbados weather," Connie laughed as she darted for cover under a shop awning.

They ran between the raindrops, avoiding expanding puddles, through the narrow streets flanked by some old-style colonial buildings.

"The local authority is considering renovating these," Connie called back over her shoulder. "They reckon they will be another kudos to the tourist trade."

Jackie glanced up briefly through the watery curtain at the intriguing architecture of the properties, they were scurrying passed, with their balconies overhanging the footpath and lattice shutters attached to the windows.

"Very interesting," but her words were lost on Connie who had leapt her way to the doorway of the museum housed in Arlington House.

"Wow!" was Jackie's first reaction as a radiant vision in white stucco burst into sight. "Another 18th century colonial building?" she asked as she almost collided with Connie who was shaking her dripping coat. "Yes, but let us get in the dry to discuss it."

Inside, fascinated by the interactive exhibits, Jackie learned about some of the current trades local people were engaged in trying to make a living, as well as contribute to the economy of the area. Things such as pottery, using local limestone, shoemaking and the repairing of leather goods, as well as photographs of street vendors selling locally grown fruit and vegetables, were on display.

They visited the map room which had a map etched on the floor from the early 1700's, when sugar plantations and slavery were at their height in Barbados. The names of the plantation owners, as well as the towns and villages, were written on the map. Plantations were often known by the name of the owner and subsequently the area or village assumed that name.

"We can trace many 21st century place names back to that era."

Connie looked for her ancestor's names in the parish of St. Peter. Only one was there showing that a Foster owned 100 acres or more near to All Saints Church but there were also indications that other settlers named Foster resided in the St. Andrew and St. Joseph areas who were plantation owners. Equally there were records to show that not all Fosters were wealthy enough to be landowners. Some were indentured servants who had sailed across the Atlantic Ocean and worked as slave labourers on the sugar plantations. Connie had been able to research back for five generations on Daddy's side of the family with accuracy but then to her frustration the records were muddied or else missing.

As her father was clearly not of pure black lineage it led her to believe that there had either been racial intermarriage or more likely a child born out of wedlock for one or more generations. She found records concerning the lives of slaves from Africa sparse.

On Mumma Madge's side of the family it was a little clearer cut. Definite liaison had taken place between a de Vessey and one of the plantation female slaves and a child had been born. This was confirmed in one of the yellowing letters Connie had deciphered from the de Vessey archives Lord Edmund had graciously given her access to.

Jackie left Connie to peruse the records that were available and wandered into the display room depicting the production of sugar. She was fascinated to learn that there were once 500 windmills on the island grinding liquid out of sugar cane to produce the lucrative syrup that a world market craved. 'There are still 900 miles of roads that criss-cross Barbados,' she read on one of the boards, 'built initially to transport the canes to the mills as quickly as possible once they were cut before they became unusable.'

Without the slave trade there would have been no labour force to carry out the arduous work. Even after emancipation the freed people still had to work on the plantations for 4 years, very often without pay, although they were allowed to tend their own plots to raise crops to feed themselves and their families. Some freedom!

A steam railway was built in 1881 to carry the canes across the island, from Bridgetown in the west to Carrington in the east but it was always breaking down so, '3rd class passengers had to push it, 2nd class had to walk by the side of it while 1st passengers were allowed to remain on board. Eventually it was scrapped.' Jackie laughed. "More trouble than it was worth, I guess," she commented to Connie who had joined her.

"Probably!"

"Is there still a sugar industry in Barbados?"

"A much diminished one. Unfortunately, many of de former plantations have been allowed to become bushland. 'Wasted land,' Mumma calls it. However, people in Barbados do like things sweet, so sugar is dominant in most food and drink."

"Such as the sorrel and mauby drinks that I avoid?"

Connie grinned, "Yes."

"For such a small island Barbados has an intriguing and varied history."

"One could say de same about de UK."

"Touché."

"Are you ready?"

"Yes, I've taken lots of pictures and made copious notes."

From the museum they again dodged the continuing rain, sheltering in doorways and under awnings until they reached a restaurant overlooking the waterfront. Jackie chose flying fish, macaroni pie and salad with iced water. They sat under cover, but three sides were open to the sea.

"Have to watch de waves don't come over and drench our food. The whole family were here on one occasion when a large wave rolled in, and de sea water landed in Jacinth's glass. Her face was a picture! Everyone could see the funny side of the incident but not Jacinth. She was much younger then, but the boys still tease her about that event." Jackie chuckled and mechanically moved her glass to one side.

"How did your research go?"

"Fine, I have been able to confirm a number of things on Mumma's side of de family but again hit a blank wall six generations back on Daddy's lineage. However, I have discovered slave records are held at Kew, in England."

Jackie grinned. "You'll have to come back, in order to research them, won't you?"

Connie beamed, "Jackie, you know I am coming! But I do wonder if illegitimate children of slaves will have been recorded. We know about the de Vessey baby because Edmund John wrote that letter to his father boasting about his son and heir."

"That seems a strange thing for him to do."

"Reading between de lines I think EJ left England under a cloud because there was bad feeling between him and his father for some reason. EJ did not inherit the family estate even though he was de eldest son. Records suggest he was disinherited in favour of his younger brother, Ralph Richard, who at the time had only produced four daughters. The sarcastic boast of an heir was to show EJ had achieved what his younger brother could not do. He had a son."

"It seems an unusual thing to boast about, for that generation."

"Yet it seems as though the child was openly acknowledged and brought up in EJ's household."

"I wonder what his wife thought of that?"

"I am inclined to believe she accepted the situation because she was childless. There is no record of any children from de marriage. The child was well educated and subsequently inherited his father's property."

"How do you feel about your slave heritage?"

Connie looked at Jackie thoughtfully before replying. "Sad! Regret that human beings were treated so deplorably but at the same time proud that they endured their harsh treatment and hard work with resilience and fortitude and that their faith in de Good Lord brought them through all de trials of li..." Her cell phone rang.

"It is Clyde," she whispered.

"Hello." For some moments she was silent as she listened to her brother's voice.

"Oh, that is good. We will see you later, bye."

Connie's eyes lit up as she turned towards her friend. "God is so good. The magistrates have taken into consideration de immense pressure Garry was put under and de treacherous nature of de threats. After lengthy deliberation they have placed Garry on de Juvenile Liaise Scheme which is run by de Royal Barbados Police Force. Leroy Corbyn is the liaison officer, which is good. He has an excellent rapport with Garfield. As Garfield is now 18, he has also been put on 1year's probation."

"Oh, Connie, that is good news. Is he coming home?"

"Yes. Initially, Garry was kept in custody for his own protection. The police and the family have been instructed to be vigilant, report and deal with anything suspicious at all times. They have released Garfield because he has a stable family background, is gainfully employed at the cricket academy and has never been in trouble before."

"That is a relief. I had not realised threats carried out against your family were so extensive."

"Neither did I. Some of them were referred to briefly when they wrote to me, but not the seriousness of them. No one ever linked them to drug activity. I understand a letter I sent may have saved Mumma's life. She was home alone when two of the thugs walked in and attacked her. Jethro, the postie, came to deliver my letter. When he gave his usual call, they ran off. Mumma was on de floor, her head was bleeding and she had two broken fingers on her left hand. Jethro sent for the emergency services. The perpetrators were never found but de police now connect that incident to the threats that were presented to Garry."

"How awful!"

"That was the catalyst that persuaded Garry to comply with their demands to, as he put it, "to save the family from further harm." The attorney discovered that the same week as Mumma's attack was when the small explosion in de entrance lobby at the hospital occurred. It was shortly afterwards that the windows were broken at Clyde's doctor's office and the brakes on his car failed. Jacinth was accosted walking from school to the bus-stop and Joel and Frue were thumped black and blue behind one of the sheds at de cricket ground a week or so later.

"Lots of horrible happenings and who would have associated them with illicit drug activity?"

"My family did not consider that possibility. I wonder how many other families they have targeted. How many innocents are involved because they are too scared to speak out?

"Leroy has a team who go into schools to explain the danger of drugs. It was set up a few months before I came to England. Pastor Desmond also became involved when de police contacted him to speak to the young people in the church about the perils of drug taking. I remember he came to our house one tea-time and asked Garfield directly if he or anyone else had been approached and Garry spluttered and never really answered the question."

"That sounds as though they had already buttonholed him."

"It does, doesn't it? Clyde sometimes goes with the team to explain de medical implications of drugs. I can see Leroy training Garry to become a part of the team to highlight the vulnerability of youth and to demonstrate, through his experience, how to deal with persistent approaches. I am sure Leroy is already working on new strategies for protecting de young and vulnerable and catching the perpetrators."

"You seem very fond of Leroy."

"We grew up together. He is a very good friend."

"Nothing more?"

"On his part, yes. On mine, no."

"Are you sure?"

"He is a fine Christian man, an excellent policeman, but he does not have my heart."

Chapter Twenty-Seven

Fluctuating temperatures!

The young women curtailed their visit to Speightstown because of the persistent rain and because, after the call from Clyde, Connie felt an urgent need to be home with the family. They hurried to the bus station. Connie hoped the next bus out would be the one to follow the coast road.

"I would like you to see more of the delightful west coast."

But when the vehicle pulled into the bus-stand it was the ABC bus.

"Why is it so called?"

"The highway is named after Adams, Barrow and Cummings, former Prime Ministers of Barbados, and is the main road from de airport, in the south, to the north of de island which is the route the bus follows."

"And has the least number of potholes but hundreds of roundabouts!" they both laughed.

"It's true! I have never seen so many potholes in my life!"

"My uncle says it is because of de way the roads are constructed."

"Well, it certainly can't be attributed to extreme weather conditions as it is at home."

"Uncle Keith worked with the civil engineers from Holland on the road leading to the deep-water harbour, which they were constructing in Bridgetown, to accommodate the large cruise liners that wanted to bring tourists to visit de island. On that project they compacted four-inch stones and rocks into the prepared earth surface before covering it with ballast and finally putting on the top road surface. One day I will drive you on it, so you can see, and feel, the difference."

"So why do the other roads have more potholes than road surface?"

"Ordinarily, Barbadian road construction involves compacting coral into de earth but that is not a firm foundation as with constant use it breaks down into sand."

"The lovely sandy beaches are testament to that."

"Then the biggest problem is caused because there is no drainage at the sides of the roads as there is in England so that when de heavy rains come the road is washed away because there is nothing of substance to hold it together, or drain it, hence the millions of potholes."

"Why don't they copy the Dutch process?"

"Cost! Stones and rocks must be imported and although Barbados is only a small island, we do have over 900 miles of roadway as you learned in the museum.

"Some years ago Uncle Keith gave a blueprint for a workable drainage system to someone he knew in government, but it was never acted upon. He also knows for a fact, from conversations with parties involved, that there is collusion between the limited contractors we have on the island and government officials."

"But why wouldn't they want to make travelling around the island better for everyone?"

"Greed and backhanders!"

"That's so hard to believe."

"It is the truth."

"I have seen so much since coming to Barbados. Your grandfathers are a mine of information. From them, and others I have been privileged to meet, I have learned that it is an island of stark contrasts. Side by side there is beauty and devastation, plenty and poverty, care and irresponsibility, generosity and greed, healing and hurt, Christlikeness and corruption. I am aware this is the same in all communities but in the short time I have been here these diverse characteristics really stand out."

"That is so true. The Gospel message is unashamedly declared, and the name of de Good Lord is more prevalent in Barbados than in England, but our faith is being undermined from many different sources."

The bus jolted to a standstill. School children piled into the interior so that bodies were crammed in like sardines in a tin. It was a journey of stops and starts all the way down to Bridgetown, incoming passengers spraying those already on the bus with their soaked clothing.

As the bus drove passed a lay-by Jackie pointed to a parked lorry piled with something she could not identify. "What are they doing?" Young men seemed to be crouched on the bed of the lorry hacking at the objects while others were standing, in the pathway of on-coming vehicles on the highway, with arms extended holding out bottles. Before Connie could reply Jackie gasped as she saw a lad clamber up the trunk of a tall palm tree. "Oh, surely he will fall!"

Connie laughed. "No, not at all, that is his job. He is used to doing it. They climb the trees, cut down coconuts, chop off the tops and pour the coconut water into bottles to sell to those driving by in cars. I will ask Mumma to show you when we get home."

The journey took almost 1½ hours and the bus was constantly full all the way back to the city. By the time they alighted the rain had stopped, and the sun shone blazing hot from a clear blue sky with no sign of the earlier deluge. They caught a ZR to complete their journey home.

"This is an experience and a half!" Jackie exclaimed as the conductor double-crammed them into a mini, minibus.

"3 ½ dollars for the privilege!"

Blaring music and a driver hurtling down the road relentlessly braking sharply to pick up passengers, and let them off, had Jackie's heart in her mouth. Then, at one stop it was musical chairs as the conductor rearranged customers to get as many more on board as possible. Connie and Jackie eventually alighted at the top of the Foster's road with shaky legs and pounding heads as they walked to the safety of home.

Connie explained the cameo Jackie had witnessed in the lay-by and within minutes Mumma Madge was initiating Jackie into the mysteries of the coconut. She chopped the green fruits with a machete making a hole in the top, then poured the coconut water into a jug.

"You need many coconuts to make a jugful of water." After Madge had extricated the coconut water, she split the fruit. Jackie was surprised to see the inner part, that she thought she was familiar with and ate, was a jelly-like substance.

"You want to try it?" Madge held out a portion on a spoon that had been scaped out.

Jackie screwed up her face in distaste, "Ugh!"

"You do not like it? It is considered a delicacy here if people can be bothered with it. Usually it is thrown away. For us it is the liquid that is important."

"When the fruit is left on the palm tree for longer the jelly-like substance absorbs all the water and goes hard to form a kernel. The outer cream fibrous shell with its green covering is removed and the inner, outer shell darkens in colour and hardens and appears like a coconut you would recognise," Connie explained.

"I had no idea."

"So, another lesson for your pupils! In some countries oil is extracted from the kernel or copra and the remainder is used in cattle feed."

"A very useful commodity."

"Mattresses were made from de fibrous part. I remember having one when I was a girl," said Madge getting up from the step where she had been chopping. "Jackie, put this into de fridge. Connie, clear dis mess away. I must get tea on de table."

Through tears of thankfulness they enjoyed the tea-time meal with the family and a subdued Garfield. His days in a police cell had quite overwhelmed him and the disgrace he felt he had subjected his loved ones to continued to plague him.

His two grandfathers joined the family for the sumptuous spread Mumma Madge, and Jacinth, had prepared. Their jovial presence leant support to their grandson, for whom they had high hopes in the cricketing world and helped to lighten the mood. Their nonsense and banter flew across the table as rapidly as the flying fish that was handed around on a platter.

"Careful, Pops," instructed Madge as her father balanced the chicken stew precariously on the edge of the table.

Jackie was stunned by the quantity of food that was offered to her and even more surprised that she was expected to sample a portion from every dish. No sooner had she partaken from one than another was placed before her. Among them was Bajan vegetables with ginger, corn pie, Bajan peas and rice, pumpkin fritters and bread fruit, as well as chicken stew.

When plates were full Grandad Foster had them in stitches as he entertained them with stories from his youth.

"We did not have much money, but we had fun making our own pastimes, like marble cricket. We made balls with de covering that went round hams wrapped around with rubber bands."

"You must have needed a lot of bands, Grandpops," said Joel.

"Just enough to hold de covering in place then we rolled it in de road when they were being repaired with tar."

"Ugh! That must have been gross!"

"Just wiped de hands on de trousers."

"How messy!" Jacinth pulled a face.

"Got licks from Ma for doing that."

"I'm not surprised!"

"We made our own bats out of bits of wood, smaller than de normal size bat. We could not afford de bats from England or India. Kneeled on one knee to bat and bowl."

"Both at the same time?" Joel asked. There were howls of laughter.

"'Course not, boy. We had to keep de ball down. If it hit a neighbour's house, you were out. If you smashed de window, you were in trouble."

"Yeah! Many a time I was thrashed and grounded for breaking windows, but it did not stop us from playing."

"What are licks?" Jackie asked.

"When we committed misdemeanours and deserved a good-hiding we got licks. My friend, Colwyn, came from a family of 8. His mother was widowed at a young age. If we heard Mrs Hills singing 'Abide with me' we children made sure we kept out of de way. We just knew that Russell, the middle boy, who was a rogue, had been up to mischief. Word went out amongst de neighbourhood, 'Keep away from Mrs Hills, she is giving out licks,' because even though only one had misbehaved all within touching distance got a lick."

Later in the evening Jacinth portioned out a Madeira style cake she had made in Jackie's honour and served it with ice-cream.

"As you have discovered Barbadians rarely have a sweet after their meal. We made this to honour the occasion and you, our guest."

As the table was cleared and spare food put away for another day conversation continued out on the veranda. The grandfathers got into a heated discussion about the decline in West Indies cricket.

"Money governs many things in Barbados, even cricket, that is why some of our best cricketers are choosing to play in de IPL, and de like, around de world, more lucrative."

"Sobers was a team player. Wish de modern players did de same."

"De greats from de past would be doing de same if dey were playing now."

"Boy, remember de game is everything. Not de coins in your pocket!"

In her eyeline Jackie marvelled at the silhouette of palm trees just beyond the garden set against a rapidly changing fiery skyscape. Night fell as a backdrop to their conversation.

"Look," Clyde whispered softly in her ear as he pointed to his right.

"Ooh!" Jackie saw her first firefly close to. "It's incredible how the light flashes out from their backs."

"De good Lord has made all things beautiful," commented Connie.

CHAPTER TWENTY-EIGHT

Heat is rising!

Kite-surfers were enjoying the swell of the choppy sea and making the most of the pull of the wind as Connie and Jackie took an early morning stroll along the beach at Silver Sands a few days later, their footprints making a distinct path in the sand.

"How strong they must be to manoeuvre the kites," Connie stood to watch the skill the surfers demonstrated as they manipulated the strings, "and what agility they display as they move with the board, almost as though they are one."

"They're huge," Jackie remarked as they passed by some of the machines parked on the beach.

"They seem to travel at such a tremendous speed as they skim across the water."

Crabs, the colour of the silver sand, scuttled beneath the girls' feet. Blue sky spread out its canopy above them and although still early morning the sun's warmth embraced them.

"This is to be your tourist day"

"Oh?"

"Clyde has today off and has offered to drive us up de east coast to Andromeda Botanical Gardens."

Following breakfast Mumma Madge prepared a packed lunch ready for the tourists before Clyde arrived to escort them on their excursion.

"You coming, Mumma?"

"No, you young things enjoy de day on your own. De boys are at cricket practice. Daddy has operations this morning and I am meeting Aunt Fran at Sheraton Mall later."

Clyde drove in the direction of the Grantley Adams International Airport in the parish of Christchurch passing through St. Philip en route to Six Roads where he enquired if anyone required a comfort break.

"We've only been travelling 35 minutes!"

"He really wants a reason to stop at a Cheffette," Jacinth explained.

"Cheffette?"

The sisters laughed teasingly. "He has a passion for chocolate ice-cream," Connie explained. "Maybe later, brother!"

Clyde shrugged and pulled a comical hard-done-by face but continued driving on towards the parish of St. John pulling into the carpark next to the parish church of St. John. It was built quite high up and gave an amazing view out to the Atlantic Ocean.

"This is the fourth church to be built on this site. The previous three were blown down by hurricanes."

"My goodness! Am I safe up here?" Jackie joked.

From St. John they traversed some steep and windy roads. As Clyde swung round a sharp bend Jackie suddenly called out, "What are they?"

"They are buffet," Connie pointed to large herbaceous bushes, that looked like stunted trees, growing to the left-hand side of the road, "and the ones on the other side are bananas."

Clyde stopped the car. "Go and have a look."

"I didn't realise bananas grew up-side-down." Jackie jumped out of the car and took several photographs.

"What is buffet?" She asked as they resumed their journey.

"A fruit."

"It looks like a banana."

"It is smaller and tastes slightly different."

After a few more miles of hair-raising bends they reached the Andromeda Botanical Gardens.

"These are the crown of the Barbados Horticultural world."

"They are packed with plants from across the globe. This was the private home of Mrs Iris Bannochie, a keen horticulturalist."

"She travelled the world to bring back plants, shrubs and trees that she planted in the garden for her own enjoyment."

"Eventually she decided to open her garden to the public and on her death, it was given to the Barbados National Trust in 1988."

Jackie found it a fascinating place of garden design and horticultural artistry. She made copious notes and took numerous photos. The tall Bearded Fig tree with its myriad vines dangling down to the ground caught her eye.

"That is incredible!" she exclaimed intrigued by the unusual living hanging curtain.

"The vines have to be frequently taken out otherwise they would take over the garden," Clyde explained, "and kill other species planted here because each individual vine the plant sends down, roots and forms a new tree trunk and consequently another tree."

"Amazing, isn't it?" Connie commented.

"These paths are also cleverly designed," Jackie looked down to where she was placing her feet. Impressions of leaves had been implanted into concrete stepping-stones.

"All hand made by Mrs Bannochie," Connie explained thoughtfully and crouched down to look more closely at the intricate patterns indented into the round slabs.

Jackie chuckled at her action, "I can see a classroom project emerging in that innovative mind of yours."

Connie's hand lightly touched the surface of the stones. "Well, I think it is it is possible. On a smaller scale, of course. Uhm... your English Autumn leaves... modelling clay..."

Jackie turned, leaving her friend to her cogitations.

Clyde reached out to take her hand as the terrain was very uneven and at times treacherously steep.

"I'm surprised there are no hand-rails."

"Do take care, I do not want any of you to slip and fall," he instructed.

"I can see now why Mumma Madge declined to come with us."

"What are those beautiful plants with such colourful leaves?"

"They are crotons."

"The tree behind them bears blossoms of 'snow of the mountain.'"

"It is so resplendent in white."

"The plant with the upright bright red spires is 'ginger lily' and to the left is lilac 'Alamander'."

Clyde smiled at Jackie's delight in the beauty of the foliage and flowers, stepped to walk in front of her and led her by the hand down the precipitous pathway. Connie and Jacinth caught up with them then moved slightly ahead loosely following the guide sheet they had been handed on entry to the gardens.

"Oh, just look at that," Jacinth exclaimed.

"It is so beautiful."

"Cleverly planned."

An amazing vista opened between the shrubs and trees which sloped steeply down the garden towards a distant view of the blue Atlantic Ocean. "This is absolutely breath-taking." Jackie paused to take photos before following the path round to the lily pond which was full of fish.

"Are they goldfish?"

"Probably something more exotic. I am not well acquainted with ornamental fish species."

As they ascended a flight of steps Jackie, suddenly, squealed with pain.

"What is wrong?"

"My eyes are stinging, excruciatingly so." Perspiration built up on her brow. Her knees buckled and she slumped clumsily on to a step. She put her hands to the sides of her head.

Concerned, Clyde immediately stooped down beside her, gently removed one of her hands and held her wrist to take her pulse. Hearing the commotion Connie and Jacinth rushed back down the steps. "Is everything alright?"

Clyde quietly explained what had happened.

Jackie rubbed a hand across her forehead. "Please, don't stop your tour on my account," her voice faltered.

Connie and Clyde locked eyes. Consternation passed between them.

"Do you have any allergies?" Clyde enquired.

"I'm not aware of any," Jackie spoke quietly her head still held in her hands.

"The restaurant veranda is to the right of the steps," Jacinth pointed back through the trees. "Would it help if we assist you to get up there?"

"Good idea, you lead the way, Jacinth." Connie crouched beside her friend. "You might feel more comfortable if you are able to sit on a chair in the shade."

"Perhaps while you two help Jackie I could photograph the last bit of garden we haven't yet seen."

"Before you do that could you get my bag out of the boot, as you pass the car park, please?" Clyde handed his car-keys to her.

"Con, get the other side of Jackie. On three we will lift her to her feet. One, two three." With each of them holding her under an arm they hoisted her and cautiously made their way towards the light green wooden veranda Jacinth had indicated through the foliage. Slowly they reached the seating area.

"It's a relief to sit down," Jackie said as she slumped into a chair. "I'm so sorry."

Connie explained the situation to the young woman on duty as she purchased an iced lime and ginger drink for Jackie. She also provided a bowl of cool water to which Clyde added some drops of witch hazel taken from the bag Jacinth handed to him. He proceeded to tenderly bathe Jackie's eyes.

"Feeling a little better?"

"Mmm. The sting is receding, but my head is throbbing."

"Take these," he handed her a couple of pills from his doctor's bag. "Antihistamine and pain killers," he explained.

"This drink is so refreshing." She took a few more gulps. "I'm sorry to spoil your visit."

"Nonsense. We are upset for you. The young lady cannot account for why it should happen to you in that area unless it has been caused by the pollen from de palm trees."

"It's a most unpleasant experience whatever may have triggered it. Do, please, continue looking round the garden. I'll be OK."

Connie patted her hand. "Nonsense, I would not think of leaving you while you are feeling so wretched. You rest and recuperate." She picked up the guide sheet and handed it to her sister who retraced her steps. "I will see you again shortly," Jacinth called out cheerfully.

After a while Clyde felt Jackie's brow and again took her pulse.

"Getting back to normal," he smiled. "Feeling more like yourself?"

Jackie returned his smile. "Yes, thank you, sorry to ruin the morning."

"It could have happened to anyone. It is also very hot, today. That cannot have helped as you are unused to such high temperatures even though you have taken all precautions with factor 50 and kept your arms and head well covered."

"You're so kind and caring. I can see why you are such a popular doctor."

"It is my day off, Miss Cooper!" He announced in a stern voice which was so comical they both burst out laughing.

"You are so good for me, Doctor Foster. Already I am feeling much, much better."

"You should laugh more, Miss Cooper, it becomes your countenance."

Jackie coloured up. To cover her embarrassment Clyde hastened to put his things away and fastened his bag. Connie walked over to the counter to ask the waitress to replenish their drinks. Quietly Clyde said, "Do you remember what the Bible says about laughter and cheerfulness?"

Jackie slowly shook her head.

"It tells us in Proverbs that they are as good as medicine."

"I'd forgotten that. In fact, for years I have deliberately pushed aside all I ever knew about the Bible's teaching. I was so angry with God, I wanted Him out of my life and His word out of my mind. Connie has loaned me a Bible until such time as I am able to get one of my own."

Clyde removed his arms from the table as the waitress approached with a tray. As she served them a cheeky bird flew under the canopy and hopped onto the table.

"I guess he's hoping for a morsel to fall his way," Connie commented. They all chuckled at his antics.

"Our Lord used the sparrows to teach us lessons about the provision of our Heavenly Father. I find frequently there are lessons to be learned each day from the smallest incident and occurrences. This little bird teaches me that I must go to the right source of food to find nourishment for my soul."

"I find it incredible that God's love and forgiveness are still available for me even though I've ignored and rejected His mercy and grace for years."

"The wonder of His grace is that it meets us where we are and gives us what we do not deserve. He does not weigh up the pros and cons before dealing it out. His grace is given freely to all who will accept it."

Jackie's eyes filled with tears.

Clyde leaned forwards. "Your eyes hurting again?"

She shook her head. "No, I'm so overwhelmed by the change in my heart in the last few days. I truly don't deserve His love or favour, yet I know the forgiveness I feel is real and comes solely from His grace."

Jacinth bounced back. "Oh good, you have a drink for me." Jacinth flopped into the nearest chair. "I am exhausted. I need this. It is boiling out there." She guzzled down her lime and ginger.

"You are beginning to look much improved. Do you want to continue our journey, or would you prefer to go home?" Connie enquired of her friend.

"Don't curtail your plans because of me. I'm feeling much better, truly."

When they reached the carpark Jackie settled back into her seat in the car and reflected on her conversation with Clyde.

Chapter Twenty-Nine

Hot and sultry!

They moved on, from what had been an interesting visit, towards the region known as the Scotland district in the parishes of St. Joseph and St. Andrew, till Clyde was driving along a road parallel to the Atlantic Ocean. Jacinth shot up in her seat. "Let's stop!"

"This is Bathsheba, another one of the beautiful spots that are a surfer's paradise," Connie explained as Clyde parked the car by the side of the road.

As she looked across at the tossing waves Jackie remarked, "I would guess not a sea for intrepid swimmers."

"You guessed right. Before you get out it might be wise to spray on another layer of protection," Connie handed Jackie the sun lotion. "This location is rather exposed, and it is the time of day when the sun is at its hottest."

They walked across the green to view the unusual rock formation standing in the sea just metres from where the waves tossed against the shore. However, they did not stay out in the blazing sun for long but soon returned to the shade of the car. Clyde switched on the air conditioning and followed the coast road so that

Jackie could see how the terrain of the east coastline contrasted with what she had already experienced in the south and west of the island.

"It is rugged and quite hilly."

"Yes, there are two peaks which reach 1000feet."

After a short drive Clyde pulled into Barclays Bay so that they might enjoy their picnic lunch under the umbrella of palm trees. Jacinth plumped for a bench overlooking breaking waves framed by trees with intriguingly shaped branches which she encouraged Jackie to photograph.

As soon as she had finished eating her lunch Jackie strolled down to the water's edge.

"Are you sure you should be walking about in this heat?" Connie asked, concern furrowing her brow.

"I'm fine, truly, I am. I can't let one little incident, unpleasant though it was, spoil my exploration of this lovely island."

Connie tapped her arm affectionately, "Just do not overdo it."

"I won't. But you were the one who persuaded me to come here for the sake of my primary school children and this is such a contrast to the Caribbean side of the island I need to capture as much as I can to share on my return home. I mustn't let them down, must I?" She grinned.

Connie punched her arm playfully. "Well, to put a classroom perspective on this area, the next landfall to the east across the Atlantic Ocean is Africa."

"Really?"

"However, the moss being tossed up on the beach by the crashing waves is from South America."

"You're kidding me," Jackie exclaimed in disbelief.

"Remember, we were talking about that the other day when we were at Miami Beach, deforestation and all that."

"Oh yes, I remember, the Orinoco river, but I didn't realise it would also be carried to this side of the island. What's all the vegetation growing on the beach?"

"Sea Grape and Casuarina trees, a regeneration project to prevent the constant breezes blowing away the sand and causing soil erosion. There is a plaque displayed along there which explains that it is part of the Barbados preservation and re-vegetation scheme to protect the island from the ravages of the sea. Queen Elizabeth opened Barclays Park in 1966 which was a gift from Barclays Bank to commemorate the occasion of independence."

"It is a great place for liming," said Jacinth.

Jackie looked at her quizzically, "Liming?"

"Getting together with family and friends. I guess the English might call it socialising!" Connie explained.

"Is Clyde alright? He is very quiet," Jackie asked.

Having finished his lunch the young doctor was walking in the opposite direction to the girls, along the shore, hands in pockets, shoulders hunched.

Connie nodded. "I guess he is mulling something over. That is his way when he is processing problems or talking them over with de Good Lord."

"He is a very caring person and an excellent listener, but he doesn't reveal much about himself, does he?"

"He has had much to contend with over the years and closely guards his heart and feelings."

"Hard to believe you two are twins. You are so different from one another. At times he appears shy and reserved whereas you are always openly affectionate

299

and demonstrative. It took me a while to get used to your effervescent spirit, but your brother..." she gave an exasperated sigh and thrust her hands up in the air, "at times, I simply don't know where I stand with him."

"Because in many ways you are similar." Connie stayed Jackie's startled retort with a slight raise of her hand and a gentle nod. "It is true, even though you have dealt with life's experiences in different ways. You erected a hard veneer around your heart and projected an image of a strong woman, always in control, whereas Clyde has, for the most part, withdrawn inside a shell to protect his feelings and emotions. You have both suffered deep hurt and are vulnerable. Work became de focus for both of you. De Good Lord will, in His time, work a miracle of grace in both of your lives."

"I don't..."

Connie shook her head. "Clyde's story is not mine to tell."

"These crazy shaped tree branches would make fantastic pictures," Jacinth shouted as she ran back towards them, interrupting their conversation. Jackie glanced up to see her friend give a slight shake of the head. She raised an eyebrow, but Connie shook her head again, a small movement indicating the subject was closed. Jackie acquiesced and moved towards the trees Jacinth had indicated, to capture more pictures for future reference, her mind in a whirl. *At times Clyde's personality seems to be as diverse as the east coast is from the west coast.*

Connie gathered up the picnic things as the others gradually made their way back to the car to continue their journey up to St Lucy, along further hilly roads.

For a while Connie and Clyde sat in the front chatting quietly, Jacinth donned earphones and lost herself in music, but Jackie sat in the back of the car mulling over incidents and actions from earlier in the day. *I am confused by Clyde's attitude towards me. I do enjoy his company. He is an interesting conversationalist when I can get him to speak to me. He has also got a keen sense of humour. My heart does strange things when he is near me but just as he gives me a glimpse of the real man he is, he quite suddenly withdraws into himself. It's as if a curtain closes and he shuts me out, he becomes silent and remote, anxious to keep something hidden. I think this is a matter Connie would tell me to pray about.* She shook her head. *I cannot believe I am thinking like this. I never expected to have feelings for another man after losing Eddie.* She shook her head again. *I must not make comparisons because I am a different woman now to the young girl who fell in love with a dashing harum-scarum young man.*

Similar unsettling thoughts disturbed the driver sitting in front of her. A silent Clyde drove for a short while along the coast road and then travelled inland, his eyes on the road, his heart in turmoil. His mind tossing back and forth the unleashed feelings he had for this friend of his sister who had dropped into his life only a few weeks ago. For years he had guarded his heart from possible entanglement with very eligible and attractive young ladies in the church fellowship. Then out of the blue, austere Jaqueline Cooper blossoms before his eyes as the hard wall around her persona is demolished by the love of God. **Time to let go!** Clyde unbelievingly shook his head as, unbidden, words came into his mind. **Trust Me!**

"Oh, Lord, I can't," he breathed, "You ask the impossible." **With Me all things are possible!** His eyes misted over. He pulled into Farley National Park as they reached it, stopped the car, and put his head down on his hands on the steering wheel.

Connie turned towards the back seat. "Jacinth, you show Jackie the amazing view on offer here. We'll join you in a minute."

The girls got out and from the tree-lined grassy bank Jackie discovered how very high up they were. Looking over a deep ravine Jacinth pointed out the hilly landscape, the distant Atlantic Ocean and the steep coast road they had so recently journeyed along.

In the car Connie twisted round in her seat. She laid a hand on her brother's arm. "You want to tell me what is going on?"

He lifted a strained face towards his twin. "Oh, Con, I have feelings in my heart I never expected to experience again. But I feel a traitor. I am also afraid."

"You are going to have to be honest with yourself. You need to let the past go. Pray about it, de Good Lord will make clear the path you must take."

He looked directly at Connie. "That's what He said to me, 'Time to let go! Trust Me!' But it is so hard."

"You cannot hold on to past hurts for ever. They will destroy you. It has been nearly four years, Clyde. Give yourself opportunity to explore if this is a relationship that could develop into something deeper. Jackie has changed so much. She is a lovely person. Take time to get to know her. She has bloomed amazingly since that Sunday service. She will also understand your pain because she has been through deep heartache herself."

"Were you aware of her story?"

"I had no idea till de other day. She has kept that hidden deep within her heart, very much as you have done."

She clasped his hands, "Come, we will pray now before they return. The park closes shortly, and we do not want to be locked in"

"Bless you, dear Connie, you always understand."

Connie closed her eyes and, in love, poured out her heart to the Lord on behalf of her brother and friend asking for clarity and peace regarding their future. A gentle calmness settled around Clyde's heart. "Thanks, Con."

"Pastor Desmond would be a good person to talk to, you know."

"He would. I'll give it some thought and prayer."

A chilly breeze brought the girls back to the car anxious to warm up. Jacinth whisked open the door and slid quickly into her seat. "Brr it is cold out there now! I don't blame you for not wanting to venture out." Jackie briskly followed suit. They sensed a different atmosphere pervaded the car. Connie and Clyde were quietly chatting in the front. Jacinth tapped Clyde on the shoulder. "You OK, Bro'?" Clyde reached up and patted her hand. "Yes, I am fine. Thanks for asking."

He started up the car and soon conversation flowed between all four of them as they chatted about what they had seen, and Jackie made comment on comparisons between the east and west coasts of the island.

"The Atlantic side is certainly more wild, rugged and windswept."

"It is, and sadly most visitors never get to see this part of the island."

Clyde drove nearer to St Lucy, the most northerly of the eleven parishes of the island. From there he took them across to the west coast and down to Speightstown, via Port St Charles, passing many other interesting coastal places through St Peter till they joined the main highway at St Thomas which was choc-a-bloc with end of day traffic. Connie started to sing, Jacinth took up the melody as Clyde harmonised.

Jackie closed her eyes. The beautiful music drenched her heart with God's grace. The words nudged her mind to consider that God's grace was not a static thing. *It is something that flows constantly out of the heart of God to my heart. Father God, it is something beyond my comprehension. I just thank You for it and that I am included in its flow.*

"Sorry, Jackie, didn't mean to leave you out."

"No, no, please carry on. Your voices blend so perfectly together. It is such a blessing."

In a short while the singers changed to a hymn with which Jackie was familiar and she joined in.

The travellers reached Christchurch just before nightfall. Madge welcomed them home with a beaming smile and a sumptuous meal. "You's all had a good day?"

"Verra good, Mumma."

"It's been an interesting day exploring different aspects of Barbados," Jackie smiled and expressed her thanks.

"And we travelled through all eleven parishes!" Jacinth tossed in for good measure.

"My goodness, you's been busy."

Before his departure for home Clyde drew Jackie to one side and spoke softly, "I am working the next few days, but I will see you at church on Sunday. May we meet to talk?" He smiled. A smile that, not only revealed gleaming, even teeth, but radiated his face in a beam not unlike that of his twin. She noticed it also reached his eyes which appeared to no longer hold that troubled look. Jackie returned his smile. "I'd like that." Her heart gave an uncharacteristic leap.

Chapter Thirty

Tropical heat!

"We will have a few quiet days. Give you chance to recoup," Connie declared the next morning.

"I'm fine. Truthfully, I am."

"Nevertheless, we are staying nearer to home, just in case."

Thankfully, there was no recurrence of the stinging in her eyes nor the pounding in her head, for which Jackie was profoundly grateful. So, the cause of the incident at Andromeda Gardens remained a mystery but Clyde advised her to have allergy tests when she returned to England.

However, the next few days sped by packed with activities and visits which gave Jackie cause to question if these were quiet days whatever did busy days look like?

The boys and Jacinth were anxious to introduce Jackie to some of their favourite bathing haunts and insisted Connie take them out so that she could sample the delights of Caribbean sea bathing in places such as the Yachting Club, Paynes Bay and Folkestone along the west coast. These trips provided a pleasant respite from the sweltering heat and Jackie revelled swimming in the clear blue sea. Jackie also got used to unscheduled calls on family and friends which took place following sea baths at these venues.

Connie's brothers also delighted in teasing her. They initiated her into what Joel referred to as the 'correct way' to eat a mango. One of their Aunts had a mango tree in her garden which was prolifically laden with fruit, so she sent a basketful to the Foster home. Garry demonstrated the process. "Cut off the top like this and then suck." Jackie copied him but the juice oozed down her chin, her fingers and along her arms. She dashed to the kitchen sink before the liquid ran onto her clothes and the floor.

"Why didn't this happen to you?" she spluttered.

"Practise and persistence, Miss School Teacher," he chuckled.

Connie came in on the scene as the boys were rolling around with laughter.

"Quick, Con, take a photo," Joel called between bursts of uncontrolled hilarity. Garry was on the sofa doubled up with hysterics unable to say a word.

"My, this is fun." Connie quickly positioned her cell phone to snap her friend in her sticky predicament.

"Never had a mango like this before?" Connie grinned.

Hanging over the sink her face plastered with the juicy flesh Jackie mumbled, "Never! And never again! You wait Garfield Foster!" She threatened playfully, but Garry simply grinned. His eyes aglow with mischief. Released from the oppressive shackles that had bound him for the last couple of years he was a changed young man.

Jackie put the offending fruit down, turned on the tap with an elbow and proceeded to wash off the sticky mess.

Connie handed her a towel.

Jackie's dried eyes met three pairs of eyes brimming with amusement and she too burst out laughing.

"You rascals!" She began to chase the boys, but they were too agile for her and leapt down the veranda steps into the street and out of reach.

At a more sedate pace Jackie returned to collapse down beside Connie on a seat on the veranda.

"Fresh Bajan mangoes taste very different to the ones you buy in England, don't they?"

"Mmm, sweeter, softer and certainly juicier, but I think I prefer them firmer, skinned and cut up into a bowl rather than a la Garfield!"

"Yes, ma'am, I'll remember that" Garry saluted jokingly as he crept back up the steps sporting a huge grin.

Joel delighted in conjuring up ways to provoke her with 'normal' Bajan wildlife, like the lizards as well as cockroaches which were much larger than the ones she had seen in the restored cottages in Newton Westerby. She did not like the pesky mosquitos which were ever present and seemed to be drawn to her fair skin even though she constantly used the repellent spray.

"Use de zapper, girl," Mumma Madge instructed as she handed her the gadget. Seeing her bemused expression Joel demonstrated its purpose.

Jackie longed to see a hummingbird and watched avidly every time she sat out on the veranda for the colourful streak as it darted into the alamander flowers for nectar. On another day she expressed a fascination in the parasitic orchids that bloomed prolifically next to the Pom Marine carpark.

"How do they survive attached to a host tree?"

"They draw their sustenance from the air."

"Oh! How?"

"Come on, jump in the car. We will show you."
Connie, Madge and Jacinth proceeded to take her to
visit the prolific orchid display at the Barbados
Horticultural Society's Headquarters.

"This was once a sugar plantation, the Booth
plantation. Look to your right, there is the remains of a
windmill."

Jackie was fascinated by the significance of this
historic place then as they turned a corner and descended
some steps she stood in wonder, enraptured by the
beauty, structure and diversity of the plants before her.

"The colour combinations are amazing and the
flower formations incredible. And even black flowers!"

"De Good Lord knew what He was about when He
created orchids," declared Mumma Madge.

"They're suspended in the air!"

"Yes."

"No water and no soil! How do they produce such
loveliness without them?"

"There is an overhead irrigation system which
enables them to be sprayed intermittently with water or
liquid feed, but they draw most of the nutrients and
moisture they need from the air."

"They are a marvel. The flowers are simply exquisite.
Totally dissimilar to the ones I've seen in England.
Thank you for introducing me to such beauty."

"De Good Lord, He is the source of all beauty."

In her heart Jackie agreed. She savoured to the full
the pleasure of her senses.

Although, overall, days were spent nearer to home
impromptu visits continuously took place and visitors
frequently dropped by the Foster house.

"Is there anyone in Barbados you're not related to?" Jackie quipped soon after cousins, Callum and Nesta, with their boisterous sons had departed from the house. "You seem to know everyone." Connie grinned and shrugged her shoulders. "That was a fun time, wasn't it?"

"Yeah! Ish and Craig are great mates but those fraudsters and underhand dealers who clobbered Frue and me and snared Garry are no friends or family of ours," Joel spat out angrily.

"True, but we will not dwell on them nor allow their misdeeds to invade our thoughts and upset our peace of mind. Be better to pray for them." Joel eyed her dubiously and shrugged his shoulders. "Choose something constructive to do, Joel, but not video games on your cell phone or Mumma will not be best pleased."

"Righteo, Con. You want to play Phase 10, Jackie?"

"Yes, why not? It's new to me so you will have to teach me what to do." As the game unfolded, she thought what an excellent maths resource it could be for reluctant learners.

"Cooee! Cooee!" a shrill call half-an-hour later burst on the quietness that had settled on the house following Ish and Craig's lively departure when Tilda and Lennie made their way up the veranda steps. The game stopped, reading paused, as Joel and the girls jumped up to greet their guests with affectionate hugs.

"It is so good to see you."

"Jacinth, glasses for sorrel and please put on de kettle for Lennie's coffee." Madge bustled around arms outstretched in welcome. "Come, come in, sit here where it will be cooler. Joel, switch on de other fan. Connie, slice de dark cake and bring ginger cookies to eat with our drinks. So good to see you, my friends."

"Brought you limes and bananas as promised, Madge," Lennie put his load onto the table, "and the recipe for lime preserve."

Tilda sat down on the sofa next to Jackie. "How are you finding your stay in Barbados?"

"Different!"

"That is what she always says, about everything." Joel jested as he repositioned the fan.

"But it's true," retorted Jackie indignantly, "everything is so very different to what I am used to."

"Even to the eating of mangoes!" They all burst out laughing. In between the hilarity Joel recounted Jackie's initiation into eating mangoes the true Barbadian way.

"Have you introduced her to Brownes Beach?"

"Oh, Aunt Tilda, we have been wanting to go but Connie nor Clyde will take us."

"Because it is over-run with tourists!"

"You are a spoilsport, Connie."

"It is the best beach on the island, in my opinion," Jacinth confided to Jackie.

"Finish your drinks and eats. We have come to take you all to Brownes Beach," Tilda instructed decisively.

"No, no, no, that is not possible," Mumma Madge got up and wafted her arms distractedly. "I have to prepare de evening meal for de family."

Lennie walked across and placed an arm around her shoulders. "All taken care of, Madge dear. Wilson is picking up Garfield from the academy when he finishes at the hospital and will meet at our house."

"But dey need to eat."

"And so they will. At our house." He patted her hand and smiled.

"How does pudding and souse sound?"

"Oh, Lennie, what a treat!"

The following Sunday dawned with blue sky and blazing sunshine. Jackie assisted Connie with breakfast preparation to the accompaniment of hymn singing from the church on the other side of the garden. Uncharacteristic excitement fluttered in her heart as she anticipated seeing Clyde again. *Calm down, girl, as Miss Pedwardine would say. Dear Lord, guide and control my thoughts, words and actions this day,* she prayed as they drove towards the church.

The music of the piano and organ before the service drew her into worship as she moved along the row to sit between Tilda and Clyde.

They exchanged morning greetings.

Tilda placed a hand upon her arm.

"I pray you will be able to come out again with us on the meal blessing run on Friday."

Jackie's heart had been stirred out of her comfort zone on her previous visits to the poverty-stricken sector of Bridgetown. She felt compelled to return but knew her involvement depended on her hosts being able and willing to transport her.

"I would like that." *Lord if it is Your will for me to participate, I believe You will make a way.*

"We will come, if at all possible, but I am on call this Friday," Clyde whispered as the choir began the Introit.

Pastor Desmond took as his text Luke chapter 15 verse 20, "...while he was still a long way off, his father saw him and was filled with compassion for him;

he ran to his son, threw his arms around him and kissed him." My topic today is being in the river of God's will." Pastor Desmond spoke of God's perfect will being in the centre of the river where the flow is strongest and God's permissive will where He allows the individual to make their own choices, by veering off to the shallows where there is no guidance or direction.

Jackie's mind wandered off on its own course. *I know I have only recently become re-acquainted with You, but I desire more than anything to be in Your will. Please, teach me Your will. I am so used to making my own decisions and being in control of every situation. My relationship with You is so precious. Clyde has only just come into my life. Is it too soon to have these feelings for a man I have so lately met? They feel genuine or is it the enchantment of this place that has captivated me?* "...Is it necessary for you to return to God's perfect will – like the prodigal son?" Pastor Desmond's voice brought her mind back to the sermon. "The Father God is always looking out for you because He loves you. How do we know this to be so? Look again at verse 20. How did the father act? He saw... he had compassion... and he ran. He did those things out of love for his child. It is necessary to return if you are to follow God's plan for your lives. In this passage Jesus is speaking of the actions of the Heavenly Father towards you. He sees you. He loves you and is always looking out for you. These are not words solely for the young people. They are relevant to us all because as Isaiah tells us 'We all, like sheep, have gone astray, each of us has turned to His own way.' Rather, follow the advice of the writer of Proverbs, 'In all thy ways acknowledge Him and He will direct thy paths.'"

A tenor soloist, backed by the choir, sang 'No one ever cared for me like Jesus.' Tears flooded Jackie's eyes. *Lord Jesus, you have proved those words to be true over the past few weeks. You have softened my heart to such an extent that I have shed more tears in recent days than I have for years. The wonder of your grace for me daily overwhelms me. I know You care for me. Thank You for loving me so much that You were willing to suffer the indignity of a cross and die on my behalf that I might be forgiven, my life completely turned around. Thank you for welcoming me back. Teach me to walk in Your will.*

Connie and Jackie travelled with Clyde back to the house in order that they might put the finishing touches to the late lunchtime meal. They worked as a team so that by the time the others returned home the food was ready to serve. Tilda and Lennie, as well as Jehu, Pastor Desmond's son, and Cousin Esther, Jacinth's friend joined them. Madge beamed as soon as Wilson had offered grace and invited her guests to sit down. She was in her element. Having company around her table was a blessing. Conversation as well as dishes flowed around the table.

When everyone had enjoyed sufficient food Connie organized the clean-up then the groupings split up. The older people elected to sit in the shade of the sitting room to enjoy their coffees, Jacinth and Esther withdrew to work on a school holiday project, Garry and Jehu spent some while checking details on a computer program before going for a stroll to meet up with a group of friends for Bible study at the beach. Following the morning church service Joel had been invited out for lunch with his cousins, Ish and Craig, so was absent from the family gathering. Jackie sat with Clyde and Connie on the veranda discussing Pastor Desmond's sermon and the possibility of taking up Tilda's invitation to assist with the meal blessing run before returning to England.

"I can't believe our time here is almost over."

"Don't you want to go back?"

Jackie looked up in surprise. "Oh, I must return. I am expected. I need to prepare for the new school year."

"Con?"

"If you want the truth, I am torn in two. I have thoroughly enjoyed being home, but I feel an irresistible pull to return to England. I have unfinished business there."

"Such as?"

She shrugged her shoulders. "The education of certain children, family history research, amongst other things."

"Not a particular cricketer?"

She gave her brother a coy grin. "That remains in the hands of de Good Lord."

Jackie's ears pricked up and her eyebrows rose. This was news to her. She waited expectantly for Connie to elaborate. When she did not offer further information Jackie sat bolt upright and asked, "Who?"

But Connie would not be drawn and only shyly shook her head. She stood up abruptly and silently collected the empty coffee mugs. She made her way to the kitchen picking up her parent's tea-tray on the way.

"You's taking pot-luck to church?"

"Yes, Mumma."

"There is coconut bread ready for you."

"Thank you, Mumma."

"You's and Jackie travelling to the Boardwalk with Clyde?"

"I think so, Mumma."

"We will see you's there."

Connie nodded her head and walked with her load towards the sink. Thoughtfully she turned on the tap and automatically began washing the pots under the running water as her mind darted all over the place like the spurting water bouncing in the sink. Her heart raced on apace remembering precious shared moments, but she was not sure she was ready to reveal the feelings that were burgeoning inside her, with a wider audience. Not just yet. Texts and FaceTime sessions were all very well, but she wanted to see him again face to face. Be in his company. Be near to him.

Chapter Thirty-One

Sunset splendour!

"You didn't know there was a particular young Englishman she was special friends with?"

Jackie was strolling along the Boardwalk at Hastings Rock with Clyde, some steps behind Connie and the group of friends and relations they had met up with, as was the custom on a Sunday afternoon in Barbados. In the background they could hear strains of music coming from the band stand played by the Royal Barbados Police Band accompanying the gentle lapping of waves on the shore.

Clyde just caught the slight shake of Jackie's head. "I had no idea," she said quietly. "Connie was friendly with everyone. You know your sister. She mixed comfortably with male and female, both young and old. She has that lovely way with her that endears her to all who meet her."

Her companion's face creased affectionately as he nodded knowingly. "That sure sounds like my sister!"

"Groups of us meet up frequently at events in the village, as you do here, and Connie joined in with most things. As she got involved with the cricket club she met many of the members including my cousin, Stephen. Any number of the young men accompanied Connie home after choir practice, house group or church meetings, particularly in the dark winter months, but she gave no indication that she was closer to any one person than another."

"Why would they do that?"

"English custom. Men would not allow a young lady to walk home in the dark on her own."

"Really? Why?"

"Well, to ensure she reached home safely. Unlike Barbados, where darkness falls each evening at 6pm all through the year and the weather is consistently hot, darkness falls at varying times in England, late afternoon in the cold winter months. Do you not know the Robert Louis Stevenson's poem about winter and summer and daylight?"

"No, I am not acquainted with that."

"My Grandmother was always reciting it to us when we were children, so I've never forgotten it.

> In Winter I get up at night
> And dress by yellow candlelight.
> In Summer quite the other way,
> I have to go to bed by day.
>
> I have to go to bed and see
> The birds still hopping on the tree,
> Or hear the grown-up people's feet
> Still going past me in the street.
>
> And does it not seem hard to you,
> When all the sky is clear and blue,
> And I should like so much to play,
> To have to go to bed by day?"

Robert Louis Stevenson

"That is very quaint and sounds typically English."

Jackie laughed. "It simply gives a broad indication of the variance in daylight hours within the English seasons and highlights one of the differences between our two countries. Anyway, in inhospitable weather it would be considered unchivalrous not to ensure that a young lady got home safely."

"So, Connie was often alone with young men?"

"No. I'm not saying that. At home we live in a village, a small community. Unlike Barbados, where you travel everywhere in a car, in our village we walk to everything and frequently do things together. So, for instance, a cluster of people will leave choir practice at the same time. As they reach someone's home the number diminishes so that whoever is left in the group would escort Connie, or me, or any other young woman, to her door."

"Well, she has intimated that one young man has been in almost daily contact since she came home to Barbados."

Pictures of all the young men in Newton Westerby flashed across Jackie's mind. "That is quite a surprise. I can hardly believe it. I saw her almost every day and for some weeks she shared my home. Has she said who he is?"

"No, just that he is special, causes her heart to dance and together they are praying about the future."

"Hmm!" Jackie pondered thoughtfully. "Although she had a lot of contact with my cousin, Stephen, I'm quite sure it's not him, because he is so busy with all his enterprises, he has little time for romantic liaisons and anyway he is much younger than Connie. Mark Bemment helped Stephen escort us to Heathrow, but it would not be him. He's so frequently away at sea they wouldn't have met on many occasions. My cousin Justin attends most things as do the crowd in Stephen's age group."

They walked in silence along the Boardwalk, each with their own thoughts, as other strollers mingled around them. They stepped aside to allow a buggy to pass through. Jackie smiled as the proud mother passed and peeped at the new-born within while Clyde shared greetings with the parents, whom he obviously knew.

"Are you anxious about Connie dating an Englishman?" Jackie asked when they resumed their walk.

"I am concerned. Connie promised she would only be away from home for one year and now she is returning to England for a further spell and if there is a young man who has captured her heart Mumma is worried she may never return home to live."

Jackie stopped in her tracks. "Surely it's natural for adult children to leave home and live independently. You have, as have I."

Clyde did not utter a word but regarded her pensively as wild thoughts raged in his mind and tore at his heart. He fought to cope with moments of internal struggle. He could not bear to have his heart ripped out as before.

Unaware of his veiled anguish, Jackie began to walk again with her quick lilting movement. When Clyde did not follow, she turned round and looked at him askance before breaking the silence. "Don't you believe God is in control of our lives?"

"Why, ye...s, umm, no...umm, I mean, of course," he spluttered, momentarily taken aback by Jackie's response.

They stood. The silence stretched between them. His heart racing, his thoughts in turmoil. Behind him Jackie's eye caught sight of the radiance of the setting sun which caused her to gasp in wonder as it sparkled on the gently lapping ocean. But the splendour was lost to Clyde. He could only focus on his inner torment. *Forgiveness!* He only just kept from shuddering. Too many memories strove to surface. Unhurriedly, he put words to his thoughts.

"If we accept that He is Sovereign why do some things in life seem to contradict His power and authority?"

Jackie opened her mouth to reply but hesitated when she saw the pain that flitted across his face.

His eyes scanned Jackie's face intently. *An open, honest face.* She smiled. A genuine smile that reached her eyes. *Not flirtatious. She willingly helped on the meal run, although it was out of her comfort zone. She came not once but twice and is willing to return. There is sincerity about her, her conversation, actions and commitment. Her care is authentic. Her attitude unpretentious. She is so unlike...* He cut that line of thought right off. No, he would not go there again. Never! *Forgiveness!*

"When we act upon what we perceive to be His direction why do circumstances appear to develop contrary to His will?"

"I can't answer from a doctrinal perspective, I simply know from experience that when I blamed Him for my changed circumstances, my obedience ceased. I took myself out of His will and life became mechanical and intolerable. But it was my doing and was not put right until I surrendered my life again to His control."

He looked in her direction, but Jackie felt he did not actually have her in his vision. His thoughts seemed consumed with some scenario elsewhere to the exclusion of her presence.

"You obviously have a story to tell. Let's sit here." She indicated the low wall alongside the Boardwalk. Although he followed her Clyde continued to speak as though he had not heard her voice.

"I loved her. From childhood we grew up together. Our parents were friends in the church. It was always assumed we would one day marry. We did so towards the end of my training at her insistence. She elected to continue to live with her parents to save money and I returned to Canada to complete my internship. We wrote regularly, she one week and I replied the next. I came home when finances and off-duty permitted. We planned to start a family when I was established in a Doctor's Office in Barbados but when she wrote that she was expecting a child I was thrilled that I was going to be a father. She died giving birth prematurely whilst I was in Canada, or so I was led to believe." A sob caught in his throat.

Jackie moved to touch his arm, then thought better of it.

"It was not until I had been back in Barbados for nearly a year that I learned the true facts. Her sister, Marcia, called into my office one day, towards the end of the evening session, in tears. 'Clyde, I feel I must confess to you the truth. I wrote those letters. Lynette paid me to do so. That is the reason they were typed. She simply signed what I had written. She did not love you. She had been having an on/off affair with Shay Bicknell for years... the child was his. When Pastor spoke one Sunday about the deceit of the heart, her conscience was pricked, and she knew she could not go through with it. You, and everyone else, would be able to calculate the discrepancy between your visits home and the child's birth. You were always so loving and kind to her so, without telling anyone she arranged for an abortion, but she had left it too late in the pregnancy. Complications set in...you know the rest. I'm so sorry, Clyde.'

"I had believed the words in the letters, such encouraging words, about our love being rooted in the love of Jesus Christ. That we would share the good news of his saving grace as we worked together in our home, in the church and in our community. I truly believed the Lord had changed her heart. She disliked me going on the meal run and firmly refused to come with me; a decision shaped by her mother's aversion to mixing with what she termed 'the riff-raff'."

Jackie watched as anguish moved across his face. She smiled again.

Clyde's scrutiny of her face continued. Deceit? No. She is different. *Forgiveness?*

Lord, You ask hard things of me.

Forgiveness?

Dear Lord, forgiveness is difficult after such deception.

I asked greater things of My Son to obtain your forgiveness.

Oh, Lord.

When I forgive, I forget.

Clyde remembered Connie's words – *Maybe it is time to let go.* He suddenly became conscious of a desire to look at the loveliness in Jackie's face instead of the glow of sunset, which was all too familiar to him, yet both reflected God's glory. *Dear Lord, please help me.*

This time he returned her smile then grabbed her hand.

"Come, that is the National Anthem. We must catch up with the others or we will be late for Bible study." The band concert had concluded, and the crowds were dispersing.

Chapter Thirty-Two

Calm and tranquil!

At the church Connie and Jackie walked in together adding the coconut bread to the offerings placed on the prepared table. Jackie looked around her. "It looks as though your parents and aunt and uncle haven't made it."

"Oh, they and the older folks are meeting at Aunt Fran's house tonight for Bible Fellowship. The teenagers planned to meet on Hastings's beach this afternoon and then were going to an ice-cream parlour across the road from there. The owners come to church and frequently open-up for church youth activities. We twenties and thirties generally meet in the church."

Clyde parked the car then followed close behind them but veered off to speak with Pastor Desmond.

"Please pray with me, Pastor."

Desmond drew him to one side.

"Anything in particular?"

"Release from the past."

"Lynette and Shay?"

Clyde nodded. "I'm tired of the flames of rage that burn in the pit of my stomach at the remembrance of her infidelity."

"I have seen how you have struggled but God has not left you. You have held on tight to your hurt for a long time. Is the Lord telling you it is time to let go?"

Again, Clyde nodded his head.

Desmond placed his hand on Clyde's shoulder. "Gracious Father God, You know and love us better than we know ourselves and are aware of our deepest needs. I pray for this brother of mine and beloved child of Your grace. Free him from that which binds him and give him reassurance of Your Almighty power to cleanse, heal and restore. Spirit of God fall afresh on him. We claim the victory in the name of Your dear Son, Jesus, our Lord and Saviour, Amen.

He tightly gripped Clyde's shoulder. "The Lord bless you, Clyde. Our Lord does not promise a trouble-free life but take heart in the fact that He has overcome the world. Nor has He abandoned you, so go in His strength to love and serve Him."

Clyde shook his hand. "Thank you, thank you, Pastor."

"In His provision God often uses friends to help us to heal. Remember He has plans for your life, bigger than you might imagine. Trust Him to lead you, in His time, along a path that is new and different but firm and secure. Now, let us join the others and see what His Word has to say to us today."

They took the vacant seats in the semi-circle set out in front of the altar in the body of the church.

"Leroy, will you open in prayer, please.'

The hubbub died down as Leroy committed their study and deliberations to the Lord, praying for insight and understanding of the passage from Hebrews under consideration.

"Thanks, Leroy." Desmond opened his Bible and looked around the group. "I would like us to look at another aspect of Hebrews chapter 1 verses 10 to 12. Last week we spoke of casting aside worn-out garments and being wary of peripheral things that hinder and perish, now, as Connie reads those verses again for us, what in the text stands out for you?"

Her voice rose as she read the chosen passage.

> In the beginning, O Lord,
> you laid the foundations of the earth,
> and the heavens are the work of Your hands.
> They will perish, but You remain;
> They will all wear out like a garment.
> But You remain the same,
> and Your years will never end.

"Thanks, Connie. Thoughts, anyone?"

"God remains the same for ever."

"No matter what goes on around us He never changes."

"De Good Lord is always steadfast and true."

"He is consistent."

Desmond nodded. "Good. Yes, that is right, but why is it important for us that He remains the same?"

"So that we can trust Him."

"His Word is dependable, you know."

"To prove that He will always keep His promises."

"Right, it is vital that we truly believe this. Turn to the first letter of John chapter 1 verse 9. Denzil, please read for us, verses 5 to 9." Denzil quickly turned to the pages in his Bible. As he read the portion of scripture with clarity the rest of the group followed the words thoughtfully.

This is the message we have heard from Him and
declare to you: God is light;
in Him there is no darkness at all.
If we claim to have fellowship with Him yet walk in the
darkness, we lie and do not live by the truth.
But if we walk in the light, as He is in the light, we have
fellowship with one another, and the blood of Jesus,
His Son, purifies us from all sin.
If we claim to be without sin, we deceive ourselves and
the truth is not in us.
If we confess our sins, He is faithful and just and will
forgive our sins and purify us from all unrighteousness.

"Thanks, man. Now, all of you look back at verse 9.
What does that tell us about the character of God?"

Ten pairs of eyes concentrated on the text.

"He is faithful."

"Someone we can depend on."

"If He says something, He will do it."

"He is honourable, you know."

"Right! Did you notice it is written in the present
tense? He _is_ faithful. He _will_ forgive. He is actively doing
it now. Negativity is not in God's vocabulary. What He
says He will do, He _will_ do. He is unchangeable…"

The words swam before Clyde's eyes. He tightly
squeezed his eyes and pressed his lips together, a trick he
had learned to stem anguish from rising in his heart. He
had managed these last few years to hide the burning
pain as he suppressed his emotions. Yet the enigma that
was Connie's friend had crashed the barrier he had
erected and was causing an irrepressible response. He
breathed in deeply letting the memory surface instead of
pushing it down.

"Dear Lord, forgive my inability to trust Your word in all circumstances of my life. Thank You for always being the same. Cleanse me of the bitterness and anger that have taken hold in my heart. Allay my fears. Plant a willingness to view the future from Your perspective rather than my own. Teach me to accept Your will as trustworthy and true. Please, help me act as though I believe Your word, always. Your grace and mercy amaze me and Your patient, unfailing love overwhelms me. My future is in Your hands. Dear Lord, lead me. I give honour and glory to You for the salvation I have through the sacrifice of Jesus on the cros..." Clyde suddenly became aware of singing voices surrounding him. How had he missed the end of the Bible discussion and prayer session that followed?

As he stood to join his friends. Leroy passed an open hymnbook to him. "You, OK, man?"

"I am good, man, real good. Praise God!"

The burden had gone. Clyde stood tall and looked ahead. Connie caught his eyes and smiled. She knew, as only a twin can know, that all was well with him. His suffering was over. The four-year troublesome weight had been lifted. His heart soared. He had peace with God. With freedom he joined in singing heartily... "My chains fell off; my heart was free; I rose went forth and followed Thee."

At the conclusion of the benedictory prayer Connie could hardly wait to scoot across to Clyde. She flung her arms around him. "De Good Lord be praised." Clyde returned her hug. "God is good, for sure." The others, knowing the weighty problem Clyde had carried, gathered round the pair and shared in their rejoicing.

Jackie stayed in the background. She sensed something momentous had happened in the heart of her friend's brother for as she caught his eyes above the clamour, the deep-seated, anxious look was gone. The smile he gave her radiated peace and ... love. Love? Where had that come from? Her heart doubled its pace. *Does he share my feelings? I have tried so carefully to keep them hidden.*

"Come," Pastor Desmond held out his arms to shepherd the group forwards, "let us enjoy this sumptuous feast before us." He gave thanks and ushered the young people into the side room where the table was laden with pot-luck offerings.

As Connie prepared to serve the drinks Jackie moved to help her. "Is all well with Clyde?"

"Oh yes, more than all well." Conversation flowed around them, and the fellowship shared was a blessing to those present.

"All my heart to Him I give... Love lifted me, when no one but Christ could help, Love lifted me." The voices of Connie and Clyde almost raised the roof of the car as they drove home that evening.

As she sat in the back of the car Jackie felt herself wrapped in the overwhelming love of an amazing God. *Your grace is beyond my understanding but once again I have witnessed how it changes lives. It was Your purpose that I came to Barbados. Thank You for changing my mind – even though I was unaware at the time.*

The following two days were crammed with activity. Farewell visits to family, sea baths at Miami Beach and

Colony Bay and a 20/20 match at Kensington Oval to support Garry's team. They also managed to fit in a final meal blessing run with Tilda and Lennie though Clyde was unable to accompany them as he was working. Jackie felt she was on a roller-coaster.

"You must go to Cave Shepherd in Bridgetown to purchase gifts to take back to England," hustled Connie. When they returned from that trip last minute packing was supervised by Wilson and Garfield who meticulously weighed the cases. "You must not exceed the baggage limit of 23 kilograms, or you will be surcharged." Mumma Madge insisted on a celebratory meal to give the girls a memorable send-off. So many friends and family came to say goodbye it was standing room only.

Wilson and Clyde escorted them to the airport. They said their goodbyes with Caribbean hugs. "Blessings on you both." Wilson raised his hand in farewell.

"God go with you." Clyde gently squeezed Jackie's hand and slipped a piece of paper into her palm. Their eyes locked. His eyes no longer held shadows. Jackie's heart skipped a beat. Clyde bent forward and whispered in her ear, "I'll be in touch, God willing. Will you reply?" Almost inaudibly she instantly replied, "Yes." She drew back and gazed intently at his face, memorizing each feature to revisit when the miles separated them. Before she knew it, his head bent down, and his lips fluttered across her own. "Until then." And he was gone.

The hand he had held flew to her mouth to hold the moment of caress. No turning back till he reached the exit. Then he glanced fleetingly and raised an arm in farewell. She looked at the slip of paper. "Mizpah," she read and tried to recall where she had heard that before. In a dream she boarded the plane and continued to savour that final moment alongside the many memorable experiences of her stay in Barbados till sleep claimed her.

Locked into her own mixed feelings Jackie missed the glow of anticipation in Connie's demeanour as they made their way through the arrivals gate at Heathrow, nor did she witness the spark of joy that the sight of Mark Bemment ignited in her friend as he and Stephen stepped forward to greet them.

"Welcome home, you globetrotters,' Stephen reached to take his cousin's suitcase.

"You two still playing Sir Galahad?" Jackie teased.

"Of course, my lady," Stephen quipped with a neat bow.

Mark deftly moved closer to Connie and slipped a hand under her elbow to steer her through the crowd.

"How's my Constance Joy?" quietly enquired.

"She's very well, now the Good Lord has brought her safely home."

The playful banter between the cousins meant they both missed the intimate smile Connie shared with the young man who caused her heart to dance.

EPILOGUE

Clyde approached his work at the Doctor's office in a state of glad assurance and renewed vigour.

"Doc, you's mighty bright and cheerful these days," commented a member of his staff. He flashed her a warm smile. "De Good Lord be praised."

The black cloud that had hovered over him since Lynette's unfaithfulness was gone. *Thank You, Father God, for mentors such as Pastor Desmond and Uncle Lennie and a loyal friend like Leroy.*

They had been there alongside him all the time he was consumed with grief and anger, but he had adroitly ignored their wise counsel. Now, he appreciated their faithfulness and Godly wisdom. Frequent meetings with Pastor Desmond and attendance at the home group revived a desire to grow more like Jesus in thought, word and deed. *How foolish I have been to keep such good friends at arms-length.*

When work commitments allowed, he met up at Aunt Tilda's on Saturday morning for the Men's Breakfast. Uncle Lennie excelled in the food department and Clyde did not need to worry about meals for the rest of the day. He left refreshed and satisfied in soul and body. *What a lot I have missed by allowing the desolation and hurt to consume me to such an extent that I have excluded these dear people from my life!*

His lean, muscular frame was carried with a deportment that reflected the release he had so recently undergone. It was enhanced by the clean-shaven, strong jawed face, which no longer bore persistent creases across his brow, but displayed more frequently a smile that emphasized the expression of joy that radiated from his heart. *Life is good! God is good!* There was a spring in his step, an urgent desire to recoup the years he had lost battling hurt and anger caused by Lynette's betrayal and subsequent death.

Because of my discontent with life, feelings of rejection and misplaced distrust in the mercy and love of God, I have missed the true nature of God who loves unconditionally. Thank you, Father, that You always remain the same no matter how wilful Your children act.

The challenge of working to achieve health in his sickly patients kept his mind and hands focussed. And the satisfaction of alleviating suffering amongst the neediest in Bridgetown through the meal run gave him opportunity to show the amazing goodness of God to others and acknowledge His Sovereign power to change lives.

However, within days of Connie and Jackie's departure for England a drab dissatisfaction began to tinge his days and, uncharacteristically, his nights. Every unoccupied moment Jackie invaded his thoughts; thoughts which engaged his waking moments were disquieting.

She has been a part of my life for so short a time, maybe my heart is playing false with me.

Yet, from the record of a faithful memory came mind pictures of her smile, the recollection of stimulating conversations they shared, her demeanour with his family and the groups at church; the manner with which she tackled the unknown and unexpected on the meal run; the serenity that emanated from her face after she surrendered her will to the Lord; her dedication to the education and well-being of the children entrusted to her care.

The way she responded to the brothers' mischief was fun. Her eyes sparkled and lit up her face as she retaliated with cheerful amusement. He grinned as he recalled their antics. *I enjoy her company. Conversation with her is refreshing. She is a good listener. Every little thing about her, draws me to her. She has captured my heart.* He paused. *But our commitments are so diverse, and our responsibilities separate us by thousands of ocean miles.* He sighed. *Dear Lord, if this is Your plan for our lives, please make a way. And please make it known to both of us.*

Amazed at the intensity of his longing, instead of ruminating on his restlessness, he acted upon it. One evening at the close of a family meal he handed a large envelope to his parents.

"Mumma and Daddy, this is for you."

"Oh, no," Mumma Madge's hands flew to her face.

"That is mighty generous of you, son," Wilson acknowledged Clyde's gesture.

"You have nothing to worry about, Mumma. All is taken care of."

So, it was in October's radiant haze, as shafts of light cast dancing shadows across the countryside, Clyde and his parents stepped from an aeroplane onto foreign soil. Madge gasped as cold air took her breath away, air infused with the unmistakable tang of Autumn. Wilson smiled as the vibrant foliage colours of the landscape that met his gaze ignited memories from his youth. To the English the coolness of the fading season was the expected mellowness of Autumn but to the Caribbean visitors the drop in temperature was a shock to the system and the blaze of colour a shock to the senses.

Clyde had liaised with Connie when preparing this surprise visit. She in turn had arranged for Mark to chauffeur them from the airport to Newton Westerby and thoughtfully sent warm coats for each of them, which Mark held over his arm in the arrival's hall, as he held aloft a cardboard sign which read 'Wilson Foster Family'.

With blankets tucked around their knees they arrived snug and warm into the driveway of Newton Manor.

As the tyres scrunched against the gravel Connie ran out of the front door and flung her arms around her mother. "Oh, Mumma, you came. You stepped onto the aeroplane, in faith, and de Good Lord has brought you safely across the ocean."

Lord Edmund strode forward to expansively receive his guests.

"Mumma, please meet your cousin, many times removed."

Before him, Lord Edmund, observed a comely woman with a handsome face, displaying a firm chin, under a kindly expression enhanced by a broad, white smile that reached her twinkling eyes.

Madge lifted her head and saw a solidly built man with a frank, open face bearing a large moustache beneath a prominent nose in a head sporting heavily peppered brown hair.

As Lord Edmund graciously escorted Madge towards a blazing fire in the drawing room Connie grabbed Wilson's arm.

"Daddy, this is Mark."

"But..." Wilson scrutinized Mark's wind-beaten face and looked him squarely in the eye. Understanding dawned. "You are the young man who makes the heart of my daughter dance?"

Mark inclined his head. "With your permission, sir."

"And, if the Good Lord wills, my blessing, too."

"Thank you, sir."

"Thank you, Daddy," they spoke in unison, as Connie reached to kiss Wilson's cheek and Mark slipped his hand tenderly around her waist and whispered for her ears alone, "My Constance Joy."

In the meantime, Clyde walked quietly through the front door into the hall and followed the sound of a voice he recognized. He peered through the door of what was obviously the kitchen.

Unaware of his presence Jackie and Lettie were engaged in last minute preparations for a meal.

"So, this is how you spend your time when you're not teaching or travelling the world," he teased.

Jackie jerked her head round. Her astounded response caused her to drop the spoon into the pan she was stirring. She stood and stared at him in disbelief.

"What are you doing here? How come...? I thought this was a meal, um, incorporating a school staff planning meeting. How did...?" Flustered at the sight of him appearing so unexpectedly, she absently brushed a hand through her hair.

Clyde moved quickly to her side and took hold of her hand.

"I could not get you out of my mind. I had to see you again and find out if you truly feel the same as I do. I love you, Jaqueline Cooper. I cannot bear to have so many miles separating us. Facetime is a poor substitute. I want to be near you. Barbados is empty without you. You bring me joy, a joy I want to share with you for the rest of my life."

Unnoticed, Lettie turned down the gas under pans on the hob, placed dishes into the oven then slipped quietly from the room.

"I didn't believe I could fall in love again but so much happened in my heart during those weeks in Barbados. I thought at first it was simply holiday excitement or the ambience of the location, but I find my life is completely turned around. You have captured my heart, dear Clyde. I cannot live without you but how are we going to work it out? We live and work so far apart."

Gently he cupped her face in his hands. A wave of surging tenderness overwhelmed him as he leant towards her. "The Lord will make a way, my dear Jacqueline. Barbados joy cannot be thwarted when we are in His hands." A featherlight kiss caressed her lips. "We will trust Him, together. After all, we have discovered He is the source of all joy."